Somewhere In France There's a Lily

Anne Arrandale

Copyright © 2022 Helen Chapman

All rights reserved.

ISBN: 9781983777745

Cover Art by SelfPubBookcovers.com/JohnBellArt

DEDICATION

For all those who served, and those who also served who could only stand and wait.

Disclaimer

This is a work of fiction. Names, characters, places and incidents are either products of the writer's imagination or are used ficticiously and are not to be construed as real. Any resemblance to actual events, locales, organizations, or persons, living or dead, is entirely coincidental.

Furthermore, should you desire to sue, remember it will only increase book sales, and give it tons of publicity. Besides, I'm pretty poor.

Part One

Chapter One

September 25, 1914

Lily Barnett stood on the deck of the troop ship *Caronia*, surrounded by British soldiers and their officers. She wore the blue-gray uniform suit and red-lined cape of the British Territorial Force Nursing Service. The men around here stood a respectful distance away. She looked at the French coast, unconsciously scanning the nearby water for a German mine. One had sunk the *Caronia's* sister ship a few months ago. Lily didn't expect problems, but she wasn't willing to take chances, either.

Two months ago, she was happily working at the Baltimore City Health Department as a visiting nurse, delivering babies as necessary and making sure homes where communicable diseases were present were quarantined.

Contagion was something about which Nurse Barnett felt strongly. Dr. Joseph Barnett, her late father, had taken her to a home to assist him with a sick child. That visit caused both Lily and her mother to contract diphtheria. Mrs. Barnett, unfortunately, had succumbed to the illness less than a day after falling ill. Lily, however, lay in the throes of the disease for weeks, in and out of consciousness. The treatment, painting the throat with a solution containing arsenic and strychnine, helped her survive, for which she was grateful.

The treatment also caused her hair to fall out. When she regained her senses, not only had she lost almost a month, but her head had been cue-ball smooth. She had returned to classes wearing a turban to cover her embarrassment.

Her hair finally regrew. In place of the brilliant auburn it was white. Her father assured her it was temporary. Five years later, Lily's hair fell down her back, still in its snowy glory.

She brushed some imagined dust from her uniform. By the time she reached the field hospital, she would be coated in mud and who knows what. For now, it made her more secure in herself to keep her newly obtained uniform as pristine as possible.

Nine weeks ago, Lily had parked her bicycle in front of her office on Canton Street, and was stopped by a telegraph messenger before she could unlock her door. The telegram was short.

LILY BARNETT

BALTIMORE CITY HEALTH DEPARTMENT, HIGHLANDTOWN

LILY—

PLEASE COME

CAPTAIN GALEN STEWART

THE MARNE, FRANCE

Galen Stewart. Dr. Barnett's colleague. Lily had known him forever, it seemed. As soon as Britain got into this stupid war, he took ship to England, signed up for the medical corps, and had been posted in the field within weeks.

Lily didn't know what conditions were really like. Only that he had sent her a second telegram the next day asking her to bring as many supplies as she could find. Lily had "borrowed" several cases of surgical supplies and drugs from her office. A quick call to the Cunard steamship company confirmed what she saw in the shipping news. She had little time to spare. She had loaded into a cab, telephoned her superior to tender her resignation, and headed home.

Her brother Josey had been there alone when she arrived. He was two years Lily's senior, and acted like her father. "Lily, where do you think you're off too? And what are all these boxes?"

Lily gave her divinity student brother a quick explanation, handed him Stewart's telegrams, then ran up the stairs and slammed her door before he could pepper her with more questions.

She had packed serviceable clothing into two portmanteaus, making certain to have one fancy dress for the voyage in case, then tossed in two books for good measure. *The Adventures of Sherlock Holmes*, an old favorite, and a new Conan Doyle book with Professor Challenger should serve her well. Finally, she dropped in four balls of crochet thread, a steel crochet hook and a small pair of scissors. She could make doilies or mittens, then pull them out and make something else. Anything to combat boredom, if a field hospital was anything like the hospitals where she'd worked.

"Josey, call a cab for me please. I've got to go."

For once Josey hadn't argued with her. He had gone out onto Washington Boulevard and hailed a motor taxi, then rode with the driver back to their rowhouse. He had helped the driver load everything into the trunk and tied the rest on the roof, then climbed into the back seat of the taxi and rode with Lily to Locust Point where the *RMS Mauretania* had been docked.

A week later, Lily was standing on the Southampton Dock. She had left directions for her boxes to be held at the freight office until she called for them, then picked up her two carpet bags and made her way toward a rank of hansom cabs. The cabman had let her off at the door of Royal Victoria Hospital.

Lily looked around the deck of the ship as they waited for the lighter boat that was rowing out to ferry them to the French shore. She remembered her first day of "official" medical education that led her here. Gawd, that had been a fiasco.

*****

Eleven men milled about the sidewalk in front of the Pathology Building, unsure of what to expect, clearly nervous. From the amount of tobacco littering the walkway, there were more than a few trembling, nervous hands.

A pair of tall, gangly blonds approached her. "I'm Jimmy Zeblinski. My friend here," he gestured to his taller companion, "is my cousin Michael Lazusci."

"Glad to meet you, gentlemen. I'm Lily Barnett." She looked up when she heard the heavy metal doors swing open. "And I believe that is Doctor D'Alba."

A figure stepped out onto the street. His voice was thin and reedy when he spoke. "Come inside. You don't make grades standing out here."

As Lily got closer, she could see the man was considerably smaller than she. Bent and hunched, he could have played Richard III in Shakespeare's tragedy. She knew outward appearance was not necessarily the measure of the man, or of his skill.

"You there. What are you doing here? This class is only for medical students." He blocked her passage before she could pass through the double doors.

She stopped. "I'm Lily Barnett, Doctor. I am a member of this class."

"No you are not. The registrar knows I don't take any female students in this class. You'll have to go somewhere else."

Lily stared at him, shocked. "Doctor D'Alba, I take it you *are* Doctor D'Alba? I was accepted at this school on merit. I was also accepted at Johns Hopkins. I decided to come here, to this school. The least you can do is allow me to begin my studies."

How dare she stand up to him. The few female students that tried backed down as soon as he gave them his speech. D'Alba never had a female student, and didn't plan to start now. "Tell me, Miss Barnett. If you were in fact accepted at Hopkins, why on earth did you decide to come here? Please don't try to tell me our curriculum is superior. I know better."

She smiled, sure she had him. "My father is on staff at Hopkins. James Barnett. Perhaps you know him? I wanted to attend a different school, where I wasn't a professor's daughter."

"James Barnett? Oh, I know him: we went to medical school together. It is because of him I am stuck in this damned morgue. I was well on my way to being a surgeon, when your father told our proctor I had cheated on an exam. It was none of his damned business whether I did or not. But he couldn't keep his mouth shut. I was sent down, and the only position left open to me was pathology. Do you know how much I hate this place?" He was raising his voice with every sentence, until he was shouting. "You want to cut up dead people? Fine. But do not expect any special treatment just because of your daddy. You will be treated as any other student in this class."

"Very well, Doctor. So long as you treat me as every other student, I will be happy." She smiled sweetly and breezed past him into the cool, dark building.

Inside, the stench of formaldehyde was enveloping. It was cool, far cooler than outside. Lily noticed wooden boxes underneath the windows, filled with what she suspected was wet Excelsior. The method worked well for some of the newly opened moving picture theaters, she supposed it would work here.

The other students were waiting inside a large room filled with half a dozen surgical tables. There were large enamel chests lining the room, holding what Lily suspected were their cadavers. The young men were donning white aprons that were laid across each table. Lily found herself paired with Jimmy Ziblinski by default as he was the only one without a partner.

D'Alba entered the room in a flurry of coat tails and clapping hands. "Gentlemen, gentlemen, if I could have your attention please." He purposely ignored

Lily. "We will be selecting your cadavers in just a moment. First, we will go over the instruments."

The pathologist pulled a wooden box from beneath one of the autopsy carts. He undid the hasps and laid it open lovingly. He began holding up various tools of his trade and announcing their names to the class.

"This, gentlemen, is a scalpel." He held up another. "This is a clamp." Then a third. "And this, gentlemen, is a retractor."

Lily's hand shot up.

D'Alba went on without pausing, naming instruments. Lily's hand continued to be aloft. Finally, with a deep sigh, he recognized her. "Yes, Miss Barnett? What is it?"

"I'm sorry, Doctor. You said the third instrument was a retractor. I'm afraid you're mistaken. It's a rib spreader.'

He sucked in his breath. It took all he had not to strike her. "Miss Barnett, if you are only in this class to contradict me, you may leave now. If you are here to learn, be quiet."

"But Doctor D'Alba, you said..."

"I know what I said. And I said it is a retractor. And if I say it's a retractor, by God it's a retractor. If you disagree, I suggest you take it up with your precious father."

So that's the way it would be. He was going to taunt her at every turn, trying to force her to resign the class. Let him keep trying. She merely gave a brief nod.

D'Alba stared at her, a malicious grin on his face. "Again, gentlemen. This is a retractor. It is used to pull an organ out of the way without causing damage."

The lecture continued for thirty more minutes, with more errors on the doctor's part. Lily kept her mouth shut. She merely absorbed the information, and stored it for later use.

"Very well, gentlemen. It is time to select your cadavers." He looked at Lily again, grinning maliciously. "I'm sorry, Miss Barnett. We only have male cadavers this term. You will not be able to participate in this class."

Lily began to sputter. "What do you mean, I can't participate? I am a member of this class. I have a right to learn just as much as the men."

"As I said, Miss Barnett, we have no female cadavers. I cannot allow your tender sensibilities to be offended by the sight of a nude figure. Therefore, you will have to learn from photographs, just as the other females who passed through these doors have done."

This was beyond the pale. "You mean I will be given a set of French postcards, and be permitted to point out breasts and mons?" She could tell the doctor was shocked at her choice of words. "I'm sorry, Doctor D'Alba. That is totally unacceptable. I will be expected to treat men when I enter practice. Therefore, I should be afforded the same opportunity to learn. Will the men be restricted to performing autopsies only on males?"

The professor smirked. "Of course not. That's completely different. Surely your father didn't permit you to work around his male patients."

"Certainly he did. Many of his patients were men who were hurt at work. They came to the office, and frequently I assisted. I have seen nude men before, Doctor."

"That, Miss Barnett, is nothing to brag about. I suggest you go see your father. Tell him I said if he thinks he knows better than I, you should attend your classes with him." He knew she was seething silently. He moved in for the coup. "Should you decide to stay, that rag you wear on your head will have to go. I allow no headwear in this class."

Enough was enough. If this school, this doctor, didn't want her, she would go elsewhere.

Lily took up her satchel and stormed out of the room. Before she allowed the door to slam shut, she turned to address D'Alba one last time. "All I can say, Doctor, is that I hope you never require my services."

Lily didn't bother catching the streetcar. She didn't even begin the walk up Russell Street towards home. Instead, she turned toward downtown. She had no idea where she was going, she just knew she had to walk.

She walked to Lexington Market. Street arabs stood outside, calling their wares out to passers by. "Can-eee-loupe, Straw-berr-ees, Wood-er-mellllon, ripe to the ry-ind!" Their melodious calls melded together in a symphony of the street. For some reason Lily found the cacophony soothing.

She bypassed the old market, where the Waskey's sold fresh meats, and the arabs hawked their produce. Instead, she headed for the new market across Lombard Street. John Faidley's fish market was at the upper end. The smell was strong, but not unpleasant. Live crabs clicked their claws in bushel baskets filled with seaweed to the counterpoint of the fishmongers crying their wares.

Nothing Mr. Faidley offered interested Lily today. She made a stop at Conrad Tiebes' stall to buy a piece of Swiss chocolate, and nibbled on it as she wandered through the stalls of fresh tomatoes and sweet corn and strawberries. There, just ahead, was her destination.

Neddick's counter was empty this early in the morning. Two women labored behind the counter, readying food for the day. Lily leaned on the counter and waited until she had someone's attention. She asked the counter girl for an orange drink, and proffered two pennies in exchange.

The drink was served in a paper cup in a freezing cold metal holder. The icy cold drink quickly made sweat bead on the outside, and left a ring on the counter top. Lily ignored it and took a deep swallow. It was so cold it hurt her teeth, but to Lily it was the nectar of the gods. The orange flavored sweetness took her back to when she was a small girl, and Mrs. Zill would bring her to the market on Saturday morning. As their reward for "helping" with the shopping, the housekeeper would treat Lily and Jack to an orange drink. She didn't realize until this moment that she missed those brief, innocent days.

Lily finished the last swallow and walked out onto Eutaw Street. She was calmer now, but knew she didn't want to go home yet. Now was not the time to face her father with her disappointment. So she kept walking.

Howard Street and its myriad stores held no interest for her. Lily had no real destination, she just knew where she didn't want to be. She walked down to Cathedral Street, turned the corner and kept walking.

The Basilica of the Annunciation was in the middle of Saint Paul Street and Cathedral. Its Byzantine dome created the optical illusion of towering over the surrounding buildings.

Lily made her way up the steps and through the iron gates, then inside the vestibule. The church smelled of cool air, old perfume and incense. She thought of the elderly women who would attend the early morning masses here, and the families who came to midnight mass at Christmas. This church was never her home parish, but it was someplace to go for special occasions. Lily had been confirmed here, and her mother had hoped she would marry here rather than at St. Martin's, where they normally attended mass.

The frescoes inside the sanctuary were glorious. Lily sat in the last pew and absorbed the beauty of the place. It had always been a favorite place to come whenever she wanted to be alone, or to think. Today the church offered no solace.

Lily left the church, and wandered to the Enoch Pratt Free Library. She didn't go inside. Books held no interest today. She looked across Cathedral Street. She had lived her whole life in Baltimore, and had never really paid much attention to the dark stone and brick building. Several girls her age were milling about outside.

Lily crossed the street and blended in with the crowd, to see what exactly was going on. Finally, unable to stand the mystery, she asked the girl closest to her why they were waiting.

The red-haired girl smiled when she answered. "We're here for a lecture. Sister Kathleen Flannaghan is going to talk about her studies with Miss Clara Barton."

Lily knew Miss Barton's work, and had grown up listening to her father's stories about the woman's work during the Civil War and later. "Why is Sister Kathleen speaking? Is this a special occasion?"

A blonde in the group responded this time. "Sister Kathleen is starting a special nursing program."

"Why should that require a lecture? All the hospitals train nurses." Lily couldn't understand what the attraction was about a three month course in changing bedpans and washing bottoms.

"This is something new. It is a two year course. Graduates will become what they are calling 'registered nurses' and will be qualified to do everything but perform surgery." The red haired girl smiled again. "I'm Catherine O'Roark by the way." She held out her hand to Lily.

"Lily Barnett." Lily smiled and offered her hand in return.

"And I'm Joanne Dombrowski." The blonde offered her hand as well. "Will you be signing up for the class too?"

"I really don't know. This is the first I've heard of it. Do you think Sister would mind if I attended? I don't have a reservation."

Catherine laughed. "None of us do. We just found out about this yesterday in an advertisement in the American. It said that all interested young ladies were welcome to attend and take part in a question and answer session."

Lily was intrigued. She had never known something like this existed. These women, these registered nurses, would graduate with more training than some men who learned their doctoring skills through apprenticeship. She smiled broadly and joined the line that had begun to form. "Yes, Catherine, I believe I will attend."

*****

May 1913 came sooner than any of the nursing students anticipated. The year and a half at Saint Joseph's Hospital so far had been intense. The students lived on campus at the hospital, and were only permitted to leave the grounds one half-day a week. Their first year was spent strictly in the classroom, learning anatomy, terminology, solutions, and the theoretical workings of a hospital. The Hospital Sisters of Saint Francis were strict task masters, and brooked neither disobedience nor sloth in their students. About half of the women dropped out, while a few others transferred to the programs at other hospitals, where the instructors weren't members of a religious order, believing the course load wouldn't be so strenuous.

The school's second year was filled with hands-on, intern training in the hospital itself. While the young women began by scrubbing the wooden floors with lye soap and brushes, then treating the floors with a mixture of salt and sawdust before sweeping it up. It was hard, blister-causing work, but it was important for them to learn the basics of cleanliness before they could begin to assist in patient care.

Their work with patients began slowly. They began by carrying food, making beds and assisting with personal needs, then graduated to assisting with post-operative care and discharging patients. All their work was strictly supervised by Sister Kathleen.

Finally, after eighteen months of backbreaking physical labor, groups of three student nurses were selected to assist in surgery. Lily was in the first group, along with Joanne Dumbrowski and Catherine O'Roark. They were to observe one operation, then would begin to assist in subsequent operations, all under the purview of the same surgeon.

Sister Kathleen stood with her clip board as she called off the names. "O'Roark, Dumbrowski, Barnett. You come with me. Dr. Stewart will need your assistance in the scrub room."

The students followed the white "sailboat" coronet of the nun's down the long corridor to the surgical theater, it dawned on Lily she had said "Dr. Stewart". No, it couldn't be Dr. Galen Stewart. He was a researcher and surgeon with her father at Hopkins. Could it? Unlike some of the girls, she wasn't trying to snag a doctor. She wasn't interested in a husband at all right now. She wanted to get an education and to begin treating patients.

She and her fella students removed their waist pockets and student caps, donned their aprons over their gray uniform dresses, wrapped their hair and masked their faces. They would scrub with carbolic soap in the next room. Lily leaned her back into the door, pushed into the scrub room then walked to the sink, ignoring the tall male figure at the adjoining sink. She picked up the brush and went to work vigorously on her nails, using the soap liberally.

The man scrubbing next to her looked to his left when he was joined by her two fellas. He didn't say anything, as, in his experience, any attention from the surgeon could make for an uncomfortable situation later. He preferred to keep everything businesslike in his theater.

Lily and her friends finished their own scrubbing, dried their hands, powdered and gloved, then waited for the doctor. He turned off the water, and turned to accept a sterile towel from Joanne. He wiped his hands dry, extended them for Catherine to apply powder, then she and Joanne each held a glove open for him. Finally, he turned, and ducked his head so Lily could put his apron around his neck, then turned so she could tie the back, and tie up his surgical mask. He decided to break his own rule. As she was tying his mask, he said, very softly, "Good to see you, Miss Barnett."

Lily smiled beneath her mask. "You too, Dr. Stewart."

*****

June 20, 1914

The morning was dragging. Lily and her fifteen classmates waited in the narthex of the Basilica, attired in their white gowns, each carrying a bouquet of white roses with a single red blossom in the center. Once Bishop Murphy finished his invocation, the young ladies would walk in two lines down the side aisles to the altar, where they would receive their pins and caps, and would recite the Nightingale Pledge.

Lily didn't know why it had taken her weeks to memorize the Pledge. She had been able to name off all the human bones and to recite Mr. Longfellow's *Wreck of the Hesperus* without prompting before she finished high school. But this Pledge had her flummoxed.

Finally, the Bishop finished, the organ music swelled, and Sister Angelica pointed to the two girls in front of the queue.

Lily turned down the epistle side of the nave. The group walked slowly while the organ played some march she couldn't identify. Once at the crossing the sixteen candidates arranged themselves around the rail, from transept to transept.

Sister Kathleen had been seated on the side of the altar beside one of the acolytes (one of the few times a woman was permitted on the altar). She walked to the epistle side and stood behind the rostrum. "Today, we welcome into our esteemed art of nursing, sixteen young practitioners." She went on, but Lily couldn't focus her mind on the speech. All she could think of was that damnable Pledge she'd have to recite.

Finally, Sister Kathleen finished. She motioned to the two sisters seated in the front pew, who stepped to the altar rail behind where Lily stood, each carrying trays holding pins and small, ruffled caps. Once their names were called, the candidates were to step forward, kneel at the rail, where Sister Kathleen would award them the symbols of their new positions.

"Lily Barnett."

Lily jumped when she heard her name called. She looked about to see if anyone had seen, then took the step forward to kneel before her instructor and mentor.

Sister Kathleen lifted a pin from the tray held by one of the younger nuns and affixed it to Lily's bodice, careful not to prick her shoulder. When Sister placed the cap on her head, Lily felt the comb slide into her hair, surprised how quickly the nun managed the procedure.

Once all sixteen women had been "pinned" and "capped", they assembled in a group in the crossing before the altar. This was the moment Lily had been dreading. At Sister Kathleen's nod, they began reciting the Nightingale Pledge, written by Nurse Lystra Gretter five years ago.

"I solemnly pledge myself before God and in the presence of this assembly: To pass my life in purity and to practice my profession faithfully. I will abstain from whatever is deleterious and mischievous, and will not take or knowingly administer any harmful drug. I will do all in my power to elevate the standard of my profession, and will hold in confidence all personal matters committed to my keeping, and all family affairs coming to my knowledge in the practice of my profession. With loyalty will I endeavor to aid the physician in his work and devote myself to the welfare of those committed to my care."

There, she managed to get it all out without stumbling over her words or screaming out loud. She wanted to laugh. Lily was standing in the center of the Basilica, the mother church of Catholicism in the United States. She had to show a modicum of decorum.

The students turned and filed into the second and third pews on the gospel side of the church. Bishop Murphy finished mass, which to Lily seemed to take forever. She could barely manage the sitting and standing and kneeling in her long dress with the necessary corset. In the hospital, she was able to wear a looser, more utilitarian undergarment. This steel-ribbed monstrosity was something out of the Inquisition.

Finally, mass ended. The nuns began filing out, and the students followed. Lily looked up and held back the urge to wave at her brothers in the balcony. She turned back just in time to see a hand reach out from the pew. She turned quickly and saw the hand belonged to Dr. Galen Stewart. He pressed a piece of paper into her palm. Lily couldn't read it until she was outside. Was it congratulations? Or something more personal? She wasn't sure which she wanted.

On the Basilica steps, the nurses were posed for photographs. Mr. Morrison arranged them in various formations around the nuns who administered their program, sometimes standing, sometimes sitting on the cold marble steps. Ten group shots later, he began taking individual portraits of each new nurse. Lily was first, as he called their names alphabetically.

At last she had the chance to read the note. "Leaving for France in the morning. Have supper with me."

Chapter Two

Nurse Lily Barnett allowed Lieutenant Colonel John McCrae, of the Canadian Expeditionary Forces, to assist her from the small boat when they reached the French shore. The two had become friends on the crossing. She found herself a little disappointed that, even though he was a physician, he was going to be serving as a gunner in a fighting unit. At forty-one, he was older than many of his contemporaries. He told Lily it was the right thing to do, and knew he would be able to administer treatment to his men in the trenches, alleviating the need to transport many of the all but the most gravely wounded.

The two exchanged mailing directions, and parted company.

An older non-commissioned officer was waiting on the beach. He approached Lily. "Are you the only nurse on this boat, Sister?"

She wasn't sure how to address him. "I am."

"Very well, come with me." He headed out across the sand at a quick march.

"Wait!" He turned and stomped back to her.

"What? Ya don't expect me to carry your bag, do ya?"

"No. I have boxes of supplies aboard that haven't been unloaded yet. Things that the hospital will need. Dr. Stewart asked me to bring them."

'They'll be sent on with the rest of the freight. Stewart sent me to fetch you, and it's a two hour trek to his duty station."

Again, he quick-marched across the beach. Lily hurried to keep up. At the end of the long coarse sand beach a truck waited. About a dozen Canadian soldiers had already piled in and were leaning on the staked sides. The one closest to the tailgate spotted the older man first. "Here. Sergeant-Major! We've been waiting for you. The Huns won't wait forever, ya know."

The Sergeant-Major wasn't putting up with his nonsense. "Enough out of you, Corporal. We have a lady present. Here, you. Lend a hand."

Without being told, Lily set one bag down, and heaved the other up into the waiting truck. The second bag followed. Her time in nurse's training, and her practice with the Public Health Service had built her strength far more than she had anticipated. She may have been small, even tiny by some standards at just barely five feet, and almost painfully thin now. But she could still move a large patient by herself, and, if necessary, put a grown man on the ground if he got too frisky. She'd done it once or twice on the troop ship, and had no reason to think she couldn't do it again.

The Canadians in the truck were only too glad to help her board. They made a show of allowing her to squeeze in between them to lean across the cab. One of the more rowdy ones tried to slide his arm around her waist.

Lily looked up at him, her smile wide and sweet. "Private, do you normally attempt to embrace your first lieutenant?"

He smiled back. "Now why would I want to do that, darlin'? When I can put my arm around you?"

"Because, Private, I am a first lieutenant. And if you don't remove your arm right now, I will. At the shoulder. Clear?"

He did indeed remove the offending arm, then snapped to attention. "Yes, ma'am."

She turned to lean on the cab, and braced herself as someone cranked the engine to life. They were off.

As they drove to the hospital, Lily was nervous about seeing Galen Stewart again. She had hardly gotten any mail from him, even though she had written him weekly. One letter when he had first arrived in France, then two cables hardly made for an intimate correspondence.

It took two hours for their truck and the convoy to reach the hospital compound at the rear of the British lines. Men rushed to the other enclosed trucks to off-load boxes brought from the ship. The Canadians in Lily's truck jumped out by twos and threes, until she was the only one left. She picked up her valises and shuffled to the tailgate, then tossed the bags out. She grabbed the corner stake and turned to try and climb down, in the most ladylike fashion she could manage when she felt a pair of hands at her waist. She was lifted from the bed and set on the ground. She felt the grip loosen slightly, but he maintained contact. "You can let me go now."

"What if I don't want to?" His voice was deeper than she remembered, gruffer.

"Galen!" She threw her arms around his waist and hugged him, then remembered where she was. "Excuse me, Captain Stewart. Lieutenant Lily Barnett, reporting, Captain."

He seemed taller. Thinner, too. Yet his arms felt stronger, more muscular. His dark hair was longer than was military-approved. But his eyes were still the same dark chocolate brown as she remembered.

Captain Galen Stewart, Surgeon RAMC, utterly ignored protocol. He released his hold on Lily's waist, then cupped her face in his two hands and kissed her, quite soundly, to the great amusement of the enlisted men.

When he stepped back, Lily's normally pale face was beet red. She straightened her black uniform hat, studied her shoes, and nervously brushed the dust from her two piece dark gray travel suit. His greeting was so different than when she had last seen him.

*****

As soon as Lily had returned home from her graduation ceremony at the Basilica, she'd hurried to change her clothes. She still had the white, pink and lavender creation her mother had ordered before she died, the one that Lily had intended to wear to the annual Cotillion at the Lyric Opera House. Diphtheria had canceled those plans, and the gown had never been worn. She pulled it from the box where it still rested on the shelf top of her wardrobe.

It was times like this she missed her father most. A mere three months ago, her strong, handsome father, the man who had cared for the poor, and taught future generations of doctors, had suddenly succumbed to dropsy. It wasn't that she expected anyone to ask what a man's intentions were. She needed to figure out her own, and it wasn't something she could ask her brothers.

She laid the dress out on the bed. First things first. She pulled a corset from the bottom drawer. It was lighter than the one she wore now, the sort necessary to hold up the heavy skirts of her graduation gown. This new dress was a bouffant creation of organza silk, and needed something lighter, more freeing. If Lily had the nerve, she would have worn one of the new brassieres some of the girls had. Not tonight.

Tonight, Galen Stewart, MD, was calling for her. Tonight, Lily intended to look her very best. Tonight, tonight she would see the man she just might love.

The doorbell rang at exactly six thirty that evening. Lily was putting the finishing pins in her Gibson Girl hairdo, and praying it stayed. She heard Josey open the door just as she stepped into the hallway and began to descend the stairs. Josey was chattering away at the tall, distinguished man, who was utterly ignoring the young man and staring raptly at the young lady he intended to escort for the evening. She reached the bottom step as Galen stepped around Josey, who was still talking, and extended his hand. She accepted it.

"Nurse Barnett, you look lovely."

She blushed. "And you look rather dapper tonight, Doctor."

"Shall we go? I have seven thirty reservations."

He helped her with her pink and purple jacquard shawl, took her arm, and guided her out to the waiting carriage. She had expected him to arrive in a motorcar, but a carriage seemed so much more romantic. He handed her up into a coach, climbed in and rapped for the driver to go ahead.

"I'm..."

"You..."

They both started speaking at once. They laughed. Galen said, "You first."

"Your note said you were leaving for France in the morning. Isn't it odd to take a holiday in the middle of a war."

"I'm not going on vacation. I've joined up."

"Joined up! America isn't in this war."

"No. Not yet. I've joined the Royal Army Medical Corps. I have to catch the train first thing in the morning to get to Montreal. The ship leaves in three days, and I have yet to collect my uniforms, or get my orders."

"So, you'll be an army doctor, a surgeon?"

He nodded. "They wanted me to train other, young doctors. I said no. I'd be more useful at the front."

Lily fumbled in her purse for a handkerchief. She finally managed to get her fingers on it, and pulled it out to wipe the tears from her eyes.

"Lily? Are you crying?"

She nodded, sniffed and blew her nose in a rather unladylike manner. "I don't want you to go. Not now."

He put his arm around her shoulders and gave her a squeeze. "You darling girl. I will write to you, I promise. And you shall write to me. And tonight, I am taking you to the Thirteenth Floor of the Belvedere. We'll dine on terrapin soup, stuffed rockfish, roast duck, and dessert upon peach cake and whipped cream. Do you have to be at the hospital tomorrow?"

It took her a moment to realize he had asked a question. "Uh, no. I start Monday, at the City Health Department." She realized his arm was still around her.

"Good. Because I wanted to walk around Mount Vernon with you tonight after dinner. And maybe, if we can find enough to talk about, to see the sun come up over the harbor."

She leaned into him ever so slightly, as his hold on her tightened. "That sounds absolutely lovely."

It was lovely. They held hands and walked around Mount Vernon, the spring flowers scenting the air so delicately. They strolled slowly up Charles Street to Howard, then to Pratt. She held his hand, their fingers entwined, his hand dwarfing hers, and making her feel even smaller, coveted.

He found a bench at a streetcar stop. They sat, and watched the sun come up over the Patapsco River. The smell of freshly ground nutmeg from the McCormick plant made them forget the smell of fish and fuel oil from the dockside. She rested her head on his shoulder, not wanting the night to end.

Finally, he stood and pulled her beside him. "Come on. Time to get you home, and I've got a train to catch."

He hailed a motor taxi that was headed up Pratt Street. He handed her into the back, climbed in after her, and gave the driver her address. When they reached her house, he told the cab to wait. He walked her to her door, hugged her, and kissed her lightly on the cheek. "I'll write." Then he was gone.

Chapter Three

Yes, this meeting was far different than when he left on the marble steps of her family home. Now, standing in boot-sucking mud on a battlefield in France, she had gotten her first real kiss. But she had work to do.

"I managed to get the supplies you wanted. I hope they are in one of the trucks that came in with us."

"I'll find them. Later. For now, you need to meet the Major, then get you settled in. You're in a tent with three other nurses."

He put his hand under her elbow and steered her around potholes and mud puddles, toward the base office.

"Major Dennison?"

"Come in, Captain. I see you've found our new nurse."

"Major Alfred Dennison, this is Nurse Lily Barnett, one of the best surgical nurses I've worked with, and well versed in communicable disease."

"Good, good." The little major stepped around his camp desk and walked around Lily, as if he was judging a horse at the fair. "Not much to her, is there?"

Galen was standing behind Dennison. He leered at her comically. "No, sir. I think there's just enough of her."

Dennison accepted Lily's written orders, and sent her off with Galen to find her quarters.

They passed two soldiers who were waist deep in a trench. Lily looked at them as they passed. "They're not digging graves this close to camp, are they?"

"No, no. Latrines. You'll be glad of them when the field complaint hits."

They finally reached the nurses' tent. "We only have three other nurses right now, and two nursing assistants. They're in your tent, too. They're all on the ward now. Your bunk is there, on the far end. Get changed, and I'll take you in and make introductions."

He waited outside while Lily shucked off her jacket and skirt, pulled on her gray uniform dress and pinned her apron in place. Her small veiled cap completed her uniform. A quick check to make sure her hair was still firmly pinned in place and she was off.

She strode beside Galen now, no longer hindered by her confining travel suit. She was careful to keep her distance. It was one thing to be greeted by an old friend. It was another to have an open display in the presence of other nurses. She knew how cruel women could be when competing for a man, and Galen Stewart was prime beef on the front.

They reached the hospital tent. Galen held the tent flap back for her to enter. She slipped in quickly and stepped to the side, knowing she was subordinate to every other member of the medical staff here.

Galen cleared his throat. "Sister, a moment of your time, if you please."

A tall, ramrod straight woman in her late thirties made her way to where they stood. "Yes, Doctor?"

"Sister Leora Myers, this is Nurse Lily Barnett. I want her assigned to surgery."

"Certainly, Doctor." Her voice was high, verging on squeaky, and went through Lily's head like a knife. "Tell me, Miss Barnett. Exactly what training do you have?"

"I studied nursing at Saint Joseph's hospital. I matriculated as a Registered Nurse, then worked as a visiting nurse for the Baltimore City Health Department."

Sister Myers gave one short, sharp nod. "Very well, *Nurse* Barnett. The orderlies are bringing the men's afternoon meal in soon. There are two men back there," she gestured over her shoulder, "that will need help. Go introduce yourself and we will see how you do."

Wonderful. Not only was she thousands of miles away from home. The nursing sister seemed to take an instant dislike to her. Oh well, she had patients to see to.

It was easy to find her two new patients in the sparsely populated ward. She grabbed a chair and set it between the two beds. A quick look showed why they'd need help: each one had an arm amputated; one above the elbow, the other below the elbow.

"Good day, gentlemen. I'm Nurse Barnett. Sister Myers has asked me to look after you. Is there anything you need before the orderly brings your lunch?"

The man whose arm was amputated at the shoulder merely groaned and turned away from her. The other patient grinned at her sillily. "Well now. Ain't you a looker." Judging by his accent, he was British.

She laughed lightly. "Well, I try not to be. You know my name. What's yours? I can't go on calling you 'Soldier'."

"Private Lucas Howland, Miss. That grumpy cuss in the other bed is Corporal Larkin Crownover."

"Tell me, Private Howland, is he always this sociable?"

"Just for the last two days. He's been complaining of pains. He can't understand why his arm still hurts when it isn't there anymore."

"Oh. I'll see if I can get him something for the pain. And how are you?"

"My arm's a might tender. And I would kill for a fag."

"Don't you have any?"

"I've got the makin's. But, you know, it's kind of hard to roll."

She grinned mischievously. "Where's your makings?"

He pointed to the small table between their beds. Lily pulled open the drawer and took out rolling papers and a small pouch of tobacco. She opened the pouch, folded a paper in half, sprinkled the tobacco in it, then deftly rolled a tight cigarette. She held it out for Howland to seal. He stuck out his tongue to lick the paper. Lily quickly crimped the ends, then put it between Howland's lips. She retrieved a match and struck it on the side of the table and lit his smoke.

He took a deep drag. "God that's good. Thanks, Nurse."

The orderly arrived, pushing a trolley holding lunch trays. He passed them out as he worked his way down the row of beds. He got to the last two, where Lily's patients were. She stepped out to meet him. "Just leave the cart. I'll feed these two, and you can pick it up when you come back this way."

She checked the trays for their contents. Soft food, milky tea, and custard. Everything was easy to digest and utterly boring. Howland was already sitting up. She decided he'd eat first. Then she'd tackle Crownover.

"Alright, Private Lucas Howland. It's time for your afternoon meal." She laid the tray across his lap, and tucked a napkin under his chin. She held the cup for him and offered him a sip. "I can manage myself, Nurse. But thank you for getting me started."

She set his cup down, and stood. "Very well then." She leaned in conspiratorially. "Is that as bad as it looks?"

He took a forkful of the mashed white conglomeration on his plate. He made a show of chewing and swallowing. "No. It's worse."

"What is that, exactly?"

"Exactly? I have no idea. It tastes like rutabagas, tatties and neeps. It wouldn't be bad if it had some salt and maybe some butter. But this is like wallpaper paste."

They both laughed. She retrieved the second tray for Corporal Crownover. "Corporal?" She spoke softly. "Corporal, it's time to eat. Let's turn over so I can feed you."

He had been lying on his left side, his right shoulder, the amputated arm with its little stump closest to Lily. He raised up slightly to turn on his back, and Lily got a whiff of something: the sweetish smell of the beginnings of putrefaction.

"Corporal, when was the last time your dressing was changed?"

"Yesterday morning, I guess. When the doc first cut off my arm." His voice was hoarse. Lily wasn't sure if it was from disuse or infection.

"Can you wait a while to eat? I want to get a look at your wound and change your dressing."

"Can I have the tea? I'm dying of thirst, but I'm not hungry at all."

She went to the supply cart and picked up fresh dressings, alcohol, a scalpel and a basin. This didn't look good at all, and she'd have to find out who was the sluggard on staff who allowed patients to go without dressing changes.

It took a little time to peel away the layers of cotton. The closer she got to the wound itself, the more intense the stench became. At the last layer, she stopped. The bandage and cotton wool was stuck to the skin all around. It would have been understandable had it adhered to the suture line. But to stick all around was peculiar. She pulled, ever so gently. There seemed to be some sort of salve that had been smeared all over his stump and shoulder. When she pulled at the cotton wool, he flinched and drew away, but didn't cry out.

"Tell me, Corporal. Did the nurse use something on your shoulder when she changed your dressing?"

He nodded. "Jelly. Petroleum jelly. Great gobs of the stuff, all over."

"Well, I need to clean your shoulder very well. It may hurt. Are you up to it?"

Crownover looked at her, really for the first time. "I guess. Will the doctor give me something after?"

"Does he usually?"

"Sometimes."

"Let's get this changed first. Then we'll see if you need something for pain, all right?"

He nodded.

Lily went to the stove and retrieved the kettle. She poured some into the basin, and added alcohol. She used a linen square to wet the remaining bandages, then peeled them off.

The skin underneath was swollen, tightly stretched. She wiped it with a cloth, and heard the tell-tale crackle. The amputation site had a peculiar gray-green pus oozing between the sutures. No doubt about it. Gas gangrene, caused by some slaternly nurse who was apparently more interested in her leisure time than caring for her patient.

The standard treatment in field hospitals was amputation. There wasn't much left to amputate here, and the infection had gone up into his shoulder. Some hospitals would just push this man aside and wait for him to die. Lily wasn't having it.

The Orderly returned to collect the lunch trays.

"Orderly. Is there any meat hanging in the kitchen?"

He looked puzzled. "Yes, miss. Why?"

"Are there any maggots on it? Have the flies blown it yet?"

He leaned in. "We're not supposed to talk about that, Miss."

"Orderly, I didn't ask you about sanitary conditions. Whenever meat hangs in a kitchen, there are flies around it. I need some green bottle maggots. Are there any in the kitchen?"

"Yes, Miss. Shall I fetch you some?" He didn't know what the hell she wanted with maggots, and he wasn't about to argue with her.

"No. Take me to the kitchen. I need to make sure I get the right kind and size."

She followed him out the tent flap, and across the tent flap to the cook tent. She could hear the men still at their afternoon meal inside. Lunch was the last thing she was interested in. She needed the kitchen.

The kitchen was in full swing, with cooks and their helpers running from pot to pan, getting everything ready for the next meal. The Orderly leaned inside. "Hey, Stevens. Nurse wants to talk to you."

A tall, burly man wearing a stained apron came to the doorway. "What can I do for you, Nurse?" He leered at her.

"I need some maggots."

He spat into the dirt. "What kind of kitchen do you think I keep? My kitchen is clean."

"Listen, Stevens. I've got a man with gangrene,

and nothing left to amputate. There's a chance some good, fat maggots can clean out the infection. I know you don't have access to ice boxes here, and you will have meat hanging, waiting to be cut. Meaning there will be maggots. So, Mr. Stevens, take me to your maggots."

He didn't believe it. But he wasn't going to argue with this little woman. Chee-rist, she was as bad as his Da's rat terrier.

Stevens led her behind the cook tent, where a drawn and dressed sheep hung from a gamboling stick. Flies were thick around the head. This was exactly what she wanted.

"Get me a cup and a spoon, please."

Stevens rushed to get her what she wanted. The sooner he got her out of his way the better. Besides, he intended for part of this freshly butchered mutton to be part of tomorrow's supper.

She used the back of the spoon to scrape newly hatched maggots from the mouth of the sheep carcass, letting them fall into the metal cup. She took more than she needed, in case some didn't survive. A napkin from the officer's mess served as a cover lest any crawl out on her way back to the ward.

Lily grabbed the orderly, who had been watching open-mouthed. "Stay with me. I'll need your help."

"Yes, Nurse."

She thought it was time she introduced herself. "I'm Lily Barnett."

"Glad to know you, Nurse. I'm Robert Scott. The boys call me Scotty."

"Happy to know you, Scotty. Do you know what we are going to do?"

He shook his head.

"Crownover has gas gangrene. Generally, the doctor could amputate to eliminate the spread of the infection. Crownover has already had his arm amputated; there isn't much left to cut off. So I'm going to scrub it and make some incisions to get the pus out."

"If you don't mind me asking, what are the maggots for?"

"After he's scrubbed and scored, I apply the maggots to the incisions. They eat up the infected tissue, and keep the infection from spreading. "

He looked ready to puke. "Doesn't it hurt?"

"Apparently not. When someone has gangrene, there's usually no pain. That's why it's so dangerous."

"Then why is Crownover hurting all the time?"

"Because the nerves in his arm are screaming at him from the surgery. Some doctors back home are trying to find some help for it. Meanwhile, the best we can offer is some Morphia."

Back in the hospital tent, Lily went right to her patient and set to work. She used a series of cloths to scrub the affected area and to remove any last traces of petroleum jelly. The more she scrubbed, the stronger the stench. Poor Scotty looked ready to either pass out or throw up. Fortunately, Crownover was oblivious to any sensation in the gangrenous area. His previous pain had been from where the dressing had stuck fast to the incision.

She handed the basin of soapy water to Scotty, with instructions to empty then refill it, then picked up a sterile scalpel. She carefully made incisions of various depths over the infected area, to more easily access the pusy tissue, then began to scrub again.

Once she had thoroughly excavated the gangrenous tissue, she told Scotty to fetch her the maggots. He curled his lip as he picked up the cup gingerly, with only his fingertips. She laid back the linen covering, careful to tap any stray larvae back into the receptacle.

Lily used the tip of her scalpel to lift out the maggots and place them in the wound. She arranged them in the cuts she had made, as if she was planting little fly seeds. Finally, when she was finished, she placed a single layer of gauze over the area.

"Corporal, I'll try to get you something to help you sleep. You should start feeling better in a few days. Don't let the treatment get to you. They're really necessary, and we've used this in my hospital in Baltimore with great success."

She began to gather up the soiled dressings and passed them to Scotty. "Get rid of those dressings, please, then you can go ahead and finish collecting the lunch trays. And Scotty," He looked into her eyes. "Thank you. You did a fine job today."

Suddenly, the orderly seemed taller, more a man than a teenager now. "Thank *you*, Nurse Barnett." He went about his chores with a new found sense of purpose.

He was leaving the ward when Lily called after him. "Scotty, see if you can find Captain Stewart, ask him to see me here, please."

Lily was changing the linens on Private Howland's bed, while he sat in the chair nearby. He told her this was the first time he had been allowed out of bed since his amputation three days ago. Lily knew strict bed rest after an amputation was the theory some medical professionals followed. Lily prefered her father's method, encouraging circulation to the affected limb to stimulate healing.

"What the hell do you think you're doing, Nurse Barnett?" Sister Myers' voice carried across the post operative ward like a mortar shell.

"I'm changing Private Howland's bed. His linens didn't appear to have been changed today."

The nursing sister strode the length of the ward and stood at the foot of Crownover's bed. "And what have you done to this man? Who gave you permission to change his dressing?"

"Sister, you told me to look after these men. I am. Did you know..."

"Ladies, ladies, what's going on?" Galen Stewart walked up behind Sister Myers.

"Doctor, Nurse Barnett has allowed Private Howland out of bed only three days after his surgery. And just look what she's done to Corporal Crownover!"

He still stood behind the sister, and smiled over her head at Lily. "Nurse Barnett, Scotty said you wanted to see me?"

"Yes, Doctor. I had to debride Corporal Crownover's gangrenous shoulder, and, for want of anything better, applied maggot therapy. As to Private Howland, his linens were soiled, so I changed his bed.

I got him out of bed, because there's nothing wrong with his legs or his back."

"Maggots?!" Sister Myers' face was a peculiar shade of puce. "How dare you put fly larvae on a patient."

Stewart stopped her. "Sister, aren't you familiar with using maggots to treat gangrene?"

She sputtered. "Certainly not, Doctor. Any patient with gangrene undergoes amputation."

"Un-huh. And what if there wasn't anything to amputate? What if there isn't any place to amputate? Like on the chest or the belly? I've used this treatment myself, and it's quite effective."

"Yes, Doctor." Myers was staring at her shoes by now.

"Now, Sister. I have a question. Why was Corporal Howland's condition not discovered sooner?"

"Well...well...I..."

"Nurse Barnett, tell me please about the condition in which you found the patient?"

"His dressing had been applied with a thick coating of petroleum jelly, then the entire shoulder covered with cotton wool and a heavy gauze dressing. It makes a perfect breeding ground for anaerobic bacterial infection. His dressing had not been changed recently, until I did it around noon. He thought it was applied yesterday, but he wasn't sure in his state."

"Sister, have you any explanation?"

"Doctor, I only have three nurses to cover this ward and surgery."

"Sister, that is no excuse. You only have eight patients. If you had lent a hand yourself, that's two patients per nurse. Quite manageable. Allowing for shifts, even four patients per nurse is below average. You don't mention your orderlies or nursing assistants. There is no excuse."

"No, Doctor. But in my defense, it has always been my practice to apply a layer of petroleum jelly, mixed with some sulfur, to new amputations."

"New amputations?" Galen was fairly roaring now. "You mean you put that dressing on Crownover three days ago, and it hasn't been changed since?"

Myers didn't answer. Instead, she stormed off, stomping through mud as she walked away.

Galen leaned toward Lily. "Thank you. If not for you, this boy would have died. He's still not out of the woods. Tell me, do you think you could handle Myers' job?"

She shook her head. "No, Galen. I'm only a few months out of school. There's no way I have the age or experience to supervise other nurses."

"Understood. But in the operating room, I want you to be in charge. You learned more from your father than most doctors know coming out of medical school. I don't know more than two or three would have thought to apply maggots. By the way, where did you get them?"

"From the mutton that's slated for tomorrow's supper. I wouldn't advise eating it any way but stewed."

Chapter Four

It was just after dawn when they heard the first cannon barrage. The entire staff was out of their bunks, dressed and assembled for duty within ten minutes. Lily learned in nursing school to always keep her chemise and corset on when she slept, so that dressing took minutes rather than hours. It appeared her sister nurses felt the same, as they beat many of the men outside.

Lily was already getting on well with the three other nurses in her tent. Verna Broadwell was Lily's age, engaged to a soldier. She had been a nurse in London before the war started. Eliza Clevenger was more experienced, from Canada. Like Lily, she did her training in a hospital nursing system after she was turned away from Medical school. Molly Duling, on the other hand, had been a field nurse during the Boer War. By rights she should be the ward sister, and Elora Myers should be mopping floors.

Galen was already scrubbing for surgery when she got to his side. She and Molly scrubbed, while the other two waited to assist with gowning.

"Ladies, scrub very well, and use a carbolic solution in your hands. Our order for surgical gloves hasn't arrived yet. There's a basin already set up."

As Verna and Eliza tied their gowns, Galen told them, "This is a big push today. Lots of casualties. There are two men on the tables right now, waiting for us. We have a long day ahead of us."

Major Dennison joined them and scrubbed in. Behind him was Sister Myers.

"Major, will Sister Myers be in theater today?"

"Yes, Captain. Why?"

"Major, am I chief surgeon?"

Dennison laughed. "Well, right now you're the only surgeon. I'm the anesthesiologist here. But I always found Sister to be competent."

"She may be, Major. But I worked with Nurse Barnett in Baltimore, and find her more than competent. I want her to be surgical charge nurse."

Myers was sputtering. Dennison ignored her. "Fine by me." He turned to Lily. "What's this I hear about you tending a patient with gangrene on your first day?"

She was in the middle of getting her mask tied. "Yes sir. I've done it before, when I worked with my father."

Galen saved Dennison the trouble of asking. "Her father was Joseph Barnett, of Hopkins. Lily started assisting him when she was around fourteen or so."

"Excellent. Now, ladies and gentlemen, we have patients waiting. Sister, will you take charge of triage?" It wasn't really a question, merely a veiled order.

"Yes, Major. As you wish." Myers' disapproval was obvious, but she went out to supervise the staff deciding which of the shortly arriving wounded would reach surgery first.

Their first patient was waiting for them. This one seemed simple. He apparently had been caught in barbed wire and needed to have his face and chest sutured back together. Galen checked the other patient, who had been deemed even less urgent.

This second, "less urgent" patient had a suppurating wound on his belly. He seemed to have ripped the flesh open several days ago, and not treated.

"Major Dennison, I believe this man is more urgent. Will you start the anesthesia, please? We will see to the other gentleman next."

Dennison had administered an injection of atropine and morphia about half an hour ago, to calm both patients. It would keep them calm, if not stuporous, while awaiting surgery. Now, he started a slow drip of ether over a cloth cone. In a few minutes, he would change cones and switch to chloroform.

Once the patient was under, Galen began by first cleaning, then debriding the wound. He managed to cut away the infection and repair most of the damage.

"He was lucky." Galen spoke to no one in particular. "As bad as this was, the damage was only superficial."

Lily was applying a wet-to-dry dressing. She looked up from her work. "Superficial. But enough to kill him."

She pulled off her apron in preparation for their next procedure. She called, "Molly, bring the basins and clean aprons, please."

Molly Duling and Eliza Clevenger carried in the three compartment basin, already filled with hot water for washing and rinsing, and a third with carbolic solution. "I'm sorry, Lily. There aren't any more clean aprons. We've looked all over, and all we can find are the ones waiting to be washed."

Oh, this was too much. "Dr. Stewart, can you manage with Nurse Clevenger, while I try to remedy this situation? I suggest you change aprons with Major Dennison, as his hasn't been soiled yet."

She and Molly Duling stormed from the tent. Lily spotted Sister Myers, staring into the distance, waiting for the ambulances.

"Sister Myers! Where are the sterile aprons?"

"Where they always are. On the shelves in the scrub room."

Lily didn't have time to argue. "Molly, where are excess linens kept?"

"In the supply tent."

"Let's go."

They ran to the supply tent, near the mess tent. Inside, Molly lit the kerosene lamp. Molly looked around. "Bloody hell. The kitchen aprons are all clean, and what we need for surgery are in the laundry still."

Lily started grabbing an armload of aprons. "Run and get as many people as you can who have an iron. We don't have time to put these in the sterilizer. Get them ironed with a hot iron. That should kill any wayward germs. Best get to the kitchen to work. There isn't enough room on the little stove we have. And make sure they're wrapped in a sheet before they're brought back across the compound."

She hurried back to the operating theater, where Galen was just beginning to clean the wounds on the young man's face. She put the six clean aprons on the table by the door.

"I found our aprons in the supply shed. These will do for less serious cases. Molly is seeing the rest get sterilized, and will keep us supplied during the day." She didn't give him the chance to answer, but plunged her hands into the wash basin, so she could return to her surgical duties.

Lily stepped in to relieve Verna, so she and an orderly could remove their previous patient to the ward.

They were finishing up. Major Dennison left his position at the patient's head to check on any incoming patients.

Lily leaned toward Galen. "Who is in charge of the laundry, of seeing it gets done, and that it gets sterilized?"

"Elora Myers. Why?"

"And who dressed Crownover's amputation?"

"Elora Myers."

"Galen, what do you know about her?" She prepared a dressing for the boy's face.

"Nothing, really. She was assigned ward sister the day I arrived."

"By Major Dennison?"

He shook his head. "No. By the commanding officer of this district. We were setting up the hospital when the truck carrying the four nurses came in. General Southard pointed at Myers and told her she was the new ward sister. That was it."

"Do you know anything about the other nurses?"

"Just that they are trained nurses."

"Molly Duling served with the Army Medical Corps during the Boer War. She's far more qualified than Elora Myers. Can you demote Myers, and promote Molly?"

He pulled his apron off and started scrubbing his hands again. "I'd have to transfer her out. There's no way she could work here after being demoted."

Scotty came in with another orderly to remove the patient. Eliza whisked off the sheet from the surgical table and quickly replaced it with another.

Dennison held back the tent flap so the orderlies could bring in the next patient. This one had a long open cut on his arm.

Lily could hear ambulances arriving, and could hear the cries of the wounded outside.

"Galen, do you think this is the most seriously injured patient?"

"No, I don't. "

He turned to Dennison. "Major, will you check the triage, please. I think there is a problem outside."

Dennison walked out, then right back in. He went to Galen and began a whispered conversation.

Galen went to the other door. He called, "Nurse Clevenger!" Eliza ran to him. "Nurse, I want you to take over triage from Sister Myers. She's being relieved of duty."

Eliza dashed to take over her new post.

Dennison returned, with Elora Myers following him. Her face was a mask of hatred and contempt. She aimed herself at Galen.

"Captain, I must protest..."

"And I must protest, *Sister*." He emphasized the last word, his implication clear. "You've been responsible for everything that happened here, and you are obviously incompetent. You will no longer be permitted in my theater, nor in my ward. I will be asking Major Dennison to have you sent back to London on the first transport."

"Well I...But...How..."

"Now, get out of here, and return to your quarters until you are needed to assist in the kitchen with butchery duties."

Myers stormed out of the theater, almost knocking Scotty over as he brought in the next patient.

"Major, we have too many wounded for you to confine yourself to anesthesia. Scrub in, get this patient under, then show Nurse Duling what to do. Then start the next patient and hand off to Nurse Duling. And as soon as we're done, cable headquarters we are dreadfully understaffed."

Dennison did as he was told. Stewart was in charge in the operating theater. The Major may be a doctor, but he was a much better administrator if he was allowed to do his job. He didn't like makindecisions about the patients' care, and left everything up to his staff.

Molly Duling and Verna Broadwell did as they were told. They took direction from Major Dennison easily. Dennison called for Eliza to send in their next patient, and to have the first, with the simple laceration removed to be treated later.

Lily rushed to get a sterile surgical tray to Dennison's table, then replaced Galen's. She grabbed Scotty, as he passed through, to find her two of the smartest nursing assistants to handle the instruments for the doctors. Meanwhile, she prepared herself to manage everything else.

The first two patients Nurse Clevenger provided were belly wounds. The doctors scrubbed, Lily helped them with masks and aprons, then gave the two aides a quick lesson in surgical nursing.

*****

Fifty two hours after they started, the last patient was recovering. Seven gastric end-to-end anastomoses, twenty four amputations, some double, one triple. Two men lost eyes, and seventeen died awaiting treatment.

The doctors and nurses had taken turns catching thirty minutes to an hour sleep twice during their long stint. Dennison agreed with Stewart they couldn't go on like this. The Battle of the Marne had shown them how grossly understaffed and under equipped they were.

The nursing assistants were set to minding the post-surgical patients, so the nurses and doctors could get some much needed sleep.

Five hours later, orderlies were running through the camp, rousing Galen, Lily and Molly. An ambulance had arrived, bearing a survivor rescued from No Man's Land.

Lily stretched, yawned, and pulled on a clean dress. She hurried across the compound, meeting Galen at the door to the scrub room. He handed her a mug of black coffee.

"It tastes horrible, but at least it's hot."

She took a sip, then a long swallow. "It's no worse than what my brother Josey calls coffee." She drained the cup. "So, Doctor, what have we?"

"A soldier was found buried under the dead. No injuries other than deep lacerations behind the knees. It appears his legs were sliced open by one of his mate's bayonets."

"And he wasn't able to get up to get back to his line."

"I'm pretty sure his tendons are severed."

She set her cup aside and started to scrub in the basin Molly had set out. "Do you think they can be reconnected?"

"The army's standard procedure is to recommend amputation."

She shook her head. "Awful thing, to leave a man that young with no legs, especially after being trapped under all those corpses."

He came behind her and started to scrub. "I know. That's why we are going to try to reattach the tendons. At least we don't have fifty other casualties waiting their turn."

They worked together for three hours on the young man. He was impressed at Molly Duling's skill. She could suture and tie as well as most surgeons, and followed direction to the letter. She asked appropriate questions, and knew the appropriate answers to Galen's questions.

Lily was putting on the final dressings when Galen asked Molly, "Nurse Duling, how would you feel about being made ward sister?"

She was just a little surprised. "What about Sister Myers?"

"She'll be headed home on the first transport."

"Then, yes sir, I'd like that just fine."

Chapter Five

For a little over a month, they struggled along with two surgeons and four trained nurses. Everyone was exhausted, unable to tell one day from the next. But they kept more than the average number of their patients alive, getting some back to their units, and some back home to their families. Since the exit of Sister Elora Myers, their survival rate had increased exponentially.

Lily slogged her way through the boot sucking mud of the compound. It had rained for five days straight, and this was the first break all week. The mud was ankle deep, with large puddles and occasional surprises left by the camp's mules.

Dr. Wismer was coming toward her, on the same direct path. Wismer was one of the new physicians who arrived today from St. Barts in London. It didn't seem to matter that she carried trays of surgical instruments to be sterilized. He expected her to step out of his way.

They met almost face to face and stopped dead. Lily said, "Excuse me, Lieutenant Wismer."

"Nurse Barnett." His voice was cold. "Are you going to move?"

"A gentleman would stand aside."

He thought he'd be funny. "But I'm not a gentleman. I'm a doctor." He smiled beneath the heavy mustache that looked as if it came from a kid's disguise kit.

"Be that as it may, Lieutenant, I have my hands full, and am going about my duties."

He took a half step aside, then walked forward at great speed. He purposely jammed his shoulder into hers.

Lily tried hard to keep her balance. With her boots stuck firmly in the mire, she had nowhere to go but down.

She sprawled on her side, her precious instruments strewn in every direction. She tried to gather herself to get up. When she turned her head, she came nose to knee with a pair of puttees.

"Nurse Barnett, is there a reason you are lying in the mud?" It was obvious Galen was trying hard not to laugh. He held his hand down to her.

She grasped his hand with hers, and he took hold of her wrist with the other hand and hauled her to her feet.

"Yes, Dr. Stewart, there's a reason I was in the mud." She picked up one of the trays and started retrieving instruments.

"And what was the reason? I've never known you to be clumsy."

"I was in the mud because your newest doctor is an abusive ass."

"Oh, Wismer again? I know he's been rude, and I've spoken to him about it."

"He's gone too far this time. He saw me walking, carrying trays of instruments, purposely rammed into me, and knocked me into the mud. You want to help me pick this mess up?"

"I have something to take care of." He looked over the top of her head. "Private Scott! Over here please. Help Nurse Barnett pick this mess up, and see everything gets washed again."

Before Lily could say anything, Stewart strode off, in the same direction taken by Dr. Wismer. Galen found his quarry in the officers' mess.

The tall American got a cup of tea at the end of the tent, then headed to Wismer's table. He stood beside him, waiting. Finally, Galen had to clear his throat to get the younger man's attention.

Wismer looked up, then jumped to his feet when he realized he was being addressed by a superior. "Good day, Captain."

"Lieutenant. I'd like a word with you."

"Certainly, sir. Just let me finish my meal..."

"No, Lieutenant. Now."

"Very well, Captain Stewart. May I sit?"

"No, Lieutenant, you may not. What I have to say won't take long. I just saw Nurse Barnett."

"Oh. The other American." The disdain in his voice was obvious.

"Yes, Lieutenant. The 'other American'. Who holds the same rank as you, and has been in the army longer than you, and therefore outranks you. If you physically abuse any female on this base, you will answer to me, and it will not be pleasant."

He snorted derisively. "Just because Barnett is your personal piece of fluff doesn't mean the rest..."

He never got the chance to finish. Galen's fist connected with Wismer's mouth.

Wismer was still spitting blood when Galen left the mess tent.

*****

Lily was in the scrub room, preparing to begin sterilizing the newly washed instruments. She heard the door open and looked up.

"Dr. Stewart! What happened?" Lily thought he looked ready to bite the head off a live snake.

He grabbed a stool and pulled it next to the table where Lily was working. "Not much. But you won't have any more trouble out of Wismer."

He reached to take his cap off. That's when Lily noticed his knuckles, with cuts from the man's teeth. She grabbed his hand. "Oh, Galen. What did you do?"

"I didn't like what he said. So I made him eat his words."

"Oh, you didn't. Yes, I bet you did. You'll get in trouble, won't you?"

"I doubt it. He wasn't raised that way. He won't tattle to Dennison. I have to tell you, he accused us of having an affair."

She blushed up to her hairline, her white hair accentuating it even more. She looked down at his boots. "I wish you hadn't."

He slipped his other arm around her waist and pulled her to him. He lifted her chin and kissed her. Not the kiss she had received when she arrived. That had hard and fast. He took his time, exploring her gently, encouraging her to join in his pleasure.

Lily stepped in closer, winding her arms around his neck. She pressed against him, conscious of his excitement.

Galen drew back, still holding Lily in his arms. They were both breathing heavily by now. He rested his forehead on hers. "I shouldn't have done that."

She tried to push away, but he held her fast. She didn't object. "I shouldn't have either. So, what do we do now?"

He kissed her forehead. "I don't know."

They heard voices outside the tent, and they broke apart. Lily took his hand again. "Let me clean this up. He might have had rabies under that brush."

She took his abused hand in hers and started washing his injury with the hot water and carbolic solution used to rinse the instruments. "Did anyone see you punch him?"

"Only two of the other doctors, and three of the nurses."

"Jeez, Galen, you really do know how to get yourself into a mess. You're worse than Raymond ever was."

He kissed her cheek. "I like it when you scold me."

She poured a liberal dose of iodine over his cuts, causing him to draw in a sharp breath.

"Jesus, Lily. You should warn a fellow before you do something like that."

She only laughed, and wrapped his hand in a length of gauze.

Galen had a mind to kiss her again, and from the look on her face as she gazed up into his eyes, she wouldn't have minded a bit. Before he could make contact, Scotty opened the door.

"Captain Stewart, Major wants to see you, sharpish he says."

Lily turned away and busied herself again with the sterilizing. Only loud enough for Galen to hear, she sang, "Galen's in trouble. Galen's in trouble," as she used to when her brothers were little.

Had they been alone, he would have slapped her behind. As it was, he donned his cap and whispered, "I'll see to you later."

"I hope so," she whispered in return as he headed toward the door.

*****

"Captain Stewart, come in, come in." Dennison sat behind his small desk, a stack of papers in front of him.

Galen stepped inside, removed his hat and tucked it under his arm. "You sent for me, Sir?"

"I'll get right to the point, Captain. Lieutenant Wismer was in to see me a little while ago. He made certain accusations against you, which I feel I must address."

"Major, I…"

"Sit down, Captain." Galen sat. "Wismer said you struck him."

"Yes, Sir. I did." There, that was out in the open. No sense trying to make excuses.

"Care to tell me why?"

"Because he purposely knocked down one of our nurses who was in the performance of her duties. I called him on it, and he not only became obscene, he sullied my personal honor, and that of our nurse. My choice was to punch him or shoot him, and I found myself without a pistol."

Dennison was trying very hard not to laugh. "About time somebody knocked that poppinjay's dick in the dirt."

Galen gave up trying to maintain military bearing. He howled. Dennison joined him. Still laughing, Dennison reached into a file drawer behind him and took out a bottle and a pair of heavy bottomed glasses. "Captain, I can't tell you how much I dislike that nasty twit. He's a snitch, the worst kind. I knew it was only a matter of time before someone set him back on his heels. I'm just sorry it had to be you."

Galen accepted the glass, and took a sip. "Excellent Scotch, Sir." He took another sip. "Why are you sorry it was me?"

"Because I need to reprimand you." Dennison drained his glass in one long drink. "So, consider yourself reprimanded." He poured himself another drink, and offered the bottle to Galen. He refused. "Now, get out of here and get back to work. And remember, if you need to punch him again, make sure there are no witnesses."

"Yes sir. Thank you, sir."

"Oh, and Captain?"

"Yes, Sir?"

"If you are going to snog the nurses, make sure they wipe their face powder off first. Your uniform jacket looks like you were in the bakery."

"Yes, Sir."

*****

Galen made a beeline back to the scrub room. He had to see Lily. When he opened the door, he stopped short when he saw she wasn't alone. Molly was helping her sterilize the instruments. He decided he could be discreet.

"Good afternoon, ladies."

Lily started, hoping she didn't blush this time. Molly answered for both of them. "Good afternoon, Dr. Stewart."

Lily finally gathered enough courage to speak. "Did you see Major Dennison?"

He leaned his hip on the table beside where she was dropping instruments into a pot of boiling water. "Yes, one of Major Dennison's concerns was that nurses are wearing facial powder. He brought up that it has a tendency to rub off, and may be unsanitary. So, Sister Duling, would you ask your nurses to please refrain from wearing powder whenever they are on duty?"

It was then Lily noticed the smudge on Galen's jacket. This time she knew she blushed. Oh crap, Molly was looking right at her.

"Nurse Barnett, you've had enough I think, what with that run in with the looney lieutenant earlier, and now standing over a boiling pot. Why doesn't Captain

Stewart escort you back to your quarters so you can have a rest? Remember, you have ward duty tonight."

"I do?" She was surprised. Last time she checked the roster, she was scheduled for the evening shift.

"Yes, I'm quite sure. Ask Captain Stewart. He's on the same shift."

"Yes, of course, Nurse Barnett. Remember, I remarked to you earlier how we'd managed to draw the same rotation for the ward. Come on. I'll escort you to your quarters, then I'll get some rest myself."

They walked out of the scrub room together, careful not to touch. If he put his hands on her, he was afraid he might utterly embarrass them both, right here in the middle of camp.

When they reached the nurses' quarters she looked inside. Good, it was empty. She spotted a parcel wrapped in brown paper and tied with twine on her bunk. "Galen, look. A package from home. Want to help me open it?"

He grabbed two folding camp stools from inside the tent and set them just outside the door, careful not to put them too close to the ever present mud puddles. "Let's sit out here, so no one gets the wrong idea."

"You mean the same idea I've had for the last hour?"

"Exactly."

She grabbed the package and sat down. Galen pulled a penknife from his pocket and sliced the twine. Before she tackled the brown paper, she reached in her pocket and pulled out her handkerchief. "Here. Wipe the powder off your jacket." She looked at the address. "It's from

Raymond." She worked at getting the paper open. "By the way, it's not really powder. We use cornstarch. It soaks up the sweat. But I'll pass the word."

The paper was off. Now she had a tin box, a bit larger than a cigar box. Under the tin was a book. "*The Lone Star Ranger* by Zane Gray. Maybe the patients will enjoy reading it. She fiddled with the tin, then handed it over to Galen. "I can't open the fool thing. Maybe you can."

He turned the tin on its side, and began sliding the blade of his knife under the lid. "What do you think he sent? It rattles."

She snorted. "Knowing Raymond, it's shiny rocks."

At last, the lid began to shift. It slid upwards, and Lily reached forward to hold the bottom, lest the contents spill.

The lid came off with a *POP*, and the fragrance of deep, rich fudge wafted out. Without looking, Galen said, "Is that what I think it is?"

She looked inside. "I don't know. Do you think it's from Berger's?"

He nodded. She reached in and took out one round shortbread, with a heavy, thick smear of fudge ganache on top.

She held the cookies out, offering him one. Rather than take the sweet from her, he held her hand in his, and nibbled the cookie around her fingers. It was the most sensual thing she had ever experienced. Not that she had experienced that many. In nursing school, some of the doctors and patients had tried to flirt with her, one or two had tried to steal a kiss. But this, this simple act of the feel of his lips around a cookie was driving her absolutely mad. She wanted to rootch in her chair, to squeeze her thighs together to try and make this feeling last, or to make it stop. She didn't know which.

When he released her, Galen was in much the same state. He shifted slightly on the camp stool, trying to hide his erection behind his uniform tunic.

Lily looked at the hand holding the cookie. There was still a piece left. She took a small bite, then held it out to Galen again. He shook his head. He didn't dare. He stood up, tugging at his jacket. "I'll see you tonight. He started to walk away, then stopped. "And Lily, bring the cookies."

*****

That night they barely had time to talk. They lost two patients, including one who had to be taken back into surgery with intestinal bleeding.

By the time they were relieved by Dr. Wismer and Adele Beemer, the two were exhausted. Wismer gave Galen a wide berth when they passed.

As Lily was briefing Nurse Beemer about the night's event, Adele asked, "Did Dr. Stewart really give Wismer that fat lip?"

Lily tried hard not to giggle. She nodded.

"And was it really because Wismer said something ugly about you?"

Best to squelch any gossip before it got started. "It started when he knocked me into the mud."

"Oh." She seemed disappointed at first. "Wait. He hit you and knocked you into the mud?"

"I was carrying trays of washed instruments. He purposely rammed me with his shoulder when I couldn't step aside. Dr. Stewart found me, and went to 'have a talk' with him."

This time Adelle giggled. "Good enough for him."

Lily finished her briefing, and went to gather her things to leave. Her tin of Berger's was gone. She looked around, and spotted Wismer leaning against a tent pole holding it, stuffing one of the cookies into his mouth.

Lily stormed across the tent and snatched the tin from his hands. "Those are mine, Lieutenant. MINE! I will thank you not to touch my property again."

He swallowed what he had in his mouth. He tried to sneer, but his mouth wouldn't cooperate. "What's the problem? Aren't I as good as your captain?"

She didn't care what the gossips made of it. "No. And you never will be."

"Maybe you and your other whores should hang a red light in front of your tent to advertise your 'cookies'."

This time, Lily didn't care what happened. She used her training from her first week at St Joseph's, when they were taught to fend off amorous advances. She brought her knee up, swift and hard, into his unprotected groin.

*****

When Adele's shift was finished, she was sent to awaken Lily. "Major Dennison wants to see you."

"Lovely. Did the little weasel run and tattle again?" She rolled out of bed and started getting dressed.

"Yeah. But I told Dennison what really happened. He still needs to talk to you. You know, procedure."

Adele helped Lily pin her apron in place. "You want me to come with you? Wismer is still in his office."

" I don't expect anything to happen, but I'd feel better having a witness."

The sun was getting low as they got to Dennison's office. The Major sat behind his desk, waiting. He didn't look happy. Wismer sat at attention against the wall, his hands on his knees.

"Sister Barnett, come in, please. Would you like Nurse Beemer to remain?"

"Yes, Major, if you please."

"Very well." He shifted some papers, pretending to look for something. "Lieutenant Wismer told me you assaulted him. Is that true?"

"Yes, Major."

"And what exactly brought on the assault?"

"When Captain Stewart and I were being relieved this morning..."

Wismer snorted. "I bet you were relieved during the night already."

Dennison turned on him. "Wismer! I told you to sit quietly. I will deal with you later." He turned back to Lily. "Go ahead, Sister."

"As I was saying, when Nurse Beemer and Dr. Wismer came in to relieve us, I was relating relevant information to Nurse Beemer, then went to gather my personal things to leave. I had received a package from home, a book and some cookies. I realized the cookies were gone. I saw Dr. Wismer holding the tin, eating my cookies. Had he asked, I would have shared. But he took all of them. I took them back. Then Lieutenant Wismer accused me and all the other nurses of being whores, and suggested we should hang a red lantern in front of our tent. That was when I kneed him in the groin."

Dennison was staring at his desk, trying hard not to laugh out loud. "Thank you, Sister."

"Will that be all, Major?"

"No, Sister. I'd like you and Nurse Beemer to remain." He directed his attention to Wismer. "Lieutenant Wismer!"

Wismer stood and snapped to attention. "Yes, Sir."

Dennison pulled a paper from his desk drawer. "Lieutenant, you are a reasonably competent doctor. You're young, and have a lot to learn. One of the first things a doctor should learn is that nurses are the life's blood of a hospital. They are far more compassionate than we doctors, have skills we don't possess, and some of them are a damned sight smarter."

"But Major, they're women." He whined like a three year old.

"Of course they're women. Because most men couldn't do what they do." He looked at Lily and Adele and nodded. "Now, Lieutenant, I'm going to transfer you to an ambulance unit. You will no longer have to contend with women, and will no longer have to fear you are being emasculated because a mere female demands respect. Although if you don't change your attitude, you'll have more to fear from your comrades and patients than a Hun's bullet."

Chapter Six

July 1, 1917

Sister Lily Barnett sat on her bunk, waiting for her hair to dry. She and her nurses were in Flanders now, a small town called Poperinge. The generals were calling for a big push soon. Lily and her nurses were setting up inside a local church.

A year ago, Major Dennison and Molly had been victims of a gas attack. It had left Molly blind, and the Major had died choking his lungs up. Molly was in a hospital in Sheffield, receiving treatment.

Three months after Lily's encounter with Wismer, Galen had been promoted to Major, and had transferred to another unit. They wrote to each other as often as they could, but their time together was limited. They had yet to really explore their feelings for each other.

Yesterday's mail call brought another letter. Galen was being reassigned to Poperinge. He was scheduled to assume command tomorrow, but he arrived today, and wanted Lily to meet him at the cafe off the town square. It was Saturday, and she already had a pass.

She would go to town with Alyce Roddy, then Alyce would go elsewhere.

Nurse Roddy was Scots. She'd trained with a rural physician, and was as skilled as many doctors. Her lack of formal education would have kept her out of most nursing programs, more's the pity. Best of all, she was understanding.

Since coming to Europe, Lily had eschewed the fashionable corsets in favor of the more comfortable brassiere and knickers. By now, she was so thin, there was hardly anything to hold up, just to keep them out of the way.

Today she was seeing Galen for the first time in more than a year. Today she would wear her corset and her good dress. She had hardly worn it at all since buying it in France. She hoped it still fit.

Oh, she hoped he liked her hair. After trying to wash it in freezing cold water last December, she had convinced Alyce to cut it off above her shoulders. She'd been surprised when it dried curly. Today she had washed it then added a drop of bluing to the rinse water to make it shine. While it dried, she bathed, and put on her chemise.

In Poperinge, Lily was granted private quarters as Sister. It was a rare privilege, and one of which she took full advantage. She laid down on the bed and reread Galen's letter.

She heard Alyce's knock at the door. Lily stuffed the letter into her purse and let her in. "You're just in time. Lace me up, will you?"

Lily stepped into her corset, while Alyce fiddled with the laces. "Lord have mercy. When was the last time you wore this? They're all tangled."

"We were still in France. I bought my first brassiere there, and I've worn them ever since."

"They're wonderful, aren't they?" Alyce put her hands under her breasts and adjusted them comically. She continued to work on the laces, at last getting them in order to start to tighten. "This may be too big."

"I don't care. Snug it up good and tight."

In the end, the corset still fit, and Alyce managed to draw the waist in fashionably narrow. Next came the narrow petticoat, and the corset cover, all in lavender. Alyce was impressed. "Where'd you find these?"

"Same place I found the dress. It matches, so I had to have it.

She helped her get into her dress. True enough, it was the same lavender as her underclothes, with wide, dark purple collar and lapels. Her hat was lavender, with purple dyed feathers, and she wore gray shoes to match her gray handbag and gloves.

"Now, you have everything?"

Lily nodded.

"What about...you know...what you talked about with Dr. Kent?" Dr. Byrd Kent was sent as Dennison's replacement. He was older, a career army doctor. He had served in the Boer War with Molly Duling, and had left part of his leg in Africa. He was a fine anesthetist, and could still work in surgery when the need arose. He made sure the nurses were supplied with what was euphemistically called "Dutch Caps". The rubber diaphragms were inserted by a doctor, and were left in place until the woman menstruated. They were illegal in England and the United States, but readily available on the Continent. Kent believed his nurses were more valuable working than home caring for children.

"Yes, I saw Dr. Kent. He was very understanding about it, and even gave me an overnight pass. He said he's ready for Dr. Stewart to take over command, too. He wants to retire, but is willing to stay on for anesthesia work, so long as they'll have him."

Alyce fastened her shawl about her shoulders, and handed Lily hers. They grabbed their bags and headed out toward town.

It was all Lily could do to stroll at a leisurely pace with her friend the few blocks toward the town square. Alyce would be going to the lace market while Lily went to meet Galen. Alyce chattered non-stop, nonsensically, all the way.

At long last, they were in sight of the town square. The sun was high overhead, the air heavy. It was too hot for all these clothes. But decorum decreed they wear a cape or shawl in public.

The cafe where they were to meet was on the far side from where the two women stood. Lily hugged Alyce, who wished her luck.

Lily fairly danced across the square, aiming for the tall, slim officer she saw sitting at one of the tables. She stopped when she reached the curb.

"Galen?" Her voice was breathy, tremulous.

He stood and turned toward her. There were several tables and chairs between them. He looked her up and down, approvingly. "Lily. You came."

She moved forward, weaving her way to him. When she stood in front of him she touched his mouth gently. "You grew a mustache." It was pencil thin, not at all like the brush sported by their earlier nemesis.

He smiled. "Do you like it?"

She grinned. "Depends on how it feels."

He kissed her cheek lightly.

"Ooh. It tickles."

He grinned wickedly. "Wait a while. We'll see how it feels elsewhere."

She blushed. It seemed that all she did around this man.

Galen ordered wine and some dish with shrimp for them. Not that she was interested in eating. She wanted, needed to be alone with him.

Would he think she was a slut, that she did this sort of thing with anybody?

He was making small talk, chatting about his duty station on the hospital ship, and his new assignment in command of Lily's unit.

She interrupted. "You know, Galen, I'm not really hungry."

He took a swallow of wine, and wiped his mouth. "Neither am I. I have a room in a hotel around the corner."

Lily picked up her wine glass and drained it. Galen gestured to the waiter and paid, then picked up the half filled wine bottle from the table.

He stood, and held out his hand. Lily took it and stood. She felt a frisson of excitement when they touched. He led her through the tables and out to the street, then around the corner to a narrow lane.

Lily knew they had to be careful. There could be serious repercussions for any fraternization between doctors and nurses, and between a superior officer and one under his command. They were off base, off duty, and she wasn't in uniform. They should be all right, so long as they didn't run into Dr. Wismer.

Galen was still holding her hand when they reached the hotel. Lily stopped before he opened the door. "Will they say anything if I go in with you?"

He smiled. "The concierge spends most of her time in the kitchen. She only comes out when someone calls her. Besides, I don't care. And I doubt anyone else does." He took her other hand in his. His voice was concerned. "Would you rather wait?"

She shook her head. "Galen, since the day you came to our house, when I had no hair, I've waited for this moment. I want this, I hope as much as you."

"Oh, darling girl." He strode through the door, and up the stairs, making Lily run to keep up.

"Galen! Slow down." She was breathless and giggling.

"I'll be slow later. Come on." As soon as they reached the second floor, he opened the door to his room, and swept her up into his arms. He kicked the door shut and leaned against it, cradling her against him as they kissed. She wrapped her arms around his neck and held on for dear life, not out of fear that he'd drop her, but because she didn't want it to end.

He carried her across the long, narrow room and stood her on her feet at the foot of the bed. He pulled the pin from her hat and tossed both on the dresser. He bent to kiss her neck, nibbling from her shoulder to her ear.

Lily was struggling to unfasten Galen's uniform jacket. Her trembling hands couldn't seem to manage the buckles on the Sam Brown belt or the buttons on his jacket. He took her hands in his and kissed each palm and wrist. "Here. Let me." His voice was husky with desire.

He made short work of his belt, tunic and blouse. Apparently in deference to the weather, Galen wasn't wearing any undershirt. Lily had never seen him without a shirt. He was almost painfully thin, but his arms and chest were muscled from the power needed to manipulate bone in the human body, his hands were gentle enough to stitch a blood vessel.

Lily undid the belt and dropped it on the floor. Her dress was held closed by three buttons. She released them, and Galen stepped closer and slipped his hands into the opening. He clasped her waist, his hands warming the silk and cotton. He whispered, "Are you sure?"

She put her hands against his bare chest. Rather than answer right away, she kissed a spot between her hands. "Oh, yes, yes."

The dress slipped from her shoulders and it pooled on the floor at her feet. He untied her petticoat and it followed. He tried to unbutton the corset cover, but his fingers couldn't manipulate the small buttons. Lily pushed his hands aside and tried to help, but was shaking so badly she couldn't manage either.

Galen grinned at her. "Oh, hell. I'll buy you another one." He grabbed the neckline of the thin cotton cover and ripped, sending six pearl buttons flying across the room.

He stared at her, never imagining her like this.

She was the picture of both innocence and seduction. He knew the corset and fancy underclothes had been to please him. But her modest pose, with her hands folded in front of her, protective of her most private area.

He asked again. "Lily, are you sure? We don't have to do this.?

Suddenly, she became even more shy. "If we don't, I'm afraid I shall explode." She looked into his eyes. "Galen, I've always wanted you. But I didn't know how, or why. Not until that night we walked the City. Then in the scrub room, after you defended my honor. That was when I first felt like this. I've been burning alone since Raymond sent those damned cookies, almost three years ago. I need you, Galen. I want you. Right here, right now."

Later, when they were both sated, he pushed himself up on his elbow and looked down into her face. "Oh, my darling girl. Why didn't you tell me?"

She kissed the side of his throat. "Tell you what?"

"That I was the first?"

"Because it didn't matter."

He propped himself up on his elbows, still deep inside her. "It mattered to me. I would have done things differently. I should have taken precautions."

"I told you, I understand the biology. I went to see Dr. Kent. He took care of everything."

"Are you all right?"

She giggled. "Better than all right. But I need to breathe."

Galen started to laugh, a deep, throaty laugh. "I just realized, you're still wearing your corset, and I still have my trousers around my ankles. And we've both still in our shoes."

"This isn't normal, is it?"

He leaned over and kissed her lightly. "It is when the parties are burning alive, and can't wait."

He took her in his arms again, this time gently, stroking her back. Then he stood and pulled up his trousers. "I don't know about you, but I'm starving. I'm going down to the cafe and get something to bring back. I won't be long. While I'm gone, you can get dressed." He leered at her comically. "Or whatever."

He finished dressing and almost ran out of the room. Lily managed to get off the bed, even though she only wanted to crawl under the covers. He had suggested she dress. Lily had other ideas; she didn't think Galen would mind.

She unclipped her stockings and rolled them down, then removed her shoes and stockings. Next, she unhooked her corset, using the hook-and-eye closure down the front. She left on her knee-length chemise, gathered up her clothes, folded them neatly, and laid them on top of the dresser beside her hat.

She turned back the bed covers, almost ashamed of the tell-tale marks their recent activity had left. At least she hadn't been one of those virgins who bleed when deflowered.

The bed was too high for Lily to climb into without a step. She found a tumbler half filled with water on the bedside table. She dumped it into the basin, wiped out the glass with her handkerchief and poured herself some of the wine they'd had at lunch.

She was in the process of arranging the pillows when Galen returned. He had paper wrapped parcels, another bottle of wine, and two proper glasses.

He stopped short when he saw her bent over the bed, wearing only the light cotton chemise. The light streaming in the window made it almost transparent, leaving little to his fevered imagination.

He put the parcels down on the bedside table and wrapped his arms around her waist. He kissed the nape of her neck. She turned in his arms. He said, "you could have gotten back into bed."

She giggled. "No I couldn't. There aren't any steps, and the bed comes above my waist. Maybe I could get a running jump at it?"

He laughed, wrapped his hands around her waist and lifted her, setting her down in the middle of the bed. He untied his shoes and climbed in beside her, sitting crossed legged next to her. She copied the way he sat, tucking her chemise between her legs. It felt good not to have to be lady-like all the time.

He handed her a wine glass and poured her a drink from the bottle from lunch, then began to unwrap parcels. "Let's see what we have. A nice baguette to start with. We have some cheese. Some pâtè of some kind. Best not to ask. And some meat. I think it's pork. Again, it's best not to ask. Oh, and I found some Liege waffles for dessert."

She broke off a piece of the loaf. He pulled the penknife from his pocket, and handed it to her. She cut a piece of cheese and a small slice of meat. "Well, the cheese is good. The meat? I think it's mule. So long as it isn't one of ours."

They ate, drank and laughed. Once they had eaten their fill, Lily unfolded her legs and slid off the bed. She gathered up the food and put it on the window ledge. She returned to the bed, and stood looking at Galen.

She was right. She couldn't get on the bed without help. Or a step stool. He slid off the bed and lifted her yet again, depositing her in the center of the mattress. He started stripping off his clothes again.

Lily giggled. She had laughed more this day than since she left nursing school. There was something comical about watching this man rush to get naked. "Galen."

He looked up. "Yes, darling girl?"

"You don't need to rush. I'm not going anywhere."

"Don't you have to be back tonight?"

She shook her head. "Nope. I have an overnight pass. Dr. Kent is very understanding."

"I shall have to thank him. Tomorrow. Today, I have better things to do, particularly since I know I can take my time."

She picked up her wine, and took a sip. "I've been doing some research."

"Really?" He folded his trousers and laid them across the chair.

She giggled again. "Yes, I've discovered your mustache does tickle, all over. But I like it."

During their time together, she found a scar on Galen's forearm. "What's this?"

"From a patient. I was examining a patient who had undergone surgery. He took offense when I had to debride his wound. Bastard stabbed me with my own scalpel. And what's this?" He pointed to three marks on her wrist.

"About the same. They brought in some German wounded. I was trying to put him under so he could have surgery. The so-and-so bit me."

He kissed the injured place, and, before she knew it, he'd pulled her astride his hips.

Chapter Seven

By the time the sun rose, they had finally fallen asleep. They were awakened by a knock on the door. Galen slipped from the bed, drawing the covers over Lily. He called out to wait, and pulled a robe from the wardrobe. He opened the door just enough to see who was there. He reached through the opening and came back with a ceramic pitcher of hot water. He thanked whoever had brought it and closed the door.

"The concierge brought us some hot water. There's a *pot de chambre* in the bedside table. Hot water, towels, soap. Take your time. I'm going to the bath down the hall to shave."

He bent to kiss her one last time before they dressed. She took advantage and slipped her hand inside his robe. He grasped her wrist. "Oh no. Start that now, and we'll never get out of here."

Lily waited until he left to climb out of bed. It wasn't until he mentioned the chamber pot that she realized how badly she needed to relieve herself. She pulled the ornate ceramic pot out, did what she had to do, then pushed it under the bed where the maid would find it when she cleaned the room.

She made good use of the hot water. She was amazed how tender her nether bits were. She supposed if she looked with a mirror she'd find bits of her person bruised. Lily didn't mind at all.

Her chemise was halfway across the room where Galen had thrown it. She padded across the room to retrieve it and slipped it on.

She was able to put her corset on without retying the laces. She merely wrapped it around and fastened the hooks. Stockings and shoes were next, then petticoat. Her corset cover was a lost cause. She looked at it and smiled, remembering how it had met its end. She tucked it into her bag. It may be a ragged mess, but it was a reminder of her first time with the man she loved.

Galen returned as she was buttoning her dress. "Damn. You're dressed."

"You told me to get dressed."

"Yeah. But I didn't think you'd listen to me."

She put her arms around his waist and laid her cheek against his chest. She whispered something he couldn't make out.

He put his fingers beneath her chin and tilted her face up. He bent and kissed her. "I couldn't hear you."

She tried to look down but he wasn't having it. "I said I love you."

He put his arms around her and lifted her so their faces were level. He kissed her again, more deeply this time. "Lily, darling girl. Marry me."

She pushed away from him, and he set her down. "What brought that on?"

"Well, I did deflower you. I took utter advantage of your innocence."

"Oh please." She was angry, and she wasn't sure why. "I knew exactly what would happen when I sat down in that cafe. Why do you think I got a Dutch Cap?"

"Well, I just thought..."

"Don't think. Just love me. I'm not about to give up nursing for the privilege of being a doctor's wife. We both have jobs to do, now more than ever with America entering the war."

Her back was to him. He put his hands on her shoulders and kissed the back of her neck. He whispered in her ear, "I love you, Lily. Will you at least promise to promise me later?"

She turned back into his embrace and kissed him. "I promise to promise. Later. When we are back in Baltimore. I promise. Not now."

"Will you at least wear my ring?" He sounded so hopeful.

She shook her head. "No, my love. It would raise too many questions."

He looked so crestfallen. "What if I give you a necklace? Something that only has meaning to us?"

"No lockets."

"Agreed. No lockets."

*****

They returned to camp Sunday afternoon. They behaved very circumspectly, careful to have no physical contact lest someone ferret out their relationship.

As they reached Major Kent's office, Lily whispered, "I have private quarters now, the room off the sacristy in the church."

"Mm-hmm."

She could have sworn he blushed this time.

Galen knocked on Kent's door.

"Come."

Galen opened the door and allowed Lily to enter first, then followed, closing the door behind them.

"Good afternoon, Major Stewart, Nurse Barnett. I trust you enjoyed your time off base."

Lily giggled behind her hand.

"Very much so. Thank you." He sounded so self-assured, but his cheeks were red. It made Lily giggle even more.

Kent looked very pleased with himself. "Nurse Barnett, you may return to your duties. I'm sure Nurse Beemer needs to update you on what's occurred."

"Thank you, Major Byrd." She looked at Galen. "Good day, Major Stewart."

As soon as Lily closed the door, Kent stood and limped around the desk. He shook Galen's hand. "Damned glad you're here, Galen. I am not an administrator."

They both sat in the club chairs Kent had managed to find for his office. "Neither am I. But I think, between the two of us, we can manage." He paused while Kent lit his pipe. "How did you ever come to be providing...shall we say 'planning services' to the nurses?"

Kent puffed in silence before he answered. "Which is better? To bend regulations, to ensure there are no unwanted pregnancies, or to send pregnant nurses home in disgrace after some man refuses to take precautions. We provide men with 'French letters', but most of them 'forget' until it's too late. Our nurses are human, and it's foolish to demand they remain celebate while providing the men the freedom to fornicate at will."

"I wish the rest of the army felt that way. I expect we're in for some trouble shortly. The Americans have arrived. They'll be coming through here shortly. Many of them are brash, forward, and have little respect for anyone who hasn't been to Times Square. I think it would be a good idea if the nurses had a security detail at their quarters, and perhaps escorts to and from their duties."

"Good. We have several men who are supposed to be transported back for rehabilitation, but London hasn't sent the orders. They've nothing to do but shoot dice and play cards. Until we get some replacements, that would be an excellent job for them, and would give them exercise as well."

"How many surgeons do we have on staff?

"Five, including the two of us. I can't do much surgery now." He knocked on his prosthetic leg. "I can manage short stints, and do well with anesthesia. But for long operations, or anything that requires feats of strength, I'm pretty useless."

"And how many nurses?"

"There's Sister Barnett, who is in charge of everything. Sister Grace Longworth. She's as competent as any of these new doctors. The woman worked in a country doctor's practice, and can suture as well as other women embroider. She is also skilled at setting small bones. I've placed her in charge of the theater. Five other trained general nurses, and ten nursing assistants. Then there's the usual complement of orderlies."

"Major, I propose we share the duties in this post. You'll be staying on anyway. What would you say to being in charge of the nurses, and supplies, and I'll handle the theater and the day to day operations? The nurses already respect you, and you know what we need and when we need it. Plus, you are familiar with the supply chain. I've spent the last year on a hospital ship. I know where to find the head and how to keep from getting seasick in front of patients, but not much about actually running a military base."

Byrd Kent leaned across between the two chairs and offered his hand. "I think that's a fine idea, Major Stewart. Now, get the bottle out of the bottom drawer of my desk. We've got a big push coming, and we may not have time for it later.

*****

Lily didn't see Galen again until three the next morning. A soldier came past her room, pausing only long enough to pound on her door and yell, "incoming wounded".

She pulled on her uniform, set her veil in place, and headed to the scrub room. Before the ambulances arrived, one of her jobs was to assist the doctors scrubbing in and gowning.

She was putting out soaps and filling the basins when Galen came in. His smile flashed, then disappeared just as quickly. She dropped the bar of soap in his hand. "Dr. Stewart."

"Good morning, Sister Barnett." He whispered, "You okay?"

She whispered back, "A little tender. But I did get a nap."

"Good. Because I expect we'll be here a long time."

As he scrubbed, he said to Lily, and anyone else within earshot, "I haven't had time to prepare the memorandum. Major Kent will be second in command, and will continue to be in charge of the nurses, supplies and quartermaster stores. If the nurses have any concerns, they should address them to Major Byrd."

"Thank you, Dr. Stewart. I'll see the word is passed."

Surgery was brutal. Dr. Kent and Sister Longworth were kept busy with anesthesia duties, until Grace collapsed from being too close to the ether. One of the orderlies carried her out and set her in the fresh air until she recovered. Lily took over her duties for the next two hours while Sister Longworth remained outside to clear her lungs.

They amputated limbs, removed shrapnel, repaired damage to organs as best they could. Sometimes, it wasn't enough, and the patient succumbed to his injuries. It was upsetting to members of staff, but there was nothing they could do about it. Regardless of the heartbreak, regardless of how exhausted they were, the doctors and nurses continued to work.

This time, there was no chance for rest, or to relieve the hardworking doctors. An orderly brought in a tray of milky tea every few hours, to keep them on their feet, and after twelve hours, he delivered some fish paste sandwiches. Lily would have prefered the roasted mule they had at the hotel.

Thirty one hours after they began, the last surgery was finished. Galen walked from the operating theater into the sun and had to shade his eyes. It was now ten in the morning, and he had things to do.

Lily came out behind him. "Good morning, Dr. Stewart."

"Sister Barnett." He wanted so much to hold her to him, to fall asleep with her in his arms.

She walked past him, headed to her quarters. He started to follow her, then caught himself.

Galen returned to his own quarters and dressed. He left word for Byrd Kent that he was going to walk into town and would be back in an hour.

*****

Lily awoke in time for supper in the mess. Everything she had hurt. Running non-stop for all those hours took a toll on her body. She groaned as she climbed out of bed. She pulled on her clean uniform. When she reached for her veil, she saw the small carved wooden box sitting on top of it. It bothered her a little that someone was in her room, but when she realized who had been there, she relaxed.

She opened the box carefully. Inside, there was a fine gold chain with a tiny gold key. A handwritten note was under the box. "For when you are ready to unlock your promise. G."

Lily lifted the chain and fastened it around her neck. She tucked the pendant inside her uniform. Nothing showed, unless she was wearing civilian clothing. It was perfect.

Her pains forgotten, she headed to the mess ready to eat, and would even welcome some roasted mule. Anything but fish paste.

Dinner was boiled cabbage and potatoes with bacon and onions. It wasn't what she'd hoped for, and there was a peculiar taste; something odd about the onions. After one or two bites, Lily pushed them aside and ate only the cabbage and potatoes.

About an hour after their meal, more than half of the staff was in the latrine with explosive bowels. Lily had a slightly upset stomach, but nothing came of it.

She checked on the patients. They had been fed clear broth, and those able to handle solid foods were given beef stew with only meat and potatoes. None of them had symptoms. The tainted food had to be the onions or the bacon.

She had to get to the bottom of it, but first she needed to check on Galen. She knocked on his office door. The call of "Come" came from inside.

She stepped inside, and suddenly felt very small and vulnerable standing alone in front of this man. "Major Stewart."

"Come in, Nurse Barnett. Close the door."

She pushed it shut and waited. She would allow him to set the tone.

Galen came around the desk and put his arms around her. His kiss was soft, welcoming. She wanted to crawl into his embrace and stay there forever.

She laid her head against his chest. "I found your gift. Thank you."

"You're welcome, darling girl."

She pushed away. "That's not why I'm here."

"I didn't think so." He sat in one of the chairs and gestured for her to take the other. "At least half of our medical staff is in the latrines. Either the bacon or the onions at supper were tainted. Thank god none of the patients were fed what was in the officers' mess."

"Let's go see our cook. There has to be an explanation. I doubt he'd purposely serve tainted food."

They walked across to the kitchen tent. The cook was still working, preparing broth for patients and prepping food for breakfast. Galen asked, "What's his name?"

"Sergeant Harlastan. He's been with us about a year."

Galen called out, "Sergeant Harlastan!"

Harlasan dropped what he was doing and met Lily and Galen at the door to the cook tent. "Yes, Major?"

"There was a problem with today's evening meal. It seems something you served the officers is causing stomach issues. We've narrowed it down to the bacon or the onions. Can you tell me their source?"

"Yes, sir. There's a young woman from the village who sometimes brings fresh vegetables. I trade her tinned meat, sometimes salt beef for them."

"And what about the bacon?"

"That was from a tin, Sir."

Lily asked, "Was the tin intact, or was it swollen?"

"No, Miss. I know better than to use a swell-headed tin."

She asked, "Do you have any more of the onions?"

He went to a bowl on a work table. "Here's a few. I thought I'd put these in the stew tomorrow."

Lily picked one up, poked her thumbnail into it. "Sergeant, didn't you notice this looked more like garlic than onion?"

"No, Miss. I figured they were some fancy French thing. The girl called them 'chariots' or some such."

"Was it 'eschalot'?"

"Yes, Miss. That's it."

Lily sniffed the bulb in her hand, then held it out to the cook. "Smell."

He did. "Smells green. Kind of like peas."

"Sergeant, I'm pretty sure you fed us lily bulbs."

"Oh, is that good?"

She shook her head. "Not really. Had you put any more on our plates we would have had a dozen dead people on our hands, rather than in the latrines crapping themselves."

"I'm so sorry Miss. Major. I never meant any harm."

Galen patted his shoulder. "I know, sergeant. From now on, don't buy anything from the locals without checking with someone first."

As they walked away from the cook tent, Lily asked, "Do we go after the woman who brought the bulbs? I mean, she could have killed people."

He shook his head. "I think she's just trying to put food on her table. The next time she comes around either Major Byrd or I will talk to her and see what she's about."

As he walked her to the church where she had duty in the ward, he asked, "Did you really like it?"

"I'm wearing it. What do you think?"

"I was afraid it was a little...I don't know...silly? Old fashioned?"

She stopped and looked up into his face. "It's neither silly nor old fashioned. It's perfect. When I'm ready to collect on my promise, I'll send you something to match."

Because they knew what the staff had ingested that caused the upset, Lily organized a treatment. No one liked it, but Galen agreed it was the best course of action that everyone afflicted have a mild purgative to get the suspect product out of their systems. By lunch the next day stomachs were back to normal, and some unlucky privates were digging new latrines.

Lily was on overnight duty on the ward. The nursing assistants were taking on much of the work now, leaving her time to fill out reports and prepare schedules.

She was seated at her desk near her quarters behind the sacristy when the side door opened. Galen slipped in, and pulled the door closed behind him. He looked around the room until he found Lily.

He made a show of checking on various patients as he made his way to her. "How are you, Nurse Barnett?"

"Well, Dr. Stewart. You?"

He had his back to the room. He leaned down so only she could hear. "Randy as hell. Want to go into your quarters for a while?"

Lily looked past him, to make sure no one was nearby. "Why yes, Doctor. I'd enjoy that very much. But I don't think it advisable at the moment." Then softer, for his ears only, "I'm done at four. Meet me then.

Anne Arrandale

Chapter Eight

August 7, 1917

Telegrams arrived that morning for both Lily and Galen. They were requests of the U.S. Army Medical Corps that the two meet with the commanding officer of the local hospital.

Lily ran across to Galen's office. This time she didn't bother to knock. "Galen?"

He was sitting at his desk, his feet propped up, drinking a cup of coffee. His tunic was hanging on the coat rack, his tie was undone and his shirt unbuttoned. He jumped up like he was caught doing something naughty.

"Oh, sit down. I've seen you in less."

He sat. When he did, he patted his lap, inviting her to sit. She shook her head. "Not now. We need to talk."

He sat bolt upright. "You're not..."

"Pregnant? Don't be silly. No. This telegram came today."

He held up his own. "I know. I got one, too. What do you think?"

She sat in the chair. "I'm not sure. I love what I'm doing here. I like the people. But I believe I could do even more."

"I know. I had the same idea. What say I arrange passes for us to go to their unit tomorrow? It's on the opposite side of Ypres, so it won't take us long to get there. I can requisition an ambulance to drive us over."

"When will we need to be back? I don't have ward duty tomorrow."

He knew what was on her mind. "I think we can swing a twenty four hour pass. Major Kent can see to things while I'm away."

"Good. Now, Major Stewart, if you'll excuse me, I need to go wash out a few things."

"Certainly, Nurse Barnett. You are dismissed."

She turned to leave, but stopped when he called her name.

"And Lily, wear the corset."

*****

It was just past seven in the morning when Lily and Galen tossed his instrument bag and their small overnight bags into the back then climbed into the front seat of the ambulance. Their driver had directions to deposit them at U.S. headquarters, then to return for them in the morning.

Galen wore his dress uniform, while Lily was left with her traveling costume she had worn on the ship coming over. He looked so handsome, while she felt she looked frowsy. She would have preferred to wear her purple walking outfit. At least she had done as Galen asked.

The commanding officer's tent was well marked. Galen helped Lily across the rutted road, then asked, "You ready?"

"I swear Dr. Stewart, you seem to ask me that every time we're together."

He started to laugh, then caught himself. He was supposed to be a sober, serious doctor, not a silly man courting a girl. Besides, he should know better. He was fourteen years her senior. Yet every time he was near her, he behaved like a schoolboy.

He straightened his jacket, brushed an invisible speck of lint from his sleeve, and knocked on the door. The voice inside called, "Come." Galen pushed the door open."

They entered, and Galen saluted. "Good morning, General Feeny. Major Galen Stewart and Sister Lily Barnett reporting as requested."

"Major Stewart. Sister Barnett. Take a seat, please.

Feeny was a man of indeterminate years. He could have been forty, or sixty-five. He was slight, thinning hair, a waxed mustache, and a baritone voice that seemed too big for his body. Behind him was a tall, whip-thin woman with red hair, wearing the uniform of the Red Cross.

Feeny offered Galen a cigar, which he refused. The general selected one, snipped the tip, and took his time lighting it. He blew a halo of blue smoke, then leaned across the desk. "I appreciate you coming. Major, I'd like to make you an offer. As you know, the Americans have set up hospitals across this sector. Our doctors are kept busy night and day, and we're not used to this sort of warfare. Or the wounds that come with it. We need your expertise. I'm prepared to offer you a promotion to Lieutenant Colonel, retroactive to the date we entered the war."

Galen didn't know what to say. "What about Sister Barnett?"

"I'll let Nurse Cortizi speak to that."

The tall, thin nurse propped her hip on the side of the general's desk. "Lily...May I call you Lily?"

Lily nodded.

"Lily, I'm Irene Cortizi, Supervising Nurse of the American Red Cross. We have a problem recruiting trained nurses for this detail, because of the danger and the harsh working conditions. You've already been here three years or so. I also understand you have some expertise in contagious diseases. There is a strange influenza that has been cropping up in pockets, and seems more contagious than anything we've seen before. I'd like to offer you a position as supervising nurse for our sector. It would mean some traveling from one camp to another, but you'd be based here. It would be a substantial increase in pay as well."

Lily knew how she had to answer. "Nurse Cortizi, may I think about it? This is a big change, and a huge responsibility. I also have responsibilities to my nurses, as Major Stewart has to his doctors."

"Yes, General." Galen finally said. "May we both consider it, and give you our answer later today?"

The General agreed they could return at suppertime. They would take their meal with him, and they'd discuss it then.

Galen and Lily walked back to the edge of town. They found a small cafe, where they ordered coffee and croissants.

Lily tore off a bit of the roll and dunked it in her coffee. "What do you think?"

"I really don't know. I don't like the idea of you going from unit to unit."

"Well, do you think you'd be traveling as well?"

He shook his head. "I'm not sure. Feeny didn't go into any details. I need to ask."

"It would be nice if they let us travel together."

"I doubt that would happen. But I'll find out. I'm sure General Feeny will dine separately from Nurse Cortizi. You ask her, I'll ask him."

She finished her pastry, and drained her coffee cup. "Galen, do you suppose anyone nearby rents rooms? And if you ask me one more time if I'm sure, I swear, I'll scream."

"Let me find out." He went to find the waiter to pay the bill, and asked if there were any rooms available nearby. Ten minutes later, he came back to the table, where Lily was busily sweeping crumbs into a saucer. He held out his hand. "Come with me."

He drew her to her feet, and led her down the alley beside the cafe. At the rear of the building was a staircase. He said, "Up here. The owner has two rooms he rents out upstairs. He said we may have both of them until tomorrow."

"Both of them?" She giggled.

"Of course. Don't want to give anybody the wrong idea. Besides, they're adjoining, and share a real bathroom."

She stopped him on the stairs. "You're not teasing me? A real, honest to god bathroom, with running water and a tub and everything?"

He laughed. "I'm not going to promise everything. But the landlord said it has a 'real bathroom'. Why don't we quit talking about it and see?" Galen unlocked the door at the top of the stairs and pushed the door open.

The room was large, with windows that opened onto the alley below. The bed was high, as it had been in Galen's previous room, but this time it had steps. He tossed his cap on the dresser and tried to take her into his arms. She pushed him away.

"I need to see this bathroom."

He opened the door and looked in. "Nope. This is the second room." He went to the next door and turned the knob. "Here you go. Look, a flush toilet, tub with running water and a sink."

"Imagine. A real tub. A real bath."

This time he succeeded in getting his arms around her. He kissed her throat, her cheek, as he undid the buttons on her traveling suit.

"Oh, no, Major. The last time you tried to undo my buttons they wound up all over the room. Let me do these."

*****

Later, Lily explored the bathroom. She loved the thought of a real bath, but first, she insisted she be able to close both doors and use the first real toilet she'd seen since she left London.

As soon as she'd pulled the chain to flush, Galen knocked on the door. She opened the door.

He looked her over, as if seeing her for the first time. She stood, the picture of innocence, wearing only in her knee-length chemise. Only he knew the fire of her passions. He was glad he had pulled on his drawers. They had things to do, and he knew once they got distracted they'd be here all night.

"Is something wrong?"

He shook himself. "We have to be back at suppertime. I thought you might like help washing your hair."

She held out her hand to him. She looped her arms around his neck and kissed his cheek. "You know, if you'd been around to help me wash it last January, it would be down to here by now." She reached behind and gestured to a point in the center of her back below her shoulder blades.

"I wondered." He ruffled her curly hair. "But I like it."

"Why don't you find some towels, while I fill the tub?"

Galen found towels in the drawer of Lily's room. He heard the water running and sat down on the edge of the bed. They'd spent the afternoon in what he considered his room. He was determined they'd spend the night in hers.

When they met with the American officers he intended to ask General Feeny what the Force's position was on married personnel serving together.

He heard her cut off the water, then heard her soft sigh as she lowered herself into the warm water. He got up to deliver her towels.

*****

They walked back to the American compound in time to take supper with General Feeny and Nurse Cortizi.

Feeny led the way to the officer's mess. The four shared a table, and were served familiar foods from home: Maryland fried chicken with gravy, mash potatoes and sliced tomatoes.

Feeny opened with a simple question. "So, where are you two from?"

Galen answered, "We're both Baltimore natives. Sister Barnett's father was my mentor at Johns Hopkins. I met Lily when she was about fourteen, when she was recovering from diptheria."

Cortizi laid down her fork and looked at Lily. "Oh, you poor dear. No wonder you developed an interest in contagious diseases. What color was your hair before? And did it affect your hearing?"

Lily laughed lightly. This woman was good. "No problem with hearing or vision, ma'am. And it was red, But not as red as yours."

Lily asked, "When you said I'd be traveling to different units, how often would I be required to move?"

Cortizi leaned back in her chair with her coffee. "Depends. Every time there is an outbreak, we'd need you to go, set up the ward, and teach the staff how to control the spread. It could be every six week, or every six months. You'll start here, and then you will get a call when the need arises. But this unit will be your home base."

"I see. And if there isn't a current outbreak? What would my duties be then?"

"It depends on the needs of that unit. Sometimes you might be assisting in surgery, others you might be on the ward, or you may even be delivering babies for some of the local women."

"Just out of curiosity, what is the Red Cross' stance on family planning for their nurses?"

"Well, the Service does accept married nurses. Some of them even have husbands in the military. But should a nurse become pregnant she's sent home immediately. "

Lily hoped she wasn't blushing. "No, that's not what I meant. In Europe cervical caps are an accepted method of prevention. Some of the doctors will take care of the nurses should they request one. I wondered what your Service's stance was."

"Oh. Well, we don't have one. If a nurse finds a doctor willing we have nothing to say about it."

Feeny pushed away from the table, and the four stood. "Major, what say I give you a tour?"

Cortizi took Lily to look over the ward, while Galen went with Feeny to the theater.

The operating theater was empty when they arrived. The room was large, with six operating tables and anesthesia set ups. Galen couldn't wait. He asked, "General, what is the Army's stance on a doctor and nurse marrying?"

"Barnett?"

He nodded.

"Thought so." He smiled knowingly. "Technically, you couldn't serve together."

"Oh." Galen sounded absolutely crestfallen.

"Now, let's break this down." The General sat on the anesthesiologist's stool. "If this 'hypothetical nurse' kept her maiden name, and if neither of you were married after you accepted your commission, no one will say anything."

Galen perked up, then thought about what Feeny said. "That sounds rather specific, General."

"It should. Just ask Irene Cortizi. Our son starts Harvard Medical in two weeks."

"Let me..."

Before he could finish his thought, ambulance bells sounded outside.

"Well, Major, looks like we'll get to see you in action. Come on. I'll show you where to scrub in."

The scrub room was much like the ones they had been using: basins rather than sinks. At least they appeared to have ample supplies.

Irene Cortizi and another nurse helped them scrub, gown and glove. Irene told them, "Only one patient. Multiple injuries. He was found in No Man's Land, two days after they went over the top."

Feeny opened the door to the surgery by backing into the door. "Looks like a bad one Stewart. I hope we can save him."

Lily was already at tableside. She had already cut the clothes off the patient. She was using a bulb syringe filled from a basin to wash the damaged areas, to try and remove not just dirt and debris, but the iodine poured on wounds by field medics in an effort to forestall infection.

Lily didn't waste time with niceties. "Closed fracture of the right hand. Looks like someone stepped on it. Deep laceration of the left thigh, barely missed the femoral artery, possibly from a bayonet. Closed head injury. Left pupil is unreactive. Possible swelling of the brain. I've already administered a tetanus antitoxin."

Galen was smiling proudly beneath his mask. Damn, he was proud of his darling girl. "Thank you, Sister."

Feeny was impressed. "Very good, Sister Barnett." He turned his attention to Galen. "Now, Doctor, how do you suggest we proceed?"

"First things first. Eliminate the risk of infection. Debride and suture the leg wound. Then bore a hole to release the cranial pressure. When that's done, we can worry about his hand, if it can be saved or if it's better to amputate."

"You wouldn't just amputate to save time?

Galen shook his head. "No, General. I refuse to deprive a man of his limbs for a mere broken bone."

"Good. Sister Barnett, do you concur?"

"I almost always do."

The door opened and another white coated figure entered. Feeny said, "Dr. Stewart, this is Dr. Zeblinski. He'll be doing anesthesia tonight. Dr. Zeblinski, this is Major Stewart. We spoke about him earlier today. And Sister Barnett."

They passed the usual banalities. Zeblinski began to prepare a syringe of Morphia, to administer before surgery. Lily stopped him.

"Uh, excuse me, Doctor. Patient has a closed head injury. Wouldn't nitrous be better?"

He dropped the syringe in the tray. "It certainly would, nurse." He turned to open the valves on the two tanks. "Tell me, Nurse Barnett. Why didn't you go to medical school?"

Lily pulled the instrument tray into position for Galen to begin working on the young man's leg. "I did, Dr. Zeblinski. But I ran into a problem."

"Dr. d'Alba." It wasn't a question.

Her eyes grew wide. "How did you...oh...Jimmy Zeblinski?"

He laughed. "Guilty. I wondered what happened to you. You hear about d'Alba?"

"Did he finally die of meanness?"

He affixed the cannula to the patient's nose. "Better. He was run down on Greene Street. They carried him into the hospital, and he was operated on by one of his own students. He died after the student removed his colon, but ignored a ruptured spleen and torn coronary artery."

Lily was laughing, causing great consternation between Feeny and Cortizi. The older nurse thought it was inappropriate and said so.

Lily managed to compose herself. "I'm sorry, Nurse. The doctor in question was my one and only instructor during my failed attempt at medical school. He refused to allow me to even see the cadavers as they didn't have a female body. He expected me to learn anatomy from a pornographer's postcards." She paused, then decided to make another introduction. "Dr. Stewart, this is Jimmy Zeblinski . I met him while waiting to start my first and only day of medical school. It would appear he became a physician in spite of our former instructor's teaching."

"Pleased to meet you. Now, if we're done with the pleasantries, may we please get this gentleman put back together?"

He swore he heard her giggle as she said "Certainly, Doctor."

He held out his gloved hand to receive the first instrument.

*****

The first two surgeries went well. Galen was able to stitch the tendons together before suturing the muscle. He did have to excise a portion of the muscle to remove damaged tissue, but he was still able to pull it closed. There wasn't enough skin to close, so he had Lily prepare wet-to-dry dressings until the boy could receive a skin graft.

The trepanning was a simple matter. Galen used a tool originally designed by the ancient Egyptians that looked like a cross between a small cookie cutter and a cork screw. Lily shaved the side of the patient's head, then watched as Galen first peeled back the scalp, then twisted the round saw through the man's skull.

Finally, it was time to address his hand. Galen lifted the injured appendage and manipulated the bones. "I'm not sure we can save the hand, General. But I'd like to wait a day or two before I decide. There's too much swelling to do much of anything other than amputate now."

*****

They stood in the scrub room removing their surgical gear. Feeny decided to give them some extra time. "Major, I'm sending word to your unit that you two will be remaining with us for a few days for the necessity of patient care. I want you to oversee the man's recovery and to make the decision about that amputation."

Irene Cortizi made the offer she knew would be rejected. "And of course we will find room for you in the nurses quarters, Nurse Barnett."

Feeny grinned at his wife. "I'm sure they've already found rooms in town. It won't hurt if they remain there, so long as we know where they can be located in an emergency."

Galen gave Feeny the direction of their temporary lodging, and the pair made their exhausted way back to their rooms. They walked silently, daring to hold hands under the protection of darkness.

The cafe was closed by the time they arrived. Galen guided her down the lane, and up the stairway to their door.

He dropped his black bag just inside the door. He bent and kissed Lily's cheek lightly. "I need a bath." And he disappeared into the bathroom.

Lily went into the adjoining room. She found a clean towel in the bottom drawer, then went to find Galen's razor, shaving mug and brush.

She gave him time to relax in the hot water before she disturbed him. She needed to have a serious discussion with him, and figured her holding a straight razor to his face was her best hope for things remaining serious.

She removed her uniform and put it away, removed and carefully folded her undergarments. She slipped on a green silk robe that matched her eyes.

She took the bedside step stool and carried it into the bathroom along with the shaving needs.

She put the stool beside the tub and sat, then realized Galen was sound asleep.

She took the opportunity to prepare the soap, adding hot water to the small disk of sandalwood-scented soap, and working up a lather with the brush.

She sat back on the stool and kissed his forehead. "Galen," she whispered.

He jerked awake, splashing water over her. "Huh? What?"

She laid her hand on his chest. "Relax. Let me take care of you."

Galen laid his head back against the edge of the tub again and closed his eyes. He had expected her to reach beneath the water and take him in hand. His shock was visible when he felt the warm soap spreading over his cheek and throat.

She laughed when his eyes flew open. "Don't worry. I'll leave your upper lip to you. I wouldn't dare mess with your mustache."

He had watched her shave their patient's head earlier. He knew she could wield a razor with skill. He was still nervous about her using a straight razor on his exposed throat.

Once she had him where she wanted him, she started having her one-sided conversation. "You know, Galen, I had a long talk with Irene Cortizi. She explained I would be based at this post, and would only have to travel long enough to establish protocols. You'd be here as this would be your command. She said we can resign our commissions, then a week later accept our new commissions here. I haven't told her yes or no. But I think we should accept their offer. Make like this." She demonstrated twisting her mouth to stretch her cheek.

He did as he was told, trying very hard not to laugh.

"Anyway, I think it would be an excellent opportunity, and you would be able to save extra, in case you wanted to open your own practice when we get home."

She grabbed the cloth and rinsed the last of the soap from his face. He waited until she cleaned his razor, closed it and set it aside. She sat on the edge of the tub and reached to pick up the sponge. Galen looped his arm around her waist and pulled her butt first into the tub.

"Galen!" She squealed.

He tried to kiss her, but they were both laughing too hard.

She tried to push herself out of the water, but couldn't get any leverage to push herself up. Her feet hung useless over the edge. "How do you propose we get out of this?

He grasped the edge of the tub and pushed as far back as he could, pushed Lily to the other end of the tub, and stood. As soon as he pulled his legs from under her bottom, she sunk deeper into the tub, her feet sticking in the air, her trunk mostly submerged, as she screamed and tried to grab onto the edges. "Galen! Help!"

He was laughing as he caught her under her arms and lifted her out. "You, my darling girl, have a promising future as a barber should you decide to leave nursing."

She slapped his chest. "Oh...you...rat. I bought this robe special. Now it's all wet, and I don't know if it will ever be right." She sounded seriously put out.

"Lily, my love, I will buy you a hundred robes. Meanwhile, hang that one over the tub so it dries."

He grabbed the towel from the floor and dried himself, then handed it to Lily. He disappeared into the next room while she took care of her dripping robe.

Galen reappeared carrying his own robe, and draped it over Lily's shoulders. She noticed he was wearing a clean pair of underdrawers. He guided her into what was "her" room. The bed was turned down, the stool returned beside the bed.

Galen sat on the edge of the bed, put his hands on her waist and pulled her to him. He buried his face between her breasts and breathed in the scent of her.

Lily's hands were in his hair, clutching him to her, and he clenched and massaged and probed ever so gently between her nether-cheeks. She moaned and arched her back. Galen fell back onto the bed, taking her with him.

Anne Arrandale

Chapter Nine

At lunchtime, they made their way, very sedately, back to the American base. Galen sought out General Feeny as soon as they arrived. The General was in his office, signing off on various reports.

"General, a minute of your time, if you please?"

Feeny put his pen aside, took off his reading glasses and leaned back in his chair. "By all means, Major. Come in, take a seat."

"General, after due consideration, Nurse Barnett and I have decided to accept your generous offer."

Feeny stood and came around the desk. He shook Galen's hand vigorously. "Welcome, my boy. Welcome. We'll put you to good use, I promise."

"What exactly will the procedure be?"

"You'll complete your commission here, with me. I will send it by special messenger to headquarters, where, on my recommendation, it will be accepted without question. Your new commission will be forwarded to British High Command, where they will accept your resignation. The whole process should take a few days. The start date on your assignment will allow a week to ten days travel time, even though you may be across the street."

"And I will be at liberty for that time?"

The general smiled, knowingly, and nodded. "Now, what say we go have a look at your patient?"

They crossed the compound to the ward, where they found Lily sitting at the bedside of the young man on whom they had operated. He was still unconscious. Lily was looking away, at nothing, as she very gently probed and manipulated his injured hand.

Feeny said, "What's go..."

Irene Crozini cut him off. "Shhh. She's diagnosing his fractures."

Finally, Lily very gently laid his hand across his chest. She walked around the bed and stood beside Galen. Lily picked up the doctor's hand and used it to demonstrate. "He has two fractures of the fifth metacarpal, here and here." She pointed at two spots in line with the little finger. "And a single break here on the fourth metacarpal. The rest are intact, as are the phalanges and the arm."

Feeny was amazed. "Nurse Barnett, how did you learn to do that?"

"We have a nurse who was a bonesetter in Scotland. She taught me. Since we don't have an X-Ray machine available, it's much better than just whacking off his hand because no one knew where the break was."

He turned to Galen. "Do you think it can be repaired?"

"I think it depends on how well he recovers from his head injury. But I believe, with Nurse Barnett's assistance, we can set the hand, and immobilize it."

"And how soon do you want to tackle it?"

"We need to wait till tomorrow. He still isn't out of the woods yet."

*****

Lily spent most of the day with Private Billy Ackroyd (She learned that was his name from another patient.) She administered a sponge bath, read to him, and kept close watch for any sign of fever.

Jimmy Zeblinski came through as she was changing the dressing on Ackroyd's leg. "You're very adept working around a man's groin, Nurse Barnett."

"You should see me pop a mercury bullet up there for the men with V.D."

The young doctor had the audacity to run his hand across her backside.

"Dr. Zeblinski, unless you want to lose that hand, I strongly suggest you never do that again."

He snorted. "Why, what are you gonna do? Have your boyfriend beat me up?"

It took a slight turn and lean toward him, so her hand was behind her skirt. She put her hand over his crotch, as if she intended to caress. He leaned in. Her hand slipped lower, grabbed his testicles, and squeezed as hard as she could.

She smiled, to him a vicious show of teeth. "I don't need anyone to defend me, Dr. Zeblinski. Touch me again, and you'll lose these." She twisted, just enough to get his attention, then let go. "Understand?"

He was bent over, holding onto the edge of Ackroyd's bed. "Understood, Nurse Barnett. My sincerest apologies."

She left him standing there, breathing heavily, while she went to find Galen.

He was sitting with Feeny in the officer's mess. "May I join you, gentlemen?"

They stood. "Certainly," Feeny said, and even pulled out her chair.

Lily had to tell Feeny about her run in with Zeblinski , before word got to him through the grapevine. "General, I need to tell you what just happened. I was changing Private Ackroyd's dressing, when Dr. Zeblinski..."

Feeny seemed to be expecting something. "Did he put his hands on you?" This had apparently been an issue in the unit.

She nodded. "Yes, General. He made a rude comment, and touched my derriere. I told him not to ever do it again, and he made yet another rude comment."

Galen was smiling like an idiot. He remembered the last time a doctor made a rude comment to her.

"I'll send him off..."

"General, may I finish, please, before you decide anything?" He nodded, and she continued. "I'm afraid I may have done some serious damage to his manhood. Or may have hindered future generations of Zeblinskis."

"Nurse Barnett, what exactly did you do?"

"I grabbed his balls and twisted. Hard."

The handful of people in the mess hall looked around to see why their General and the new doctor were laughing and wiping tears from their cheeks.

*****

Word of Lily's altercation with Zeblinski spread through the camp rapidly. Galen was in the operating theater, assisting with a new two step amputation the American doctors were now performing, when the doctor performing the operation decided to gossip.

Dr. Kenneth Poplovitz was carefully demonstrating how to even the ragged tissue, trim back the bone, and close the skin over the original amputation. Apropos of nothing, he asked, "Did you hear about the run in our anesthesiologist here had with that nurse who came over from the British unit?"

Galen was laughing silently behind his mask. "No. Do tell."

Zeblinski's face above his own mask was purple. Galen didn't know if it was from embarrassment or anger. Regardless, Galen Stewart decided he deserved whatever he got.

"Seems Jimmy here got fresh with her. She didn't like it, and slapped his dick."

A nurse assisting them giggled, then murmured "Sorry."

Galen could have very easily announced that he knew Lily, that she had told them the true story. He could have threatened Zeblinski with physical harm if he put his hands on her again. He decided to let it drop; Lily could handle the little weasel on her own for the time being. If it ever escalated, or if he ever tried it again, the young doctor from Baltimore would find himself shoveling horse shit in the company's stables.

In the scrub room, Zeblinski approached Galen out of earshot of the others. "Major, I'd like to apologize for any insult I may have caused you or Nurse Barnett."

"Thank you Lieutenant. But I believe you owe the apology to Nurse Barnett. She's in the ward with Private Ackroyd, preparing to set his hand later today. If you want your apology to get around as much as what she did to you, I suggest you make it publicly, and loudly, in the ward. You know patients are like old women, and gossip with anyone about anything. Have at it."

Zeblinski stripped off his apron, tossed it in the hamper, then headed into the ward. He spotted Lily sitting beside Ackroyd, still holding the boy's injured hand, tugging gently on his fingers as she compressed his palm.

He walked up behind her and cleared his throat. "Excuse me, Nurse Barnett?"

She looked over her shoulder. "Come around to the other side, Lieutenant, where I can see you. I'm a little busy right now."

He walked around the bed and stood with his hands clasped in front of him in an unconscious effort to protect his crotch. "Nurse Barnett, I'd like to apologize for my unwelcome assault upon your person two nights ago, and for the crass words I spoke. You were justified in everything you did to me. If you never wanted to speak to me again, you would be equally justified."

Lily knew what it had taken for Zeblinski to make a public apology. "Thank you, Lieutenant. I propose we forget the incident ever happened. However, should anything of a similar nature occur again, regardless of the perpetrator, I assure you, retribution will be swift and hard." She pulled on Ackroyd's ring finger at that moment, making an audible "crack" that could be heard across the ward. She thought it was a nice touch, never mind that it set the bone in just the right place.

Zeblinski bowed and backed away, still afraid.

Galen had watched the whole proceeding from the doorway, along with Dr. Poplovitz and the young nurse. Poplovitz asked Galen, "You came over with her, didn't you?"

He allowed as the two had traveled together.

"She's pretty, isn't she? Pity she cut all her hair off, though. You know if she's seeing anybody?"

Galen wanted to laugh out loud. "She's a damned fine nurse, no matter how long her hair is. She's got a fellow, so I doubt there's much hope."

"I heard she'll be transferring here on a permanent basis. Her boyfriend will be in the British camp. So there's always hope."

Galen said, under his breath, as he pushed away from the door frame, "Don't count on it." He walked lazily to where Lily sat and stood in the place Zeblinski so recently vacated. He said softly, "You done good."

She laughed lightly at his use of the South Baltimore phrase. "I've got Ackroyd's bones aligned. Anytime you are ready to cast it he's ready." Once the hand was casted, they would be returning to their British unit. Meaning their lovely idyll would end, and they'd be thrown back into the rush and grime of patching boys back together, to either send them back into the field, or to send them home, sometimes far less than when they arrived.

"Let's splint it for now. Tomorrow, we can complete our paper work with General Feeny and the Red Cross. Then we'll cast him. If it holds, then we're done here for the time being."

The young nurse from surgery came to introduce herself. Frances Johnson was newly trained, all her work experience had been in military hospitals. She went to gather the supplies Lily requested. When she returned with stout wires and gauze, Galen helped her bend the metal into the necessary shapes, then the two held them in place so Lily could wrap and tie off the gauze.

As they were finishing their task, they felt the ground rumble, there was a flash and an explosion. Zeblinski stuck his head inside the ward. "Plane crash. Fire." The entire staff ran for the accident.

They ran toward the now-flaming wreckage. The bi-plane had snapped into two parts. The engine compartment was fully involved. Galen called to anyone within earshot, "Where's the pilot?"

Zeblinski gestured. "He's there, behind the tail. He was thrown free in the crash. I'm looking for the bombardier."

Galen and Lily ran to the pilot, to look for signs of life.

He was burned on his chest, arm, and neck. Lily stood and called for the stretcher bearers. The man was conscious, barely, and groaning in pain. The four men lifted him gently, put him on the canvas stretcher and ran for the theater.

Irene Cortizi was preparing for the burn victims already. Lily began cutting off the pilot's clothes when she heard a metallic sound. Irene was wielding an egg beater, and adding ingredients by the spoonful.

"Nurse Cortizi, it's not time to bake."

"It's for his burns. Petroleum jelly, lanolin and sulfur."

"Petroleum jelly is too heavy for burns."

"Not when it's whipped." Irene held up the beater. The mixture looked like whipped cream. "The sulfur helps the burns heal, the cream helps keep the tissue soft."

"So it's medicinal cold cream."

"Exactly. You still have to irrigate and debride the wounds. But once it's done, spread this on. Keeps out the bacteria and keeps the burned flesh from getting crispy."

Frances delivered the cart of supplies: basins of mild cleansing solution, a sprayer, sponges, forceps, tweezers. She took up a second pair of scissors and began helping Lily cut off the clothes which had become embedded in the burnt tissue.

The pilot continued moaning. Galen returned from the crash scene. "We found the bombardier. He was blown in half." He wiped his face, obviously upset. It was one thing to see death in a hospital. Carnage in the field was something else entirely.

He looked at the patient. "Is there a reason he hasn't been given an injection?"

Lily was still peeling bits of burnt wool from his chest. "I did, as soon as he came inside. I suspect he took something to keep him alert before he took off. I wanted to talk to you before we gave him more."

"Zeblinski!"

The young doctor came running.

"Get this man on gas now. I suspect he's full of cocaine. Morphia isn't having any effect."

Zeblinski did as he was told. It took a few minutes to take hold, but the pilot finally succumbed to the Nitrous Oxide.

When all his burned clothes had been removed, they were ready to assess the extent of his injuries.

Zeblinski stretched to see the extent of the damage. "He doesn't look bad. Only on his left side, so half his chest, his shoulder and arm, and part of his neck. It could have been a lot worse."

They cleaned and debrided the burns. Frances worked behind them, irrigating the now raw flesh.

Irene was ready with her sulfur emulsion. She used a wooden tongue depressor to spread on a thick layer of the mixture. Lily finished the process by laying on a single layer of protective gauze.

Galen spoke to Zeblinski . "Bring him down off the Nitrous slowly. I want him in intravenous fluids tonight, and one whatever we have for fever. What do you use?"

"Quinine is all we have. All the aspirin are stuck in Germany."

"It's better than nothing, I guess. Now, once that cocaine is out of his system, get him on Morphia, judiciously please. He may have a high tolerance, so there is a chance we could kill him trying to stop his pain."

"Yes, Doctor."

"And Dr. Zeblinski ?"

"Yes, Doctor?"

"You did a good job today. Thank you."

Lily was collecting her instruments. "I must say, Jimmy. I'm impressed. Maybe you really didn't pay any attention to Dr. d'Alba."

He grinned, glad their relationship was becoming normal. "Well, I paid enough attention to pass his tests. Then I spent nights in the hospital as an orderly, talking to real doctors and getting a real education."

"Seems like it took."

Zeblinski charted the patient's Nitrous use, so he could gradually add oxygen to the mixture. He looked up from his work. "Dr. Stewart, if you and Nurse Barnett want to take off, I believe Frances and I can handle this. Besides, you wanted to set Ackroyd's hand in the morning."

"Thank you, Doctor. I appreciate it. It's been a long day."

Galen and Lily walked back to town. They could have taken their meal in the mess, but Lily decided she'd rather have her meal at the cafe.

They dined that night on rabbit stew with mustard sauce, red wine, and a small cheese course to finish. Galen ordered a second bottle to take back to their rooms.

Once upstairs, Lily needed Galen to hold her, to make love to her long and slow. Instead of taking her in his arms as she expected, he sprawled in the chair and poured two glasses of wine. He set one glass on the table beside him for Lily. the other he drained, then refilled.

Lily knelt beside him. "Galen? Darling? What's wrong?" She'd never seen him like this.

He leaned forward, elbows on his knees, his face in his hands. His shoulders shook as he tried to hold in wracking sobs.

She didn't know what to do. Her strong, self-possessed man was beside himself, over who knows what. "Galen, talk to me. You've seen burns before, worse than today. Tell me, please."

"That wreck. The bombardier." His voice cracked, and he stopped speaking, lest he break down even more in her presence.

"You said he was cut in half. That's awful."

"That wasn't all, Lily. It was worse. Much worse. When Zeblinski and I found him, he was still alive. Mumbling incoherently, his spinal cord severed, his legs blown off. He felt nothing below his chest, and didn't know his intestines were spread on the ground. He only knew he couldn't move. Zablinski and I turned away to discuss his case, and one of the soldiers put a bullet in the man's brain."

"Oh Galen! That's horrible. Does General Feeny know?"

He nodded. "It was on his order. There was no way the man could have survived, and triage would have left him to die. Ending it quickly was a kindness, really."

"Kindness? Probably. Ethical? Not exactly. Legal? No. And I hate that you were a part of it."

He drained his third glass of wine, then pulled Lily into his lap. He held her tightly, so tight she thought her ribs would crack. She didn't care. He needed her, needed her love, her comfort, her presence. She put her arms around his neck and laid her face against his, breathing in his scent, reveling in the idea that he could turn to her in a moment of weakness. Too many men refused to allow themselves to show the least little chink in their armor.

She felt him sob once, silently, then he eased his hold and sat back in the chair. "I'm sorry, Lily. I never meant..." He wiped his eyes with the heels of his hands.

"Galen, my love, don't ever apologize for showing feelings. Not to me. You're human. It only makes me love you more."

Galen Stewart wasn't sure what he'd done to deserve this woman, his darling girl, but he never intended to let her out of his arms. He took her face between his two hands and kissed her eyelids, then her lips, softly, gently. She sighed against his mouth, and stroked the side of his face.

She stood, and pulled the second chair so their knees were touching. "Irene said we would have a week between the time we resign our commissions and we assume our new posts."

"Yes. Why?"

"Perhaps we can put that week to good use."

He raised one eyebrow, trying to look lecherous.

She slapped his knee. "That's not what I meant. I think we should go to the Register's office."

"Register's office? Did you want to buy a house?"

"No, you idiot. People in Belgium get married there."

He jumped out of his chair, almost overturning it. He jerked her up and into his arms. This time his kiss was deep, searching. By the time they broke apart she was utterly out of breath, and clinging to him for support.

He looked into her eyes. "We can go first thing in the morning."

She pushed away, walked away, and made a show of turning down the coverlet and fluffing the pillows. "No, we can't, not if I intend to keep working. Don't you remember? We have to complete our paperwork first, resign our commissions. Then we can do as we please during our week holiday. I please to get married. Now, if not you, I suppose Jimmy Zeblinski might be amenable."

Galen came up behind her and slapped her behind. She squealed and rubbed the offended area theatrically. "Don't you dare even mention that to Jimmy Zeblinski. If you do, I'm afraid I'll have to give him a lily."

"Give him a lily? You want to give Jimmy flowers?"

This time Galen laughed, a deep, throaty sound, that sounded so good after his earlier sobs. "I guess you didn't hear. It's what the men on post are calling an...external testicular torsion."

"Oh, no. You mean they've named that after me?"

He nodded, still laughing.

"Galen Stewart, you are absolutely awful."

He slipped his arms around her again and pulled her hips into his own, so she could feel his hardness. "I know. And that's why you love me."

Chapter Ten

They were awakened shortly before dawn with Poplovitz pounding on Galen's door. Lily hurried to her own room, in order to maintain at least the illusion of decorum. She slipped on her chemise and her robe, so she could make a proper entrance.

Galen pulled on his robe and opened the door. "What's wrong?"

"Zeblinski said to get you now. The pilot's gone into seizures. I've got a horse cart downstairs."

"Lily!"

She opened the connecting door. "Yes, Dr. Stewart?"

"The pilot's having seizures. Poplovitz has a cart waiting downstairs. Get dressed."

"Yes, Doctor."

"Go ahead down, Captain. We'll be down in a few minutes."

He opened Lily's door. "Any idea?"

"Brain damage? Fever?" She shook her head. "I hate to say out loud what it probably is."

"Withdrawal?"

She nodded. "When his plane came down, he was loaded full of injected cocaine. No telling how much he's accustomed to using."

Lily was having trouble buttoning the front fasteners of her brassiere. He brushed her hands aside and did the six buttons up for her. He rushed to pull on his own trousers and shirt. He didn't bother with his jacket or hat. They could court-martial him later. Likewise, Lily didn't bother with petticoats or stockings. She pulled on a pair of socks, tied her boots, and left her veil behind. If they had to go into surgery she wouldn't need it anyway.

She went back into Galen's room and they left together. The late August heat was already evident even before the sun was up. They hurried down the steps and found Poplovitz sitting holding the reins of a small mule hitched to a cart.

Galen half tossed Lily into the back of the cart, then climbed onto the seat beside the young Captain. Poplovitz snapped the reins and the mule started off at a trot.

They made it to the post in half the time it took them to walk. Poplovitz led the way to the impromptu burn ward, which was the orthopedic section of the unit, with screens put up to segregate the patient.

The young man on the bed would, by turn, go rigid then twitch violently. Zeblinski sat at the top of the bed, holding the boy's head steady, and keeping a bite stick between his teeth.

"What's going on, Lieutenant?"

"He was on full oxygen after two hours. I discontinued it all together, and administered a quarter grain of Morphia. That was two hours ago. An hour ago, the seizure activity started. He's been like this since."

"Any fever? Obvious discomfort?"

"No, Sir. Temperature is ninety-nine, so not nearly high enough for febrile activity. And he was still groggy when I hit him with the injection."

Galen looked at Lily. She said, "We were right. Is there any chance someone can get in touch with his unit, to see what and how much he was using? And why he was being allowed to fly in an altered state?"

"We'll leave that for later, after the sun's up at least." It was time for Galen to turn professor for these fledgling physicians. "Gentlemen, suggestions?"

Poplovitz decided to throw out the first suggestion. "Would it help if we administered a small dose of cocaine? To ease his withdrawal?"

"We could, but he'd only withdraw again as soon as it wore off. And we'd put him at risk for a heart attack." He turned to Zeblinski. "Any ideas?"

"I thought about giving another quarter grain of Morphia. Maybe a little less."

"Very good. Do we have any more saline solution?"

Poplovitz ran to fetch a bottle of IV fluids.

Standard treatment for severe burns included a single bottle of intravenous sterile saline. Galen decided it was time to deviate from the norm. He prepared a syringe with a quarter grain of Morphine Sulphate, and when Poplovitz returned with the bottle, Galen opened it, injected the Morphia solution into it, put the cap back on and shook it. He handed the bottle to Lily, who affixed the rubber tubing and large bore needle, hung the bottle, and established the intravenous line.

"There. He'll get a steady dose, sufficiently diluted as to not overdose him, but enough to keep him sedated. If it isn't enough, we can switch to an even smaller dose of Diamorphine. Is there any on hand?"

Zeblinski shook his head. "We had two bottles. They disappeared last month."

"For the love of god, this is a hospital! We need to keep sufficient analgesics on hand, particularly if they expect us to specialize."

That last caught Lily by surprise. "Specialize?"

He nodded. "Feeny told me yesterday. The Army wants us to specialize in orthopedics. Anybody here trained in orthopedics?"

Poplovitz raised his hand, as if he was in school. "I was planning to specialize once I finished my residency. I never got the chance. But I've got two years of hospital practice, piecing bones back together."

"Good. How many other doctors are on staff?"

"Seventeen, plus the two of us. And thirty nurses, some Army, some Red Cross."

"Good." He pondered for a minute how much he should divulge. "Has General Feeny said anything about a change of command?"

Both doctors shook their heads.

"Within a month, I'll be resigning my commission with the Royal Army Medical, and assuming command here. We need to get this place running at peak performance if they expect us to take over for other units with orthopedics. Of course, we'll still get other cases, like this burn victim. And I expect we'll have a fair number of neurological cases like our brain damaged gentleman the other day. How is Private Ackroyd, by the way?"

Zeblinski said, "He regained consciousness earlier tonight. He complained his hand hurt like hell, that his leg itched, and that he was starving to death. One of the nurses fed him some beef tea. He wanted more. I said no."

"Good man. And no breakfast for him, so we can do his hand. Will you be able to do anesthesia in the morning?"

"I'm not sure. Depends on if I can get a quick nap."

The pilot had stopped seizing. "I'll stay with him. Why don't you get some sack time? We'll call you in plenty of time."

Galen sat beside the patient. He knew he'd need to carefully monitor his vital signs. "Nurse Barnett, were there any tags on the patient when he came in? It would be nice to know his name."

"No, Doctor. I found none."

"We'll need to see if there were any with the bombardier. Someone has to know who these two are."

Lily suspected there may be something strange about these two, but she couldn't put her finger on it. "I'll go roust General Feeny. He can send a messenger to the air base and figure out who was flying that plane."

Lily left the ward long enough to find coffee in the mess tent. She brought a pot and two cups back.

They'd had no breakfast, weren't even properly dressed. She had the passing thought that it was almost like they were married already.

An hour and a pot of coffee later, the camp was coming to life. Their pilot was still sedated, but Galen was worried the seizures could resume at any time. She excused herself and went to find the commanding officer. She found him in his office, having a quiet breakfast with his wife.

Irene stood as soon as Lily knocked. "Lily, what's wrong? You look like you've been pulled through a knothole."

"Feels like it. The burn patient started seizing, and Dr. Poplovitz came to get us before dawn. We've been with him since."

Feeny set his coffee aside. "How is he now?"

"Sedated. But Dr. Stewart needs to find out what stimulants he was using. When they crashed, he was so hopped up the Morphia had no effect, so they had to use gas."

"What was so strange, he had no identification at all. No dog tags. What part of his uniform that wasn't burned was ragged. We need to know who he is. Is there any way to find out?"

Feeny started shuffling through reports that had come in overnight. "Oh, here's something." He read it. Twice. "The plane was stolen. By two Germans wearing uniforms stolen from the camp laundry."

Suddenly, it all became clear. "General, do we have anyone on staff who speaks German?"

He looked at Irene. "I'm not sure. Do we?"

She nodded. "Poplovitz. His mother's Prussian, or

Austrian, or something. Anyway, he is reasonably fluent."

Feeny said, "So, I suggest we bring him out of sedation, and have Poplovitz question him."

"General, since we will be taking positions here, would it be possible to send a cable to my brothers? I don't want their mail to be returned and think the worst."

He passed her paper and pen to write out her message.

Lily stopped by the mess on her way back to the ward. She talked the southern cook into making a couple of ham and biscuit sandwiches.

She handed one to Galen as she sat down. "The plane was stolen. He's German."

Galen stopped in mid-bite. "Holy shit! No wonder he's been so hard to sedate. Reports say many of the German troops use huge amounts of cocaine and amphetamines to remain alert, then take Diamorphine to come down. Why not? They synthesized the stuff, so why wouldn't they use it."

She took a swallow of cold coffee to wash down the biscuit. "Any idea how we manage him?"

"Once he starts to withdraw again, I guess we could give progressively smaller doses of Diamorphine. Keep him sufficiently sedated for pain, and deal with his addiction at the same time."

"So, how long do we stay? If we keep getting patients, I'm afraid we'll never be able to resign."

"One more day. We'll set Ackroyd's hand, hand his care over to Poplovitz the orthopod, spend one more night, then leave in the morning."

Anne Arrandale

Chapter Eleven

An ambulance delivered them to the British camp as planned. Their twenty-four hour trip had turned into a week.

Major Kent had kept the place operating in their absence. Upon their arrival, Lily and Galen sat in Kent's office and discussed their plans.

"You know you're both needed here. And I'm sure headquarters would push through promotions and would match whatever the Yanks are going to pay."

Galen leaned forward in his chair. "It's not the pay, Byrd. It's about our homes. We have a chance to throw in with other Americans, and it's a chance we have to take. Will you process the paperwork for us please? The new commissions should be through by the end of the week."

"Well, if that's what you really want."

Lily and Galen spoke together. "It is."

Kent agreed to send their resignations by special messenger. He was sorry to lose them, but was even more sorry he would be put back in charge.

Galen walked Lily back to her quarters, and left her at her door. She knew she'd have to reacustom herself to sleeping alone.

She changed her clothes, then headed into the ward. She picked up the reports that were done in her absence and saw it had been a fairly quiet week, as the new American hospital seemed to be getting a fair share of their patients. Lily noticed she had a lack of orthopedic cases now, but more head wounds and the occasional bayonetting.

"Nurse Roddy, pleasure to see you." The young Scots nurse finished with her patient and went to greet Lily.

"We were getting worried about you, Sister. Thought maybe you eloped with that handsome doctor."

If only she knew. "No Alyce," she whispered. If I ever elope with Galen Stewart, you'll know it."

"See that I do. I hate getting my gossip third hand. Much nicer to get it from the horse's mouth, as it were."

They discussed their patients, and the plans of treatment for them. Six of their beds were filled with closed head injuries. For those, unless there was severe swelling, treatment involved bed rest and nourishing food. Two ocular wounds were awaiting an ophthalmologist to arrive to assess the damage. A single burn patient reminded Lily of the German pilot.

"Alyce, have you ever used sulfur on burns?"

She shook her head. "No. Normally the doctors use heat. Doesn't seem to help, but it's what they do."

"At the American hospital, they are mixing six parts petroleum jelly, two parts lanolin, and one part sulfur. Then they whip it with an egg beater until it's the consistency of whipped cream. After the wound is debrided and irrigated, it gets spread on like meringue. Keep it applied, then every other day, the patient goes in a tub to wash off the cream, debride the burns, then butter him up again. It's amazing, really. Whipping it makes all the difference in the world."

Alyce was amazed. "I don't even know if the kitchen has an egg beater."

"I'll see we get one even if I have to go buy one at the local bakery. Of course, it and the bowl all need to be sterilized first."

"How long does it stay whipped? I mean, does it lose its volume if it stands?"

"What the American nurse prepared was good for at least three days. What are you thinking?"

"That we could prepare it ahead of time, and keep it on hand. Put it up in sterile jars, then keep it ready whenever we get burns in. I wonder if it would be beneficial for softening older burns? Sometimes they don't get here for hours, and by then the skin is like pie crust, all hard and flaking away."

"How about we try it, and see what happens?

Alyce agreed, and sent one of the nursing assistants to the kitchen to check the availability of an egg beater and bowl. She returned ten minutes later in tears.

Lily was the first to meet her at the door. "Maisie, what's wrong?"

"That Noble Harleston, that's what's wrong. He said he don't cut his veg with your scalpels, you don't be mixing your medicines with his beaters."

"Oh, he did."

She stormed out of the ward and across the compound to Galen's office. She rapped sharply, then opened the door before he could answer.

"Dr. Stewart, I'm on my way to the kitchen to give our cook a lily. Would you like to attend?"

He ran around the desk and followed her at a near-run to the mess. She was hot, and he wouldn't put it past her to deck the big cook. He didn't want to have to put his future bride on report.

"What did Noble do, Lily?" He was struggling to keep up with her.

"I sent an assistant to get a beater and a bowl, and he said, and I quote, "he don't cut his veg with our scalpels, we won't mix our medicine with his beater."

He tried to calm her down. "Lily, honey, I can requisition a hundred egg beaters."

She stopped, and he grabbed her when they collided. "That's not the point, Galen. You could very well have busted him for his little 'accident' with the lily bulbs. Instead, we took care of it, and educated him. Now he pulls this. It's too much."

"I agree. But..."

"Galen, I'm angry. I'm tired. Yes, we spent a glorious week together, but we also worked hard, and learned a lot. The last thing I want to deal with is a picayune argument between an incompetent cook and a poor little nursing assistant. He had her in tears."

"Why don't you let me handle it?"

"Let you handle it? Men like Harlaston have to learn that women have abilities, worth. She was sent on orders of a superior officer. Had Corporal Scott gone in and asked for a beater, or a bowl, or even a ham sandwich on your orders, would he have been turned away?"

"No. I doubt it."

"Then why does he think he can treat my nurses any different?"

She took off again. He strode after her, doing his best to keep up and utter soothing words, not that it would do much good.

By the time they arrived at the mess tent, she had worked off some of her anger. She was even stifling laughter at the way Galen acted, as if he feared she was really bent on mischief. Good. It will keep him on his toes.

She stood at the open door, where the cook was putting together lunch. "Harlaston!"

Galen stared at her. My God, she sounded like a drill sergeant. He stood to the side, ready if she needed backup, but not wanting to get involved yet.

The cook sauntered to the door. "Yeah?"

She wasn't having it. "It's Yes, Sister. Or Yes, Captain."

He came to attention. "Yes, Sister?"

"I sent an assistant here to collect some articles. You refused to relinquish them."

"Well, ya see, miss..."

"Sister!"

"Ya see, Sister, my kitchen tools are just that. Mine. I don't like to let them out of my sight."

"Sergeant, did you pay for those tools out of your pocket?"

"No, Sister."

"Were they provided by His Majesty's Army Commissary Corps?"

"Yes, Sister."

"Then they are not your property, are they? They belong to His Majesty."

"No, Sister. I mean, yes, Sister."

"Now, please hand me an egg beater and a bowl or basin. They will be returned to you tonight."

"Yes, Sister." He ran across the work area and pulled a beater from an overhead hook, and retrieved an enamel basin from beneath a shelf. "Here ya go, Sister. Keep 'em as long as you need 'em."

"Thank you, Sergeant." She took her prizes and walked away as quickly as she could, Galen again hurrying to keep up.

"Damn. That was impressive."

She slowed down a little. "As I intended. When I leave I want the men to respect the women working with them, not treat them like furniture."

"Well, I think you accomplished your ends. Although I doubt Nurse Roddy can command such respect."

"Don't bet on it. She wanted to deal with Harlaston. When she threatened to castrate him with his own kitchen knife, I decided it best I intercede."

That evening, when a company of nurses entered the mess for their meal, every enlisted man in the room snapped to attention.

Lily, seated with her nurses, got Galen's attention. She mouthed the word, "you?" asking if he had organized the demonstration.

He shook his head, no.

After their meal, Galen asked her, in front of the other nurses, to see him in his office to discuss a report.

Galen was already seated behind his desk when Lily arrived. "You wanted to see me, Major?" She closed the door.

He gestured for her to sit. "Harlaston came to see me after lunch."

"Oh, no." She couldn't keep from laughing. "Because I was mean to him?"

"He said you humiliated him in front of his staff."

"And?"

"I asked him what was the cause of his humiliation. He told me some uppity nurse wanted to invade his kitchen."

"Uppity? Have you met Maisie, the assistant we sent?"

"She's the one who cries when a patient is discharged, because she's sorry to see them go?"

"That's her. Harlaston made her cry, too."

"I asked him if he would report Captain Walkup for speaking to him the same way. Or if he would have refused to give the requested articles to an orderly."

Lily waited for his answer.

"He hemmed and hawed. 'Well, uh, ya see, uh.' I sort of felt sorry for him. But not enough to let him off the hook."

"Good."

"I cut him off. Then I reiterated the fact that nurses outrank him and everyone else in his kitchen. You are all officers and will be treated as such."

"Was that the end of it?"

"Not exactly."

"Well, what, exactly?"

"I offered him a transfer. Told him I'd be happy to send him to a howitzer unit at the front."

"So that demonstration was your doing."

"No, my darling girl. You put the fear of Lily into him. I merely added the fear of God. The fear of Lily is worse."

She changed the subject. "Did Kent Byrd send off our resignations?"

He nodded. "It went by special messenger. He believes our replacements will arrive a few days before we leave."

*****

Major Aldwin Moore, MD arrived as expected, in the midst of what the military leaders referred to as a "big push".

Wounded were scattered on blankets and stretchers in the field beside the hospital, where Alyce Roddy was in charge of triage.

Moore climbed out of the truck that delivered him in front of Major Stewart's office, and dropped off a packet of papers on the desk. Seeing the turmoil of emergency surgeries and triage, he made his way to Nurse Roddy. He wasted no time.

"I'm Major Moore, Nurse. What can I do to help?"

Alyce wasn't wasting time either. "You'll find gowns and aprons in the scrub room, Major. There are at least a dozen men who can be helped here. It will free up the surgeons inside."

He was already stripping off his jacket. "I take it Major Stewart is in surgery?"

"He is. Introduce yourself later Major. We have work to do."

He headed into the scrub room, where Maisie, the nursing assistant, was in charge. "Gown and apron please, nurse."

She didn't bother to correct him. She held the gown for him, tied it, then slipped the apron over his head. He grabbed the bag he had dropped by the door when he came in, and headed back out to the triage.

Inside surgery, word reached Galen by one of the stretcher bearers, that Moore had arrived. He wondered if Lily's replacement was on her way, or if the unthinkable had happened, and she had been declined. It would have to wait until after surgery. He had a ruptured spleen to remove.

Three hours later, Galen closed his tenth patient, and declared he needed a break after nine straight hours in surgery. Lily was assisting Teddy Ward as he resected a bowel. "Let Clevenger take over."

She stepped away and handed off her duties to Eliza.

She followed Galen outside, where the number of wounded awaiting surgery seemed to have diminished considerably. Had so many patients died and been removed? She spotted Alyce Roddy and made a beeline.

"Alyce? What happened?"

Alyce Roddy paused in administering a second Morphia injection. "The new Major happened. He's good. Can we keep him?"

"What's he been doing?"

"Field surgery. Cleaning, suturing and dressing wounds. Some shrapnel extractions. Oh, and you'll never guess who came in on the last ambulance."

Lily shook her head.

"Mortimer Wismer! He was shot in the arse by one of his own men. Accidentally, of course."

"Naturally."

"And he refused to allow me to touch him. Said he'd wait for a real doctor."

"Oh, he did."

Lily looked around and found Galen speaking with Major Moore. She decided further introductions were in order. She headed their way.

Galen pointed to her. "Major Moore, meet Sister Lily Barnett. Sister, the Major's been telling me he's been ordered to promote a current nurse to Ward Sister, as there are a dozen nurses and six additional surgeons due on the next boat."

Moore shook her hand. "Aldwin Moore, at your service. I'd like to talk to you about it later, Sister. But I already have some definite ideas."

"Very good." She turned to Galen. "Major Stewart, an old friend of ours came in on the last ambulance."

He asked who.

"Mortimer Wismer. Gunshot wound to the gluteus maximus. He's refused to permit the nurses to touch him. Demands only a doctor may perform any procedure."

Galen never had the chance to answer. Moore looked around at the remaining triage patients. "Where is the idjit?"

Lily pointed. "The lieutenant lying face down on the blanket. The one still fully dressed."

Galen thought it best he inform his replacement of their history with the gentleman in question. "Wismer started in this unit, Major. He thought it was advisable to physically assault a nurse, insult the nurses and other doctors on staff, as well as steal from a senior staff member. I fattened his lip, and Nurse Barnett kneed his groin. He lied to Major Dennison about the incidents, then repeated his slander. Dennison sent him down to trench foot detail, since he refused to work with women."

Moore was looking forward to dealing with Wismer. "Well, Sister, why don't we go meet this paragon of British manhood."

Lily walked beside him as they made their way to where Wismer lay. "Hello, Mortimer."

He didn't turn to look up. "That's lieutenant, nurse."

Ooh. She was going to enjoy this. "That's Sister, Lieutenant."

He groaned as he finally twisted to see who addressed him. "Oh, hell."

"And Lieutenant, this is Major Moore."

Wismer acknowledged him, vaguely.

Moore asked, "Nurse Roddy, why is this man still wearing his trousers?"

"The Lieutenant refused to permit me to touch him."

"Oh, he did? Nurse Roddy, take your scissors and remove this man's clothing. We must assess his wounds."

Alyce took her scissors from her apron and knelt to take hold of Wismer's uniform by the seat of his uniform trousers and started to snip. Once the fabric was cut away, and the affected area exposed, the injury was evident.

Moore leaned over and "tsk tsked", then handed Lily a pair of forceps. "Sister, debride the wound, please."

Lily knelt and began picking pieces of wool from the wound, as Wismer carried on.

As she worked, Moore asked, "Sister, have you ever extracted a bullet"?

"I have, Doctor. But I'm not very good at it. Now, Nurse Roddy, here, she's as skillful as many of the surgeons at projectile extraction."

He handed Roddy a probe and tweezers from his bag. "Nurse Roddy, evacuate the wound please, then extract the projectile."

"Really, Major. I must object!" Wismer tried to push himself up.

Moore put his foot in the center of his back and held him down. "Stay there, Lieutenant. And shut up. That's an order."

Alyce used the probe to locate the bullet, then picked it out with tweezers. She dropped it into the basin. "There you are, Major. It was hardly even under the skin. Had he waited a day or two, he could have popped it out like a pimple."

"Very nice work, Nurse Roddy. Now, I believe one or two stitches should close it off nicely."

Wismer was still complaining. "Really major. Isn't it customary to administer an anesthesia before a procedure?"

"Lieutenant, there are critically wounded men awaiting surgery. You have a little boo-boo on your bum. Get over it."

Alyce was having far too much fun. "What shall it be, Major? Two simple stitches, crossed in the middle? Or I can do a button-hole stitch around the perimeter, and make him a second anus?"

Moore covered his mouth with his hand, trying very hard not to laugh at Nurse Roddy's purposely inflammatory comment. "I suggest two simple stitches, Nurse. A button-hole stitch would take far too much embroidery floss. Just use plain gut stitches and have done with it. He's really not worth your time."

Alyce made quick work of the two stitches, doused the area with a squirt of alcohol, then put on a small dressing. "You're done, Lieutenant. You can get up now."

"Really, Major. I must insist I be examined by a physician."

Moore made a show of leaning over Wismer's derriere. He poked the fresh stitches with his index finger. Wismer squealed. "Major Stewart, I believe this is a fine job."

Galen was thoroughly enjoying the whole scenario. "Yes, Major Moore. I concur. Sister Barnett?"

"I don't believe any of our surgeons could have done a better job, Major. Nurse Roddy, please return to your patients. We'll finish up here."

Wismer finally managed to get on his feet. "This will get me sent home, won't it, Major?" It sounded more like a statement.

Galen looked at Moore. "Major Moore, you'll be in charge here soon. Would you like to answer him?"

"Certainly Major Stewart. No Lieutenant Wismer. Getting shot in the arse does not get one sent home. It gets you a week in a hospital behind the lines, while you get used to sitting side saddle. Then you are sent back to your unit. If you want to get sent home, you'll have to do better than this."

His question brought up more. Galen called Alyce Roddy back. "Nurse, at what angle was the trajectory of the shot?"

She demonstrated with his fingers. "Down and in. Like when a person reaches around to scratch their bum."

"Un-huh. Wouldn't there be stippling around the wound, Nurse?"

"Hard to tell, Doctor. The woolen trousers were too damaged to really tell, and they would have taken most of the powder burn."

"Very good, Nurse Roddy. Major Moore, do you believe this wound may indeed have been self inflicted?"

"Yes, Doctor. I concur. Well Lieutenant, it looks like this will get you sent home. But not to your cushy private practice. You'll be going to jail for cowardice under fire. You will be lucky to go to jail. Sometimes men are hanged for such an offense."

A group of enlisted men were passing, carrying supplies to the ward. Galen called two of them over.

"Yes, Major?"

"Gentlemen, this man is under arrest. He is a coward. I want him under twenty-four hour guard until he can be sent for trial. Understood?"

"Yes, Major."

Wismer was hustled away, and consigned to the tent holding the handful of German wounded.

Lily watched this all unfold. "Major Moore, this was a real education. I must say, I agree with Nurse Roddy's assessment."

"And what was that?"

She leaned in close, lest Alyce be embarrassed. "She said you were good, and asked if we could keep you."

The company ate supper late that night. Lily was asked to share the table with Galen, Moore and Byrd Kent. Harlaston served them personally that night. He placed Lily's plate in front of her, and she surprised him.

"This looks delicious. Thank you, Sergeant."

"You're welcome, Sister. A couple of the men

trapped some rabbits. I thought a good stew might be a nice change from tinned beef."

"Real onions, Sergeant?"

"Definitely, Sister. Well, dried onions, because that's what they send.'"

She took a taste. "Wonderful, Sergeant. Compliments to you and your staff."

Moore watched this exchange in wonder. He'd never seen a cook behave this way, particularly with a nurse.

Galen filled his replacement in on what had happened on two separate occasions.

Moore raised his coffee cup to Lily. "Sister Barnett, you have done the impossible. I'm sorry we're losing you."

Lily seized the opportunity. "Since I'll be leaving, I was wondering if you've given any thought to who would be named ward sister in my absence?"

Aldwin Moore took a bite of his dinner, swallowed, then said, "I am really impressed with Alyce Roddy. But since we will be taking on more nurses, we will need a sister as well as a matron. I propose Alyce be named matron. Who would you recommend for ward sister?"

Lily answered without hesitation. "Eliza Clevenger. She's more than competent. She used to work for a practice in rural Scotland where she did most of the work, and the doctor only showed up to collect the fee."

"So it's settled then."

They finished their meal, and Galen took Moore back to his office for a quick, belated tour.

"Galen, tell me, what do you know about Sister Barnett?"

"Quite a bit, actually. I've known her since she was around fourteen or fifteen. Why?"

"I was wondering how old she was. That white hair makes her look like she's in her forties, but her face and figure say otherwise."

Galen reached into a desk drawer and pulled out a bottle of whisky. He poured two glasses and passed one to Moore. "It's a strange story. She had diphtheria when she was about fourteen. It made her go bald. She was lucky that her hair grew back, but it came in the color you see, and curly. She's about twenty-four, I'd say."

"Any problems with fraternization?"

"Let's just say there have been no complaints. I can tell you I haven't had to send any nurses home for pregnancies."

Moore nodded. This was the kind of base he liked. "By the way, did you see the orders I left on your desk when I arrived?"

Stewart sifted through the reports that had been put there during the day, until he got to the brown packet. He held it up. "This one?"

"That's the one."

Galen undid the ribbon tie, and pulled out the contents. "Oh, our releases." He scanned his way down the page. "It says this is our last day. That's a surprise. Are you ready to take over?"

"I reckon. I think I saw the worst of it today."

Galen told him, "The nurses are all capable, and if you listen to them, they can teach you a lot."

Moore raised his glass. "To our nurses."

*****

It was close to midnight when Galen knocked softly on Lily's door. She opened the door a crack, then stepped back to let him slip inside. He set aside the open wine bottle he carried and bent to kiss her, thoroughly and soundly.

She pushed herself away. "Galen, you're drunk." Given the proximity of her quarters to the ward, they had to keep their voices down.

He pulled out his pocket watch to check the time. "Yep. and in ten minutes, we will no longer be members of the Royal Army Medical Corps."

She sat on the chair beside her small desk. "Any word on our new commissions?"

"I need to dispatch a message to General Feeny first thing in the morning. But you know what this means, don't you?"

All it took was one look into his eyes to figure out what was on his mind. She did her best to hold him off. After all, they were still medical personnel in a military base hospital. "It means we can sleep soundly tonight, and not worry about early calls or emergencies."

He put his arm around her waist, and pulled her against him, so she could feel his already growing urgency. "We can sleep later. For tonight, I intend to have your legs over my shoulders."

She and Galen had done many things in all their time together. She had been familiar with various aspects of sex, due to her time in the hospital, and working with the girls in the sex trades with the health department. But his comment about having her "legs over his shoulders" had her at a loss. She was intrigued.

Later, as they lay in each other's arms, he decided it was time they explore more than their bodies. "You know, I was talking to Aldwin in the office earlier. He asked questions and I couldn't answer."

She was busy drawing figures on his chest with her fingers. "Like what?"

"Like how old are you?"

"Twenty-four. How old are you?"

"Thirty-four. Do you have a middle name?"

"Mmm-hmm. Lily Elaine Barnett. You?"

"Claudius Galenus Stewart."

"Claudius Galenus? Your parents named you after a Roman emperor?"

"Nope. Claudius Galenus something-or-other was the Roman physician who pioneered a lot of the procedures we do now."

"You knew my parents. What about yours? Are they still living?"

"They are. In Timonium. And before you ask, my father is a doctor. Had their second child been a boy, he would have been named Hipocrates."

"So what did they name her?"

"Alice Jane. And she's going to medical school in Philadelphia right now, first in her class."

"I'd love to meet them."

"You will. Let's see. Parents. Siblings (I know yours). Ages. Names. What are we leaving out?"

"Well, what do you plan to do once the war is over, and we get back home?"

"I don't know. I might go back to hospital work, or I may open a private practice somewhere. How about you?"

"Well, I had figured on assisting you, wherever you are." She went back to drawing letters on his chest. "When did you first realize you loved me?"

"I'll ask you the same. When did you know you loved me?"

"Well, I decided I was going to marry you the day you came to our house for dinner. It was when Papa asked you about the lasting effects of diphtheria, after my hair loss. You were so understanding. You treated me like a real person, not some mouthy little kid. Now you."

"I could say when I came to your house, after you had diphtheria. But you were only fourteen. Your father would have taken a bullwhip to me. No. It was at St. Joseph's, when you were in school. You were so self-assured, so smart, and you questioned everything."

"Interns and doctors used to ask me out all the time. Why didn't you? I would have gone had you asked."

He raised up on one elbow, trying, and failing, to appear menacing. "Oh, really? Other doctors asked you out?"

She nodded, suddenly shy. "Mm-hm. Including Dr. Dreyfus."

"Dreyfus? Not Dreadful Dreyfus, the old bastard who used to like to corner students in the scrub room?"

"The same."

"What'd you say?"

"I didn't say anything." A beatific smile lit her face. "I gave him a Lily"

Anne Arrandale

Chapter Twelve

September 20, 1917

Galen and Lily stood hand in hand in the anteroom of the Register's office in Ypres. They were both considered civilians for the time being, and wore their civilian clothes. Galen had a simple dark suit he'd picked up in a local shop, while Lily wore the purple dress from when she first went to Galen.

As they waited, Lily laid a watch chain with an unusual fob in his palm. "I told you, when I was ready to marry you I'd give you this." The fob was shaped like a padlock that matched her gold key.

He wanted nothing more than to kiss her senseless right there. Before he had the chance, the Register opened the double doors to his office.

The ceremony was simple, direct and to the point. They were finished within an hour, and headed down the wide staircase to the street.

Lily looked up at her dashing husband. "Somehow, that seemed sort of anti-climactic."

"Should I be offended?"

She laughed. "No. But I somehow expected to feel different after we signed the book. But I feel exactly the same as I did before."

He picked up her left hand and kissed the finger where he had so recently placed the small gold band. "Well, my darling girl, we have a whole four uninterrupted days to see if we can make you feel different."

They walked slowly down the street. Lily still carried the small bouquet she'd held during the ceremony. People applauded as they passed. "Galen, did you arrange for rooms at the same cafe where we stayed before?"

"I did. Is that alright with you?"

"Certainly. Would you mind terribly if we had dinner in our rooms tonight?"

"Of course not. I can go fetch the food while you have a bath."

She stroked his cheek. "No, my darling. You need to shave. I don't want whisker burn on my thighs.

They made several stops on the way to their rooms. True to his word, Galen bought her a wrapper to replace the one he had baptized in the tub, and a corset cover for the one he had destroyed. Lily insisted they stop in a wine shop and get a couple of bottles of locally produced red.

They arrived at the cafe in time for an early dinner. Lily sent Galen upstairs, with instructions to bathe and shave, and she'd be up as soon as she had their meal.

The waiter at the cafe remembered her. She ordered their food, then asked if anything had come for her. The waiter delivered a parcel wrapped in brown paper and tied with twine, with a Baltimore return address.

The waiter brought her food on a tray. Pate, cheeses, bread, some cold meat (she knew better than to ask its provenance) her parcel, two wine glasses and a corkscrew. He started to give her a knowing wink, then saw the gold band on her left hand. In English, he said, "Best wishes to you and the doctor, lady."

She thanked him, then headed up the steps. It took her a minute to get the door open.

Galen called out, "Still in the tub." She set her tray down on the dresser and arranged the plates of food on the small table. The box she set on the bedside table for later, as a surprise.

Galen came from the bathroom wrapped wearing his robe, drying his hair. "This looks good. Dare I ask what it is?"

Pointing to individual items, she recited "Bread, cheese of some kind, including some sort of bleu, figs, meat that may or may not be beef. Something that looks like Parma ham, and pate.

He picked up a fig and popped it in his mouth. "Mmm." He mumbled around his mouthful.

She handed him the corkscrew to open the wine. He poured them both a glass, then sat opposite her as they ate and talked about nothing in particular and everything in general.

They ate leisurely, feeding each other select bites of food.

Lily still wore her elegant purple dress. She sat very primly on the edge of her chair as they ate. When they had eaten their fill, Lily rose and retrieved the paper wrapped parcel. She handed it to Galen. "A wedding gift."

"A gift? Nobody knew we got...it's...it's from your brother?"

She nodded.

Galen started unwrapping the parcel, struggling with the twine until he fetched his pen knife from the dresser.

At last he was through the paper, to the box. "This looks familiar." At last, he got the box open and extracted the tin. He pried the lid off the tin. His eyes lit up when he saw the chocolate enrobed treasures. "Bergers!"

He bit into one, savoring the bittersweet chocolate ganache and crumbly shortbread.

Lily took his hand in hers. She bit into the cookie, mimicking his actions of so long ago, when she first discovered the depth of her passion for him.

Galen closed his eyes as she sucked the thick frosting from his fingers. With his free hand he reached and drew her to him. He could feel the corset beneath her dress. He didn't need any extra enticement to desire her. Hell, he'd look at her when she was up to her wrists in somebody's gut and would want to drag her into the supply closet and ravage her. He loved this woman. But the things that bit of canvas and steel ribbing did for her were another matter entirely.

*****

Galen and Lily reported for their first day of duty following their four day sojourn as newlyweds. They still had to be guarded in their relationship, but since Lily would be part of the Red Cross contingency rather than the regular army, she would have more freedom, and they could well have opportunities not otherwise afforded.

General Feeny was in the middle of packing up his personal things in anticipation of handing over command to the newly minted Colonel Stewart. Uniforms were waiting for Galen in his quarters. He and Lily went directly to Feeny's office when they arrived.

The General stopped his packing and sat at his desk. There were still forms to be signed. He presented them to his replacement. As Galen reviewed them, Feeny went to the door and hailed a passing enlisted man. "Soldier, go find Nurse Cortizi. Tell her I need her in my office now. I believe she may be in her quarters."

Lily sat quietly in the chair, waiting for Irene to arrive, wondering how long she'd be able to stay before her first assignment. She didn't have to wait long.

The older nurse looked into the office. "Oh, good. You're back. Come with me, Nurse Barnett. I'll show you your quarters."

Lily's new quarters were behind Feeny's office. The large tents were each divided in two, so their sleeping quarters were behind their offices, and abutted one another. Lily wondered if they two had set them that way on purpose, in order to be more conducive to nocturnal conjugal visits. She didn't ask.

Irene gestured to a neatly folded stack of clothing. "Those are your uniforms. You have to provide your own undergarments. You have six white dresses, aprons, a blue dress uniform, cloak, hat, and cap. If you need more, you can ask Colonel Stewart to requisition them from London. Do you have serviceable boots?"

Lily lifted her skirt to show what she had.

"Just those?"

"These are my second pair. My original boots cracked too badly to be repaired."

"Requisition a pair of those as well, unless you have a favorite pair someone can send you from home."

Irene gave Lily a brief tour: where files were kept, how to file reports, and what specifically would be her duties. "Technically, you are head nurse. The army has charge nurses over the various wards and surgery. You are the ultimate arbiter of any differences, as well as preventing the spread of infectious diseases. You may select two other Red Cross nurses to act as assistants once you get to know them. Just don't make them your stooges. Don't use them merely to get information and gossip about other staff."

"How many nurses are on staff, both regular army and Red Cross?"

"Fourteen Red Cross nurses, assisting wherever they're needed. Nineteen army nurses. There are also twenty-two doctors, I believe twenty-two nursing assistants, and the same number of orderlies. This job is intended to be primarily administrative, but I've found it best to go on and dig in, get your hands dirty, so you know what your nurses need and when they need it. Now, I'll leave you to get changed, and take you to meet your new staff"

Lily picked up a white uniform dress. At least it was pretty close to her size. These dresses were considerably shorter than the British version, by at least three inches. It made it much easier to keep them out of the muck, and being all white, it made them easier to clean. She'd seen nurses wear the same gray uniform several days, because they didn't show dirt.

Once she was changed, she stepped out to find Irene Cortizi and Joshua Feeny standing with Galen. He was resplendent in his new American uniform. It wouldn't take much for her to drag him off somewhere.

This new uniform Lily wore fascinated Galen. The skirt was shorter than any he'd seen her wear, and the white cotton hugged her slim figure faithfully. He was glad their quarters were adjoining.

They were given a guided tour of the camp, introduced to the staff on duty, as well as those whose shift had not yet begun.

When they had seen as much as they were able, without having any active surgeries, the four returned to Feeny's, now Galen's office. The General pointed to a dispatch pouch on the desk. "That's for you, Colonel. It's your command now."

Galen opened the pouch and removed the contents. "Big push tomorrow at Polygon Wood. Lily, get your nurses ready, and get the theater set up. No telling when the first wounded will arrive."

Feeny waited until she was gone. "Do you need us to stay, Galen?"

"No, Joshua. You and Irene get out while you can. Otherwise, I'm afraid you'll be stuck here a week."

*****

The first patients arrived after breakfast. Six patients were brought in with multiple injuries.

Until Lily was sure what her nurses could do, she took triage herself. Galen assigned a doctor to work with her, much as Aldwin Moore had done his first day at his new post. It was an excellent system, she found, freeing up theater time for the more serious cases.

Lily sent two belly wounds in before the bearers could set the stretchers down. She knew it would be the beginning of a long haul so she tried to make the process as streamlined as possible. After the first few cases arrived, she devised a system of organizing the triage into areas: orthopedic, neurological, shell, and miscellaneous wounds. That way, as the specialist surgeons finished one case, the next could be more easily sorted to be sent in.

The next eight days were a living hell.

*****

October 4, 1917

Lily and Galen sat in the officers' mess, exhausted, yet too tired to sleep. The cook had spent the last eight days keeping the surgical staff supplied with coffee and soup. They had all grabbed sleep, or at least rest, as they were able, in half hour increments. Lily and Galen had taken fewer breaks than the others, feeling the need to be available to their staff. Now the worst of the work was done and it was up to the ward staff to look after their charges.

Galen shoved his cold coffee aside. "I swear to God, I never want to see another cup of coffee. Or another cup of soup. I especially never want to drink either one out of a glass straw again."

Lily looked around to make sure they were alone in the mess. She pushed her own cup back and stood. "Come on, Colonel. I need someone to tuck me into bed. And if he's amenable, to hold me while I sleep for the next ten hours."

Galen pushed away from the table and stood. He stretched and arched his back, trying unsuccessfully to work out the kinks. "Lord, I must be older than I thought. Everything I have hurts."

She took his hand and led him out of the mess. "Come along, Colonel. I'll tuck you in."

They walked slowly back to Galen's quarters. She pulled off his shirt, then unbuttoned his trousers. She aimed him at the bed, and managed to get him into it without him collapsing first. She shucked off her own uniform, leaving her underwear and chemise, and climbed in beside him on the narrow bunk with her back to him. He pulled the blanket over them both, put his arm around her, and was snoring before she had found a comfortable spot on the pillow.

Lily awoke in an empty bunk. The sun was high in the sky. She dressed hastily, and peeked out the back door of the tent. No one was in sight. She slipped through and into her own quarters. She washed quickly, changed her clothes, and headed out to start her day.

She found Galen in the mess, pushing food around his plate. She sat next to him and waited for him to say something.

He looked up, seeming to finally recognize her. "Good morning."

"And good morning to you. When did you get up?"

He took a swallow of the coffee he had sworn off only last night. "Around seven. Emergency in one of the wards. Zeblinski wasn't sure how to handle it, so he called me."

"What was it?"

"Orthopedic patient. They amputated his arm a couple of days ago. He had an apoplexy this morning."

"Oh, Galen. How is he?"

He pushed his plate back. "He's dead."

Lily wanted to weep for him. She got up and fetched a cup of coffee for herself. If nothing else, it was hot. Food was the last thing on her mind. She picked up the sugar bowl to sweeten her cup when a courier came in and handed Galen a dispatch case. He opened it, then passed one of the pages to Lily.

"Did you read this?" she asked.

"No. I just saw it was for you."

"There is an outbreak of disease at the camp near Verdun. I've got to leave tomorrow. I need to see my nurses." She took a quick swallow of coffee, made a face because it still had no sugar, and headed out to find the two young women she intended to make her assistants.

She found Melina Carlin in the orthopedic ward. "Nurse Carlin, when you're done, may I see you?"

Lily went to busy herself checking on supplies. She was writing up an order for gauze and iodine when Melina found her. "You wanted to see me, Nurse Barnett?"

"Yes, I did. I have to go to another camp tomorrow. I need to appoint two assistants. I was very impressed with your performance this past week. There's no promotion yet, only more responsibility. Are you in agreement?"

"I am. Who else will you appoint?"

"I thought Philomena Stinson. Can you work with her?"

"Sure. We share a tent already. Working together is just one more small step."

"And where do you think I can find Nurse Stinson?"

Melina checked her watch. "She'll be in the hydrotherapy room in the burn ward. She's changing the dressing on that young French officer today."

Nurse Stinson had just put a burned man into a tank of water, to clean his injuries and to remove more of the burned tissue. It was a horribly painful procedure, and he had already been given a dose of morphine in preparation for the treatment.

Lily drew her aside, out of hearing of the patient and orderlies and put the same question to Philomena.

"Of course, Nurse. Now, if you'll excuse me, I need to get back to my patient."

That was good. The girl was dedicated to her work.

Lily returned to her quarters and reread the dispatch. It said there was an outbreak at the unit in question, but claimed it was of "undetermined origin."

The next page contained a list of the symptoms and pathologies exhibited by the patients. She decided to consult with Galen before she left, and found him in his office, signing reports. "Galen, have you a few minutes?"

He nodded.

"This outbreak. It seems rather straightforward. Sudden onset pain, high fever, followed by partial paralysis and death. What does that sound like?"

He didn't even have to think. "Meningococcal Meningitis. And it sounds like they have a carrier."

"That's what I thought. I wonder why the doctors didn't pick up on it."

"Could be anything. Exhaustion. Lack of training. Stupidity."

"What I thought. Do you know if we have a supply of polyvalent serum?"

He reached into the file cabinet behind him and pulled out a folder. He ran his finger down a page. "We have more than enough. Take what you need. Sign out a microscope, slides, syringes and stains. I have a feeling the unit where you're bound is woefully understaffed and undersupplied."

The next morning, Orlando Holt pounded on Lily's door. She yanked the door open. "Wait a minute, would you?"

The big ox of a man leaned against the door frame. He didn't care how long this took. At least he wasn't digging latrines today.

Lily finished stuffing a change of uniform into her pack. She gestured to the two wooden crates set inside her door. "These two boxes go, Corporal. And don't drop them. They're fragile."

He took them one at the time and secured them in the back of the truck. He tossed her bag into the back, then handed her up into the cab.

It was almost a forty mile drive to the camp. Holt tried to make small talk. Lily barely paid attention. She was suddenly unsure of herself. In the past, she had always had Galen or another physician she respected to fall back on. Suddenly, she was on her own, and she dreaded being wrong. It could cost lives.

When they arrived, the camp was little more than a scattering of distant tents and bomb craters. A young nurse ran out to greet their truck. "Are you Nurse Barnett?"

"What happened here? And where is your commanding officer?"

The girl sobbed and wiped her nose on the sleeve of her dress. "All dead. They were all in surgery and triage when the bombardment began. The theater, triage, and primary wards took direct hits."

Lily was appalled. "So who's been caring for patients?"

She sniffed again. "We've eight nurses aids, a few orderlies, and enlisted men left. We're doing what we can, but we don't know what to do."

First things first. "Is anyone in charge?"

"We have a sergeant who's been directing grave operations."

"Good. Point me to where he is." She turned to her driver. "Corporal Holt, please unload the supplies. This young lady will show you where I can set up a lab."

Lily headed out in the direction the assistant had pointed.

Holt looked down at the tiny girl who met their truck. He smiled as sweetly as he could manage. "Hi. I'm Orlando Holt. But buddies call me Hoss. Guess cause I'm so big." He actually blushed and toed the dirt like a school boy.

The harried young woman smoothed down her stained uniform dress. "I'm Rose Oakley. Pleased to meet you, Orlando." She returned his smile, feeling hopeful for the first time in four days.

She guided Holt to an empty tent Lily could use to set up a laboratory to process samples, then helped him uncrate the microscope. She carried Lily's personal bag to the tent previously occupied by their head nurse.

Lily found Sergeant Raoul Casavetes in the field to the south of camp, supervising graves detail. She stood out of the workers' way and called to him.

Casavetes rose from where he knelt, recording names from dog tags, and noting where they would be interred. He brushed the dirt from his pants and went to meet her.

"Am I ever glad to see you!"

"Sergeant, how many were killed in the shelling?"

"Ninety three, including all our trained medical staff, patients in surgery, and those in triage."

"You still have some patients in the wards?"

"Yes, ma'am. They were operated on first, then went to the wards."

"How many patients do you have?"

"Only fifteen from that day, but twenty seven were already here when the push came. Then everybody started getting sick." He started to break down. "I'm senior enlisted man here, Nurse. I didn't know what to do."

She laid her hand on his sleeve. "You're burying the dead, and recording their information. That's the right thing to do. Now, show me where I can find your commander's tent. I need to get out some dispatches."

Casavetes escorted Lily through the cratered camp to the tent in question. He went inside ahead of her and lit an oil lamp. "I don't know what all's here, Nurse. But there's paper and ink on the desk."

He returned to his work, and left Lily to hers.

Lily sat behind the desk. She found paper, pen and the ink well, and started a dispatch. She wasn't sure how to get word to headquarters in London, but knew someone who did.

Colonel Stewart,

Medical staff wiped out, ninety three dead. Hospital gone. Require transport for forty two post operative patients, plus trucks for remaining supplies and personnel.

Lily Barnett, RN, ARC

She didn't know what else to do. She was without trained staff, and she couldn't possibly perform spinal tap on forty two men alone. For now, she concentrated on organizing what she could.

It was close to midnight when the rescue convoy pulled in. Holt drove the lead truck, with the squad of ambulances behind.

Lily directed traffic, sending non-infectious patients on ahead, with orthopedics, including amputations, going to Galen, and other injuries going to the British unit they so recently left.

She had done one spinal tap on the most critically ill patient, and discovered it was in fact meningitis. She administered a dose of polyvalent serum to each infected patient, on the theory that they were in an epidemic. If she was wrong, it wouldn't hurt. But if she was right, it just may save lives.

Part 2

Chapter Thirteen

November 11, 1918
U.S.S. Leviathan

Lily pulled the sheet over the face of the most recent soldier to succumb to the influenza. She watched as two orderlies bore their silent burden up the wide, carpeted staircase of their ship, the *Leviathan*. Originally commissioned in Germany as *Vaterland*, she had been a luxury ocean liner plying the transatlantic trade. Docked in New York when America entered the war, the Army commandeered the ship and pressed her into service, first as a troop transport, then as a hospital transport vessel, recommissioned as *U.S.S. Leviathan*. What had once been the grand ballroom was now the contagion ward. Where fine ladies in silk gowns had once waltzed with captains of industry, now infected soldiers were quarantined, to either recover or die beneath her ornate chandeliers.

She stopped to wash before going to the next patient. By the time they reached New Jersey, more than half of these men would be dead. She wished there was a way to segregate the patients more effectively than simply putting a screen between the beds. Apparently, the army didn't understand that air could carry over and under a screen. These men needed their own rooms, or they needed to be outside, where the contagion wouldn't be confined in such closed spaces.

Philomena Stinson handed her an envelope. "The radioman brought this down. He asked me to give it to you."

"Take over, will you?"

Lily was fearful of cables. Since she'd received that first one from Galen asking her to "please come", all others had brought bad news. Her brother Josey had joined the American Expeditionary Forces, and had been gassed his first day as battlefield chaplain. Raymond cabled he had lost a hand, not in the war, but in a stupid accident on his friend's boat.

Galen couldn't make this trip with her. She worried constantly that something would happen while they were apart.

She ducked into the narrow corridor that was part of the servants' passages between parts of the ship. Taking a deep breath, she closed her eyes and ripped open the envelope.

11/11/1918

LILY BARNETT

USS LEVIATHAN

IN PARIS STOP ARMISTICE DECLARED STOP NEW APPOINTMENT IN NASHVILLE STOP PLEASE COME STOP

        COL. GALEN STEWART   PARIS

She wrapped her arms around herself and leaned back against the wall. My god, the war was over! By the time the ship arrived in Bayonne, her husband would be bound for home. At last, they would be able to live as a married couple, not skulk about, stealing kisses and embraces in linen closets, like some first year intern and an aide.

Lily realized what she was holding in her hand. This wasn't news she needed to keep to herself. She ran into the ward and half-screamed, "ARMISTICE!"

A cheer went up from the staff and those patients capable of responding. Of course, they asked for details. She had to explain she had none, other than the war was over. They'd have to wait until one of the ship's officers brought the official word.

Philomena stopped Lily as she walked between the rows of beds. "Lily, is everything all right?"

Lily looked at the cable once more. Oh, what the hell. "It's from my husband. He's coming home!"

Nurse Stinson grabbed Lily in a hug and started to dance around with her then stopped. She held her at arm's length, and said, "Wait, what? Husband? What husband?"

Lily laughed. "Who do you think?"

Philomena looked puzzled, staring at Lily's face for some sort of sign. Then it dawned on her. "Not that good looking Colonel?"

"Which one? There's a lot of good looking Colonels running around."

"The commanding officer. Colonel Stewart."

Lily nodded.

"Shit fire. When did you get married?"

"Last year."

There was that puzzled look again. "Oh, you clever thing, you. All this time you've been keeping it a secret. I am so damned jealous. Now, tell me everything. Did you meet over there? How long have you known him?"

Lily shook her head, thoroughly enjoying the younger woman's delight in her news. "I met him when he was my father's research assistant, when I was a kid, and had diphtheria. I knew him when I was in nursing school, and was assigned to his surgical rotation. Then after I graduated, he sent me a cable from the front that he needed nurses, and could I please come."

"So that's how you both wound up in the British Medical Corps. We all wondered. So you worked together all that time?"

"Not all the time. We had different duty stations sometimes, like when he spent over a year on a hospital ship ferrying wounded to England. But we always managed to find our way back together."

Philomena thought that was the most romantic thing she had ever heard. "So what did he say in his cable? I know he didn't send that just to announce the war was over."

"He cabled to tell me he has a new appointment in Nashville. He wants to know if I'll come."

"Of course you will. Why wouldn't you?"

"Galen...Dr. Stewart knows I enjoy my career, that I don't want to give it up. I don't know what sort of opportunities there would be for me in Tennessee."

"Well, even if you have to stop working, at least for now, you'll have all that extra time to spend with that handsome doctor of yours." She heard a patient struggling to breathe, and turned to help him. As she walked away, Philomena mumbled, "Damn, I gotta find me a Galen."

*****

February 9, 1919
Union Station, Nashville, Tennessee

Galen Stewart paced the platform where the evening's L&N train was due to arrive in five minutes. The last five months had seemed never ending, but they'd flown by in comparison to the time he'd been waiting for Lily to arrive.

Three days ago she telegrammed she'd be on the train out of Baltimore, but there had been a hold up at Cincinnati, where she'd changed lines from the B&O. The train was three hours late already. The roses he'd brought were wilting, as was his starched collar. His face mask kept slipping. Damn, why had he never mastered tying these things? Probably because a nurse tied it for him.

Just when he was considering going upstairs to the bar for a stiff drink, he heard

the long blast of the train's whistle as it approached the station. He gripped the roses tighter, feeling more nervous than that night he'd called for her after she graduated nursing school. Here he was, an old married man, and he was nervous about greeting the woman whose bed he had shared for more than two years.

The long train pulled in and screeched to a halt. As the engineer released steam pressure, soldiers, some wearing masks, some not, rushed from the cars like water over Niagara. Galen stood, looking up and down the line. Finally, he saw a kid boot, followed by a well-turned ankle and the hem of a lavender dress. He ran three car lengths to reach her before that foot hit the platform. Her feet never had a chance to touch the ground.

Lily stepped from the L&N day coach into the arms of her husband. He grabbed her and hugged her to him. She dropped her carpet bag on the platform and threw her arms around his neck, happy for now just to breathe in the scent of him after days on trains. She wanted more than anything to kiss him and never let him go. But their masks got in the way.

He put her down, loathe to release her. At last he remembered he had a death grip on the bunch of flowers he held, and thrust them into her hands. "I brought these." Lord, he sounded like a teenager.

She looked down at the roses that had seen better days. "They need water."

He grabbed her hand. "Where are your bags?"

"I thought we'd check them tonight. I've got everything I need here." She held up her carpet bag.

"Come on." He took her bag then headed up out of the underground platform into the main station. "Can you walk four blocks?"

"Dinner?" She was starving. Because of the returning troops, there had been no dining car on the train, and she'd had to make do with an apple.

He nodded. "Room service."

Galen half dragged her the four blocks across Broadway, and up Sixth Avenue, until they reached the Hermitage Hotel. The liveried doorman tipped his hat as they came up the steps and pulled the door open. "Evening, Dr. Stewart."

Inside, he paused at the desk. "Key please, Marcus."

The clerk picked the key from the hook behind him and handed it over. "Good evening, Dr. Stewart. Mrs. Stewart."

He guided her to the elevators at the back of the lobby. While they waited for the car to come down, Lily leaned against him, still holding his hand. "Mrs. Stewart. I think that's the first time I've been called that, officially. It feels good."

The operator pulled back the gate and opened the filigreed door. "Top floor, please, William." They rode in silence, until William stopped at the requested floor, and slid open the gate. Galen handed him a silver dollar. "William, ask the captain to bring us up a bottle of champagne, some cold meats and fruit, you know. Something nice. And something for dessert."

Their room was large, with an oversized brass bed, dresser, wardrobe, and a small sitting room with table, chairs and a settee. Not only was there electricity, but there was a telephone in each room.

Galen wanted nothing more than to rip their clothes off and have his way with her. Influenza dictated they wait.

Lord have mercy, that bed looked good. Almost as good as her husband looked. But not yet. "Where's the bathroom?"

Like many hotels built at the turn of the century, one or two rooms on each floor were *en suite*. Otherwise, residents used the shared bathroom. He pointed to the door at the far end of the room. "Go ahead. I'll grab a shower down the hall."

Galen gathered his robe and towels and struck out for a quick shower, so he could be back before the bellman returned with their food.

Lily was grateful for the deep tub. She swore she had three states caked on her face. while the tub filled, she unpacked her carpet bag. It held the bare essentials-- night gown, robe, clean lingerie, and some lovely scented soaps she had treated herself to in Baltimore.

Her brothers had refused to see her at first. Josey, being Josey, said he didn't approve of her hasty marriage. Raymond was ashamed of his amputation. Lily didn't care. She walked into the family home, parked herself in the parlor, and refused to leave until they talked to her.

In the end they seemed to come around. Both young men agreed to visit them in Tennessee, once Galen had found a permanent place of residence.

She sighed as she sank her travel-weary body into the steaming water. It would have been so easy to sit in the tub and fall asleep. But that wasn't what she wanted. She finished bathing, and used the sponge to wash her hair. After cutting it twice in the field, it was starting to grow out, and was finally long enough to pin up.

It didn't take long to put away her bath things. Even though it was still early in the evening, not quite eight, she put on her gown and robe. The robe was the wrapper Galen had given her in Belgium, to replace the one ruined in the tub. This gown wasn't silk as her original had been, but fine cotton sateen, and was a lovely shade of mauve. She had managed to find a nightgown that matched it reasonably well. Both were embroidered across the bodice.

She sat on the settee, finger-fluffing her hair as it dried. The sound of the key in the lock announced Galen's return. He was carrying his clothes, and wearing his long brocade robe. He swung the door wide and admitted the bellman behind him, pushing a wheeled cart holding a magnum of champagne, a plate of cheeses and meat, bread, and an assortment of plated desserts. He took the bill from the bellman to sign, then handed it back. "What's this, George?"

The dark-skinned man grinned broadly, making it a point to avert his eyes, lest he embarrass Lily in her deshabille. "Compliments of the management, Dr. Stewart. In honor of your wife coming home."

Galen shook George's hand, passed him the bill, and a silver dollar for his trouble. "Thank you, George. Would you see we're not disturbed for the rest of the night?"

"Sure thing, Doctor. Would you like to put in your breakfast order now? Just tell me when to bring it."

"Excellent idea, George. Bring us eggs, bacon, biscuits, and some grits. And coffee." He looked at Lily. "But don't bring it until around ten."

George winked knowingly. "Y'all have a nice night. I'll see you're not disturbed."

The door closed behind the departing bellman. Lily went to the table where the food had been placed, and waited for her husband. "Galen, this is lovely. But I'm surprised the staff is so informal with you."

"I make sure I tip well, and I treat the staff like human beings, rather than being invisible like so many who stay here. It works."

The champagne cork exited the bottle with a loud "pop". Galen poured two coupé's of the chilled sparkling wine, then held one out for Lily. She stood and walked the two short steps to him and accepted her glass. He raised his glass, "My darling girl, my wife, my only love."

Lily looked into his eyes and took a small sip from her glass, took his glass and set both aside. She put her arms around his neck and kissed his cheek. "My husband, my gentle doctor, my heart."

*****

George knocked on the door a few minutes after ten in the morning. Lily pulled the covers up to her neck when Galen opened the door. The bellman had apparently made an art of averting his eyes from the lady in the room. He quickly gathered up the evening's dishes, and replaced them with the breakfast dishes. Galen pressed another dollar coin into his palm, then locked the door behind the departing bellman.

"Shall I serve you breakfast in bed, or would you like to join me at the table?"

Lily scooted across the bed and found her wrapper on the floor. She slipped it on, then sat at the round table with her husband. "What did we get?"

He removed the cloche from her plate. "Country ham, biscuits, eggs, gravy, and grits. Guess the kitchen couldn't get any bacon."

She looked at the plate curiously, picked up a fork and poked curiously at the white pile on her plate. "What are 'grits'? This looks like boiled sand."

He took a pat of butter from the bowl and dropped it into the grits. "Let the butter melt, then try them. I promise, it's better than boiled mule."

Obediently, she waited as the butter melted and ran down the sides to pool on the plate. A tentative bite. Then another. "These are nice. Better than mush, at least."

"Hospital ship mush?" He shivered theatrically at her nod. "Sheesh. The guys used to compare it to wallpaper paste, only not as tasty."

She followed his lead, pouring the bowl of white gravy over the biscuit and scrambled eggs.

He poured them each a last cup of coffee, then leaned back in his chair. "Do you feel like meeting with the Public Health Service director today? If not, it can wait until later."

"After lunch?"

"If you like."

"Galen, is this a job offer?"

He nodded. "If you'd like it to be. Would you?"

"Depends. Will I be working with you?"

"Depends. Would you like to?"

She looked over the top of her coffee cup. "What do you think?"

"The city council has decided influenza deaths won't be counted, and won't be recorded by the health department. There are a few cases being handled by the local hospitals. The rest are being shipped out, some to Sumner County," naming the county north of Nashville. "The plan is to set up a military style field hospital on the grounds where the North County Fair is normally held. Not only would it receive patients from Nashville, but from north Sumner and Macon counties. The Director wants me as medical director. I want you as nursing administrator."

"I don't know anything about the geography around here. But that sounds like it's in the middle of nowhere."

"Not exactly. It's in Coatesville, on the Kentucky line. It's a railroad hub for the L&N. In fact, your train came through there and probably had a short layover."

Lily still wasn't sure. "So, will we live in a tent? You know, like in Belgium?"

"Not exactly." He grinned, feeling he'd saved the best for last. "The position comes with a house. Of course, it also comes with a buggy and horse, because there are too many places a car can't go. So, what do you think?"

"I say call down to the bell captain and get my trunk sent up. I need to find something to wear to meet the Director."

*****

Just before two that afternoon, the motor taxi dropped the Stewarts in front of City Hospital, temporary home to the Public Health Commission.

Like most hospitals, the place was a rabbit warren, with multiple staircases and additions making it even more confusing. The pair were met at the door by a young man who introduced himself as Dr. York, who led them down two levels, past the morgue to the new Office of Public Health. He made introductions.

Dr. Happer rose from behind his desk. "Dr. Stewart, Mrs. Stewart. Welcome to my humble home away from home."

The three sat and exchanged pleasantries and made small talk, while York went to organize a pot of tea. Once they had all been served, Happer got down to cases.

"So, Galen, what do you think of our offer?"

Lily wasn't certain why she wasn't really being included in this discussion, other than as the doctor's wife. "Dr. Happer, my husband explained the offer to me. He also mentioned he is permitted to select his own staff. Is there any bar against me accepting a post in this new field hospital?"

Happer looked surprised. "Mrs. Stewart, I had taken it for granted that, as a newlywed, you'd want to keep your husband's home and keep him happy."

Galen started to speak, but Lily held up her hand. "Dr Happer, we've been married for two years. Perhaps you were unaware, but I spent two years as supervising nurse with the Red Cross, in charge of containing infectious diseases. Before that, I was sequentially a trained nurse, surgical sister, ward sister and matron with the British Medical Corps in France and Belgium."

Now she let Galen answer. "If I'm to accept this post, I want my wife as my nursing administrator. I know of no one more qualified."

The older physician shuffled papers and rooted in his desk drawer while he tried to think of an answer. At last, he stood and extended his hand to Lily. "Welcome aboard, Nurse Stewart." He sat back down, and as an afterthought, "just for our records, please bring me your nursing degree, your military record, and your paperwork from the Red Cross. Not that I doubt your word, but you know how the federal government is about their record keeping."

She was a step ahead of him. She opened her large bag and pulled out a collection of envelopes. They hit his desk one at the time. "Diploma, Public Health Certification from Baltimore City, British Medical Corps Commission, British Army Medical Discharge, American Red Cross commission. Anything else?"

Happer gathered them up and passed them to Dr. York, with instructions to have the information entered in Nurse Stewart's employment file. "They'll be returned to you in a few days. We'd like you to start Monday after next."

*****

The cab dropped them off on Broadway, near Fourth Avenue. Lily got a guided tour, walking past the Ryman Auditorium, where in better days they had put on plays, past the Customs House, and St. Mary's Catholic Church, where the nuns had cared for the diseased prostitutes licensed by the army during the War Between the States.

Knowing it really wasn't safe to eat in the few restaurants still open, they made their way back to the Hermitage Hotel.

Back in the room, Lily was pleasantly surprised that not only had the room been made up, but her trunk had been unpacked, and her clothes put away.

Lily flopped on her back across the bed. "Well, my love, it appears we are employed again."

Chapter Fourteen

"Coatesville, next stop. Coatesville in ten minutes." The conductor passed through the train car announcing their arrival at their home for the foreseeable future.

The engine picked up speed as it prepared to pull the long grade that started at Rock House Hollow.

Lily leaned back against the cushioned seat looking out the window. The wildness of this part of the country, this late into the Twentieth Century, was a constant source of surprise. She had experienced Europe during the war, and had come to expect minimal sanitary accommodations, given the age and condition of some of the buildings. What she couldn't get over here was families living in homes not fit to keep chickens, without any form of potable water, this close to civilization.

The train came to a stop in front of the depot in the center of what was referred to as a town. A dozen or so stores along a single strip, beginning with the bank on the southern corner and the Methodist Church on the northern. In between there was a barber, general store, a small hotel, feed mill, and a few others. Strangely enough, one of the first rural telephone exchanges was in the second floor front of the hotel.

The rest of downtown was taken up by the timber yard and sulfur storage, the two primary cargoes shipped by rail from that hub.

The depot wasn't large enough to hold any sort of lobby. It had a luggage room and a ticket window. Galen stopped there to arrange to have their bags held until they could be called for.

Before they could inspect their new housing, lunch was in order. Next to the hotel was something euphemistically called a "tavern", the euphemism being that the county was still officially dry. It at least looked reasonably respectable. They went inside, and Galen ordered them chicken and dumplings, which he considered the safest dish on the four item menu.

They were taking the last bites of their cobbler when an extremely tall black man slipped in the door. One quick look around the room, then he headed straight for the Stewarts' table. "I reckon you're Dr. and Mrs Stewart." It wasn't a question. "I've got your buggy outside if y'all are ready."

Galen paid the bill and they headed outside, where a polished red-wheeled Studebaker buggy, drawn by a spotted mule, waited.

Their driver introduced himself as Liberty Rogan. "I'll be y'all's driver and handyman. My wife, Miz Beatrix, she'll be takin' care of the house and the cookin'. Folks in Nashville figured, with both y'all working, wouldn't nobody have time for house stuff."

Galen handed Lily into the rear seat, and climbed in beside her. Liberty snapped the reins to get the mule into motion. He leaned across the seat to speak confidentially. "Besides, the big boss reckoned you didn't know nothing 'bout mules or drivin', being city folks and all."

Lily was grinning under her mask. She leaned forward, to express her own confidentiality. "I'll tell you a secret, Liberty. We do know a little something about mules. Horses too. During the war, we ate them. Sometimes in restaurants. "

Liberty's eyes got big. Then he asked, "You pulling my leg, ain't ya?"

"No, sir." Galen answered. "She's telling you the God's honest truth. The army had lots of mules and horses. When one of them got killed, the cooks in town would all rush and cut off as much as they could carry. It wasn't bad, either? Unless the shells the beast carried exploded. Then the meat tasted too much of gunpowder to eat."

Liberty turned back to his driving. Lily could have sworn she heard him mumble "crazy white people".

Their new home wasn't impressive by what some consider a "doctor's house". A two storey house with a wrap-around porch, with a three storey "tower" in one corner, and a few roses planted in the front. A lone hen strolled past the front steps, as if defying someone to shoo her back into the coop.

Liberty pulled the mule to a stop by the side door. "This door is to the mud room. Miz Beatrix, she keeps the boiler going all the time in there. Draw yourself off a bucket so's you can wash up, while I go back to town and get your stuff."

Inside the mudroom looked nicer than many of the homes they passed. The floors were slatted, to allow for easy drainage. Not only was there a boiler, but two heavy robes hung on pegs beside the stove.

Galen drew off two pails of hot water for them, while Lily organized washcloths, towels and soaps.

They undressed and lathered quickly, then poured the hot water over each other's heads. A quick dry, then into the heavy warm robes.

Lily pushed open the door that led to the kitchen.

A short, round black woman was busy rolling out pie dough.

"Mrs. Rogan?"

The woman looked up. "Miz Stewart! Doc Stewart! I'm Beatrix." She pronounced it *bee AH tricks*. "Miz Rogan is Liberty's mama. Come in. Set a spell. Let me pour you some coffee while my man fetches your trunks."

She bustled about the spacious kitchen, pouring coffee, putting out milk and sugar and a plate of cookies.

Galen picked up one of the sweets and took a small bite. It was sweet, tasting of sorghum, soft, with a pleasant, yet peculiar mix of sweet and salt. His wife, however, wasn't shy about eating. She bit, chewed and swallowed.

"My goodness, Beatrix. These are delicious. And so different. What's in them?"

"I used to cook for the men working in the tobacco fields. They'd have to be out at first light, and needed food they could carry. I started making these. They're just oatmeal cookies, but I add raisins, dried apples and chopped bacon. It makes a good breakfast for someone in a hurry."

Lily finished her cookie. "Such a wonderful idea. Once the hospital is open, we need to keep these on hand all the time. As you can tell my husband is very partial to cookies."

He tried very hard not to choke on his third cookie. "Yes, Beatrix. They really are delicious."

Beatrix put the crust in the pie plate and leaned on the back of an empty chair. "Ms. Stewart, if you want to do the cooking, I'll be happy to let you have the kitchen. You won't hurt my feelings none."

"No," Lily laughed far louder than she probably should have. "No, Beatrix. I spent my whole life learning medicine, first with my father, then school, then the war. I can't boil an egg. I'm afraid if I did the cooking, my husband would starve to death."

"Then I reckon it's a good thing I like to cook, isn't it? Can we talk about menus?"

Lily looked at her husband. "Galen, why don't you go make sure there's a fire in the bedroom stove? Miss Beatrix and I have business."

By the time Liberty returned with their trunks and taken them upstairs, the new mistress of the house had worked out a month's worth of menus with their cook-housekeeper.

In due time the trunks were unpacked, and the Stewarts dined on ham and fried potatoes. As she said, simple fare.

The first night in their first real home took some getting used to. Lily had never really had servants before. Oh, Mrs. Zill was the family's housekeeper and childminder when she was young. But she had been one of her father's patients whose husband had been killed working in the steel mill. Papa gave her the job to help them survive. Now, she had to plan meals, arrange deliveries, and manage a household. She realized it was easier running a hospital. No wonder men wanted women to stay home and keep house.

The Rogans retreated to their cabin behind the stable after supper. Galen slid across the sofa in the parlor and put his arm around his wife. "Well, Mrs. Stewart, I propose we retire for the evening as well. Tomorrow is a busy day. We really should go into town and introduce ourselves in the general store, then check on the progress of the hospital."

Mrs. Stewart agreed. Galen took her hands and led her up the spiral stairs to the top floor, the room he had selected for them. Windows surrounded the room, admitting light all day, and always managed to spill across the bed so long as the sun shone. And if the Rogans should be up early no one need be embarrassed overhearing anything they shouldn't.

Their room at the top of the stairs was hexagonal, dominated by the bed situated between two doors. The door to the left of the bed led to the landing and the spiral stairs. The door to the right opened into a dressing room. Lily's only complaint about the home was the lack of indoor plumbing, other than the pump in the kitchen.

The bed was an oversized iron bedstead with a thick feather tick. After years on straw and cotton mattresses in the European theater this was a new experience.

They both still wore the heavy robes from the mud room. Barefoot already, Galen pulled the tie from Lily's robe, letting it fall open. She returned the favor.

They came together, arms encircling, flesh pressing flesh, mouths plundering, as they stood beside their first true marriage bed. "Lily, love me."

Chapter Fifteen

Saturday morning, the Stewarts and the Rogans drove into town with Liberty at the reins. Their destination was the Jent mercantile where the women intended to select some household necessities. Lily had dressed carefully that morning in a simple green wool suit covered with a canvas duster. It was the first week of March, but seemed, to Lily at least, to be unseasonably warm during the day.

While the ladies shopped, and while Lily introduced herself to the other women who she knew would be in the store, Galen stopped in the local telephone company. As a physician, he needed multiple telephones in his home, including the current one on the first floor, one in their bedroom in the tower, and a third, with a separate number, in the Rogan's cabin.

Mr. Jent was unsure he could accommodate the doctor's request. He had never installed more than one phone in a residence. In the end, after a hefty exchange of cash, the telephone magnate agreed to Galen's request, knowing there would be more connections needed once the new hospital was set up.

The hospital was less than two miles from downtown on the Lafayette Road. Liberty drove the little mule at a showy pace, rightfully proud his protege was the only gaited mule in three counties.

Tents were spread flat on the ground, arranged where they would stand in just a few hours. Galen helped her from the buggy and they walked together to inspect what would soon become their new domain.

Lily noticed three men working on a trench a few feet from what would be the door of the tent. She left Galen and made her way to where they worked. Even though she had a pretty good idea what was going on, and they weren't going to like what happened next, she pasted a smile on her face behind her mask and asked sweetly, "What are you gentlemen doing?"

Already waist deep in their trench, the three men stopped their work and leaned on their shovels. The older of the three, a gangly, bearded man looked her up and down, pulled the bandana from his face and leered at her. "Digging a hole. Wanna come down and help?"

She squatted down to look into the hole. "What's it going to be?"

He spat a stream of tobacco juice over his shoulder. "For the outhouse. State's got some prissy doctor coming up from Nashville to open some sort of clinic. Foreman said to dig the latrine, so we dig."

Lily felt a presence behind her, then Galen's hand on her shoulder. "Gentlemen, I'd like you to meet my husband, the prissy doctor. Dr. Stewart, these gentlemen claim to be digging our latrines. I contend they will be much too close to the hospital, and need to be another fifteen feet away. As the 'prissy doctor', what do you say?"

He put his hand under her elbow to help her to her feet. "Well, Nurse Stewart, you are the public health expert. If you say the latrines are too close, they're too close. Gentlemen, please fill in the trench, and move your operation over there," He pointed to a spot. "Otherwise, the patients in our hospital will become even sicker. Besides," He pointed to the creek that ran behind them. "It's too close to the water. We'd wind up drinking what's dropped into your pit."

The spokesman sputtered, only slightly embarrassed by his "prissy doctor" crack. "But doc, lots of people here abouts have their shitters by the creek. In fact some folks put their backhouse over top of the creek so they don't have to dig a pit."

Well, that was good information to have. "How much typhus do you get here? Was there ever an outbreak of cholera?"

"Damn, Doc. I don't know. But the women folk say there's a lot of summer complaint."

Summer complaint. A folksy term for chronic diarrhea in infants, generally caused by fecal bacteria contaminating a food source. In the case of infants, the source was too often the water used to prepare their food or wash their bottles. There would be a lot of work to do here, in addition to their quarantine hospital.

"Well, gentlemen, we don't want any summer complaint here. The people we'll be treating will already be sick when they arrive. We need to get them healthy, not make them sicker because we're not smart enough to put the 'shitter' far enough away."

Lily knew she should have at least pretended to be shocked at the language. Four years among soldiers had killed any tender sensibilities she may have had.

"Since you already have the hole dug this far may I suggest you keep digging? We'll need a reliable well. We're in a bottom here. There's willow trees less than twenty feet away but twenty yards from the creek. I'd bet there's an aquifer here." She squatted back down to speak directly to the spokesman. "Bring in a dowser to make sure, then get a drilling rig in. Have the driller see me to get his bill paid."

"Lady, how do you know all this?"

"Because I had four wells dug during the war. One of them was dug by hand but this ground looks too rocky. You'll need a drilling rig. Do you know where to find one?"

"Yes'm. I reckon I do. Man up to Scottsville. He can be here Monday."

"Get him here tomorrow and there's a bonus for both of you."

"Well lady, tomorrow's Sunday. I don't reckon he'll want to work on the sabbath."

Lily nodded. "Fine. Then I'll find someone else who wants to earn an extra twenty dollars." A gold Double Eagle was a month's wages for most men, and for a farmer it could be a year's profit.

"Twenty?"

"Twenty."

"Yes'm. He'll be here."

"What's your name?"

"Randall Whittimore, ma'am."

"Thank you, Mr. Whittimore. I'm going to put you in charge of this project. You already seem to have taken charge of this detail. This well is your baby.

When it's done, and pumping we'll talk about what else we have for you. That is, if you want the job."

Randall Whittimore had been trying to find paying work for the last year. He couldn't get into the army when the war came. Doctor said something about one leg being shorter than the other. Railroad wouldn't hire him either, because he had done county time a while back. The Toby Shows took him on for a season as roustabout, then this damned influenza closed them down. He'd spent the last three months sleeping in barns, sometimes without the owner's permission. Last work he'd done was in January, stripping and tying tobacco. This job came up for the state and Whittimore had grabbed on with both hands. He'd worked hard, done his best, but the foreman had still given him every shit job on the site. Now, this fancy lady and her doctor husband were gonna give him a real job with some responsibility.

"Why, yes'm. I'd be right pleased to take you up on your offer." He heaved himself up out of the hole he'd been digging, and without thinking, he wiped his palm on the seat of his britches and offered his hand to Lily.

She shook it. "Welcome to our team, Mr. Whittimore. Now, will you point my husband to the foreman please."

Al Hailey sat on a nail keg, smoking a cigar as he pretended to supervise three of his laborers as they laid out canvas when Galen found him. The man had been so wrapped up in watching someone else work, he was utterly oblivious to the recent interaction with Whittimore. He looked up at the man wearing his fine city suit and fancy top coat.

"You come to gape at the yokels Mister?"

Galen looked at the man in the filthy biballs with the same rude attitude Hailey had demonstrated. "I'm Galen Stewart. *Doctor* Galen Stewart. This is my hospital clinic you are doing your damnedest to set up wrong."

Hailey heaved himself off his perch and sauntered over to Stewart. "And what exactly is wrong with how I'm setting up 'your' clinic?"

"Aside from the fact you'll never get that tent up? And that it's facing the wrong direction? And you had Whittimore dig that latrine ten feet away from the entrance? And you're sitting on your dead ass while these men do your work."

"Well, Doctor High and Mighty, if you think you can do a better job, have at it."

This was the chance Galen waited for. "Fine. You're fired. Get off this site and don't come back."

"But my pay!" Hailey was on the verge of groveling now.

"What pay? You got paid yesterday after work. From what I've seen today, you haven't done anything that deserves any more. Now get out. And if I see you back here again I'll shoot you myself."

"But you're a doctor!"

"An army doctor. An army *Colonel*. You want to try me."

Hailey looked at his boots as he kicked the dirt and scratched his crotch. "No, sir."

"Then get out."

The former foreman took off at a dead run up the Lafayette Road toward Siloam.

Lily watched this exchange from a distance, glad for the mask that covered her amusement. She knew she was more likely to shoot the foreman than Galen ever was. But no one else had to know. She put her hand on her husband's shoulder.

"Alright Lionheart. What do we do now? We've no foreman, not that he was much to start with. The tent needs to be taken up and relaid. And we've no well yet."

His arm went around her waist. "You're chief administrator. I'm just the medical chief of staff. So administrate."

"I say we have Whittimore get the men together and roll up this tent until we get a well in. Anything else would be premature. Put him in charge of the whole job, too. Do you think we can find a couple of vets who know a little about tents?"

"Randall, come over here, please." Galen called across the field to the former latrine mechanic.

Whittimore came at a trot. "Yes, sir?"

"Nurse Stewart already spoke to you about a well. Do you know any men who know how to put up a tent? That man who thought he was a foreman was making a dog's dinner of it."

The laborer seemed to stand a little straighter. "Yes, sir. I do. I worked a season for a Toby Show as roustabout."

"What's a 'Toby Show'? Is it like a circus?" This was something unfamiliar to the city-born doctor.

"Well, it's a show. We don't get much out here. The Toby Shows go from town to town and put on plays. Things like Eliza crossing the ice or the villain tying the heroine to the railroad tracks. They sing funny songs too, and tell silly jokes. It's a good way to spend a Saturday evening for a dime."

"So what does this show have to do with a tent?"

"That's where they put on the shows, Doc. That was my job. I was in charge of seeing the tent got put up when the show rolled in on Wednesday, and striking it come Sunday."

"And you say this was a big tent?"

"Yes, sir. Not quite as big as this one. But there shouldn't be much difference."

"Randall, you think these men here would work for you?"

"Me?"

"Yes, you. What do you think?"

"I reckon. I know all of them. Of course some of them, like that Purcell boy over there," he pointed to a boy staring open-mouthed at a butterfly. "If brains was dynamite, that boy couldn't blow his nose. But he can do what he's told, mostly."

Galen nodded. Yes, this man was perfect for the job. "Randall, call everybody together please. I need to talk to them."

Whittimore stuck two fingers in his mouth and let loose with a shrill whistle. "Gather round boys. Doc wants to talk to us."

The fifteen men came running across the site. Galen waited until they were quiet. He pulled down his mask so there would be no confusion as to what he had to say. "Gentlemen, I'm Dr. Stewart, and this is my wife, Nurse Stewart. The Public Health Service has sent us here to set up a clinic and influenza hospital.

That's what you've been working toward. Unfortunately, the man who was your foreman didn't know what he was doing, and almost everything you've done so far was wrong. That's why I fired him. Randall Whittimore is the new foreman. He has our full confidence and authority.

"We hope to have a well digging rig in here tomorrow. As soon as the well comes in, we can go forward with setting up the tents and digging latrines." He turned to his new foreman. "Randall, has the job been providing meals for the men?"

"No sir. Every man here gets his two bucks a day and that's all."

"How many tents do we have?"

Whittimore knew right off. "Four of the big four room tents, four two room, and one large single room."

"Any of you men know how to cook?"

The Purcell boy raised his hand.

"You know how to cook?"

He twisted his shapeless hat, worrying the brim almost to the point of separating it from the crown. "Yes sir. I cooked for the timber crew down to Graball."

This was unexpected. "Why aren't you there any more?" Had he given the crew food poisoning?

"The foreman's wife kept trying to get me alone. Boss didn't like it so him and some of his men beat my head in with a board. Then they fired me."

Well, that explained why he often stared off into space. "What will you need to cook for these men, breakfast and lunch, every day?"

Purcell seemed lost in thought, then started counting off on his fingers. "Twelve pounds of flour, a small bag of soda, a gallon of buttermilk, baking powder, and four pounds of lard. That'll make biscuits for the crew for two meals, and some extra left over. Two gallons of sweet milk, five pounds of sausage, three pounds of coffee, plus sugar for them that wants it. Ten pounds of beans and three pounds of side meat. That's for each day. Of course I'll need a stove with a good oven, and a good supply of stove wood."

Lily was more impressed than her husband. This man just rattled off the ingredients to make biscuits and gravy for an army, off the top of his head. She laid her hand on her husband's arm to get his attention. "Does Mr. Jent have a good stove in stock?"

Galen motioned to Liberty, and gave him directions to take Beatrix back to the store, and buy the stove Purcell would need and to order the supplies necessary.

"Randall, can you set up one of the two room tents please? We can make that the mess tent. The men will have hot food while they work." He returned his attention to the men. "Men, starting Monday, you'll get your regular pay plus two meals every day you are here to work. Mr. Purcell here is in charge of feeding you. Mr. Purcell, until we get a well dug you have to promise me that you will boil every bit of water you get out of the creek before you use it, whether for cooking or for washing. We'll see you have everything you need. Once the mess tent is set up I want all this other canvas rolled up and put away until we have a well." He looked around the assembled group to make sure everyone knew what was expected of them. "Questions?"

A man in the back of the group raised a hand. "If

we ain't got no well come Monday, do we still need to come in?"

Randall leaned over and whispered, "That's Mayne. He wouldn't work as a taster in a pie factory. Always wants a reason to lay out."

"No sir, Mr. Mayne. I don't expect you here Monday or any other day. You'll get your pay for today, then we won't be needing you again. Anybody else?" The men all studied the ground. There seemed to be a lot of spitting and scratching. "Very well. Mr. Whittimore, let's get to that canvas."

Before they could erect that cook tent, it was necessary for the crew to roll up the large four room tents that would be joined together to make their hospital. The floors had already been leveled there, and wooden pallets laid down. Whittimore directed his new crew in the careful folding and securing of the tents, then stacking and storing the temporarily unused canvas under a waterproofed tarp.

What would be the mess tent was set up and staked down as quickly as they were able. Galen knew they'd get quicker with each successive tent they erected. Randall was securing the last guy-rope when Liberty pulled up in the buggy.

Lily asked, "Did you have any luck?"

"Yes'm. Mr. Jent will deliver it as soon as the store closes today. Beatrix ordered the food, enough for 2 days. Hope this it's okay, but she told Mr. Jent to send enamel plates, cups, and cook pots. Said she didn't figure that Purcell boy didn't have none of his own gear."

"That's fine, Liberty. By the way, where is Beatrix?"

"She had me drop her off at the house. Said she needed to get supper going.

The crew remained on site until the spring wagon from Jent's store rolled up. They helped unload the heavy cast iron stove, then set it up in the tent. The other purchases were stored inside the tent, ready for Monday morning. Jimmy Purcell agreed to be there before sun up to start the fire and get breakfast cooking.

When Randall Whittimore arrived with his well drilling rig Sunday morning, the stacked canvas was burned to ashes, and the food supplies gone.

Chapter Sixteen

The work on the hospital proceeded at a much slower pace than was anticipated.

Lily's well came in on Tuesday. The clay well pipes were in place, and the pump set. Randall Whittimore had his crew dig three latrines, so there would always be one available.

For every two steps they managed, they wound up a step behind. Person or persons unknown apparently were making it their life's work to harass them.

First, it had been the tents being burned. Then, the day after the well was finished, the pump head was stolen. Then supply orders arriving at the rail head disappeared off the flatbed wagons before they could travel the two miles east to the work site.

Galen didn't have a choice. He called Randall to the house before work and told him they needed ten more men, and that any man on the crew could earn extra by taking on the job of armed guard.

"Couldn't we just bring up guards and hire them?"

"We could." Stewart really liked this man. "But if we use the men already on the crew in two or three hour shifts they will have a stake in what happens on the job. All our men are local too. They know who belongs and who doesn't. Can you imagine some armed guard challenging Jimmy Purcell when he shows up to start the stove?"

Randall laughed, then choked on his chaw. "No, sir. He'd run clean to Carthage before we could explain what was going on."

"How long will it take you and your crew to set up a barracks?"

Whittimore looked puzzled. "Barracks? You want us all sleeping here?"

"I know some of you don't live in town. And some of the men are sleeping in barns. If we are going to have them on the site around the clock we may as well provide a place to stay. It won't be mandatory. But if a man has guard duty at three in the morning, he'll be right here. Think about it. Those who live out of town could stay here and head home on their days off. So. How long?"

"Couple, three days. If the replacement tents come, we could use one of them."

Galen picked up a telegram from his desk and passed it to his foreman. "This came early today from Nashville."

Randall read aloud. " 'Tents loaded stop Arriving Nashville stop Arrange transport your location.' So we gotta send somebody to Nashville?"

"Mrs. Stewart will be in town tomorrow to give progress reports. She'll be able to handle things."

"Really Dr. Stewart, you think it's a good idea to let her go to the docks all alone?"

"Are you worried about her, Randall?" He leaned back and grinned.

"No, sir. Not exactly about her. I'm more worried she might try to take over the waterfront."

*****

Lily's train pulled into Union Station around ten in the morning. Outside on Broadway she hailed a taxi that would take her to the Public Health offices. The detailed reports she carried showed their progress, as well as the failings of the initial project. Even with the cost overruns Lily was still keeping their expenses within budget.

Dr. Happer met her in the conference room on the first floor rather than his office. She had made it plain in her letter when he requested the meeting she wouldn't have much time. Besides, the woman was too bossy for his taste, no matter how pretty she was.

"Dr. Happer, it's good to see you again." Lily offered her hand as a man would. Happer stared at it, then finally accepted her handshake. She set her bag on the conference table and withdrew her stack of reports. "Shall we get down to cases? I have to be on the train back this afternoon."

*****

The weather was still unseasonably warm for early March. Lily stood on the platform watching the men load her new tents. Well, they weren't new. According to the bills of lading, they originated in New Jersey, spent eighteen months in France, then wound up in Georgia. She didn't care, so long as they ended up in Coatesville.

A sudden chill blew down the platform from the Cumberland, making Lily turn up the collar on her thin cotton duster. She really should have worn something heavier, but it had been so warm when she left the house.

She signed off on the shipping form then boarded the day coach. The sun was beginning to dip below the western horizon when the train pulled out heading north. The train reached the county seat, about twenty miles from home, when the ice storm hit.

Ice pelted the windows in staccato rhythm, even blocking out the sound of the steel wheels on the rails. As the engine began its long pull up the grade toward the Coatesville' ridge, those same steel wheels began to slip. The three people in the car that evening were silent, listening to the wheels, and the engine as it strained, the engineer hoping to gain purchase by pouring more coal into the firebox.

The conductor made his pass through the car. "Sorry, folks. Looks like we're gonna be stuck for a while. There's a few people in the next car. I'm gonna bring them over here, and put some more wood on the fire."

Lily moved to the front of the car. No matter how long she was here, she was upset that the residents refused to wear a mask. Sitting in the front would at least minimize her exposure. She could put this time to good use, reviewing what Dr. Happer gave her.

Five people filed in from the second coach. Two appeared to be farmers, a young woman and her three year old daughter, and a dark, thin man carrying a Bible. Lily buried her nose in her paperwork, trying to avoid eye contact with the man who had that proselytizing look about him. Of course he sat down opposite her.

"Good evening, Sister."

Lily grunted and tried to read.

"I'm Brother Conover. First Church of Coatesville. And you are?"

She didn't look up. "Busy."

"Oh? What are you reading? Some sort of romantic novel?"

Jaysus this man was annoying. She flipped the report closed and held it so he could see the cover. She read it aloud, to make sure he got the idea. "It's called 'Dual Diagnosis and Plan of Treatment for Venereal Disease Concurrent With Influenza'."

"Oh, that's awfully serious reading for such a little slip of a thing."

He wasn't going to let her get a damned thing done. "Not for the nurse administrator for the new influenza infirmary in Coatesville."

"Oh, so that's what all the fuss is about." He sat back in his seat, opened up his Bible. "There wouldn't be any of that if people trusted in the 'Great Physician'."

Lily counted to five. Twice. "So you're saying there would be no illness if more people went to church?"

"Exactly."

"So tell me. If a child breaks her arm are her parents merely to pray over her? Or may they take her to a doctor to have it set? What about the men wounded in the war? Should the surgeons be replaced with chaplains?"

"If one simply has faith..."

Enough was enough. She grabbed her satchel and stood. Influenza be damned. "Excuse me, Mr. Conover. I have to go now."

He made the mistake of putting his hand on her arm. "Don't go. I'm not done talking to you yet."

The conductor was in the next car. If she yelled, he may or may not hear her. She fixed Conover with her best ice queen stare. "Sir, remove your hand."

He stepped closer, close enough she could smell his rotten breath. He tried to loom over her, to intimidate. "Why? What are you gonna do?" His grip on her left wrist tightened.

She was at the wrong angle to knee him in the groin. Her right hand was free. A quick look around the car let her know that the two farmers were waiting for something to happen, while the young mother tried to make herself as small as possible. The other two passengers who started off in the coach were dozing. She smiled. Had the man any sense, he would have been afraid.

Lily Barnett Stewart balled up her right fist and punched him square in the nose.

He clutched his face with both hands, trying to staunch the crimson flood pouring forth. "Ahhh! You hit me! Bitch."

"Tsk tsk. Such language. And from a good Christian. Really, Reverend Conover. I'm appalled."

Hearing the commotion, the conductor came from the other, now unoccupied car. "What's going on in here?"

Conover was still trying to stop the bleeding. "She punched me!"

The conductor looked at Lily. He had an idea what was going on. "Ma'am? Are you all right?"

"Certainly, Mr. Terry. Mr. Conover and I had a disagreement. I wanted to move away from him. He objected, and put his hands on me. I asked him not to. Mr. Conover came closer. I backed him up."

Mr. Terry, the conductor, looked from the looming Conover, to the petite Nurse Stewart. He had met her several times before on other trips, and knew she rarely spoke to anyone on this trip, other than he and her husband. "Mr. Conover, do you wish to prefer charges against Mrs. Stewart? I'll be happy to have the police see you when we reach Coatesville. Of course, Mrs. Stewart is free to file charges against you as well. And we have ample witnesses here. I'm sure they would be more than happy to testify."

Conover mumbled something.

"What's that? Couldn't quite make that out."

"No. No need."

"Mrs. Stewart, would you like to move to another seat? There's blood all over the floor here. You don't need to get that on your shoes." Terry offered his arm and led her away from the grumbling preacher.

Brother Conover sat back down, grumbling about vengeance and women not knowing their place.

*****

Seven at night, and Lily still wasn't home. She'd telegraphed what train she'd be on before leaving Nashville. Galen had an idea the ice storm had delayed her train. That didn't mean he'd worry any less. He didn't fret this much during the war, when one or the other of them had been dispatched to other duty stations.

He paced the room he had been using as an office. When he heard the kitchen door open and close, he made a mad dash. "Lily?"

"No, Sir. Just me." Liberty was standing in front of the cook stove, trying to warm himself.

"What'd you find out?"

"Train's stuck at Rock House Hollow. Can't pull the grade."

"Can we go down in the spring wagon and get her?"

Liberty shook his head sadly. "No, Sir. It's too icy. Poor mule slipped and slid all the way home from the depot. No, Sir. It's safer she stay on the train where she's warm and dry."

Before Galen could argue any further a fist beat on the front door of the house. Galen held up a hand when Beatrix started to answer. "I'll go."

A boy stood on the porch, shivering against the bitter cold. Galen pulled him inside. "What's wrong, son?"

The child's teeth were chattering so hard he could barely talk. He finally got out, "Accident. Lumber yard. Bringing him down."

"Beatrix!" The little woman bustled from the kitchen. "Get something hot into the kid and keep him with you. Liberty, I don't have an office set up yet. We'll have to use the dining table. Get me all the lamps you can."

Dr. Stewart ran for his surgical kit and medical bag. He stripped off his suit coat and tossed it on the settee, then slipped an apron over his head. This wouldn't be a sterile field, or anything close to it. His goal was to save a man's life. At this point, he wasn't even sure what sort of injury it was.

This was what Galen had spent the last five years doing. Organizing, assembling, saving lives, and when he was able, limbs. He wasn't an administrator, he was a surgeon.

Footsteps on the front porch. Galen yanked open the door. Four men carried a wooden door, holding the injured man. "Come through, gentlemen. Put him here on the table. Now, tell me what happened."

The man who had been tapped as spokesman said, "Bubba here. He was changing out the belt on the saw. The belt snapped and caught him above the eye. Then he fell forward and the blade caught him across the gut."

Oh shit. A belly wound. Maybe, just maybe, there was hope. "Let's see what we have."

Bubba Lee lay on the table perfectly still. Had it not been for the slight rise and fall of his chest, a less trained observer would have declared him dead. A quick examination showed he had a deep laceration across his midsection. Before he dared do much of anything, Galen gave him an injection of Morphine, because he was about to cause him excruciating pain.

He made short work of the ruined clothes. "Liberty, get me some boiling water from the kitchen. I need to get this wound cleaned."

It took some time to pick the shards of cotton out of the laceration. Damn he missed Lily right now. Finally he was able to see what he was dealing with.

He cleaned the cut with water, and examined the area thoroughly. Thank God, the blade hadn't penetrated into the abdominal cavity. Galen could close him up with some pretty stitches, and he'd be able to tell his kids about the time he fought a saw blade and lived to tell about it.

First to trim away the ragged flesh. Once he had even edges, he began suturing the long laceration. Stitches inside first, to prevent pulling and separation. Then twice as many sutures outside, to make a nice, even scar.

A simple gauze dressing would do for tonight. He would need to be checked for any sign of infection. That's what would kill him faster than any saw blade.

The belt had missed the boy's eye, catching him from cheekbone to hairline. Must have hurt like hell, but at least he didn't lose his eye. A little salve would help keep infection from the laceration.

"All right, boys. Can you get him into the bedroom?" They picked up Bubba and the door that still bore his weight, and followed Dr Stewart to the bedroom off the parlor. The doctor snatched back the quilt and blanket, Bubba was deposited, this time without his door, and the four men left, with directions to have their employer contact Galen in the morning.

A quick trip back to the dining room to gather up his instruments and straighten his bag, then a stop in the kitchen. "Beatrix, I'll need a pot of coffee please. I'll be sitting up."

Liberty brought in a scuttle of coal and got a fire started in the grate. Galen pulled in a chair from the parlor and took up his post by his patient. It was going to be a long night, particularly since he was also worrying about his wife.

The ice storm continued throughout the night and into the next day. Around nine, Bubba Lee opened his eyes.

"Huh? What happened?"

Dr. Stewart jumped up from where he had dozed in his chair. "You're awake. Good. How do you feel?"

Bubba started to put his hand over his belly, but Galen grabbed his wrist. "No, don't touch. You got cut up last night. Took me the better part of two hours to sew you back together. Don't go messing up my work."

He repeated, "What happened?"

"Apparently you were changing the belt on the saw blade at the mill, and it broke. Gave you a beaut of a black eye. But when you fell forward, you fell across the blade. Caught you right about here." Galen gestured with his hand in the general area of the laceration. "You are one lucky fellow. Of all the injuries you could have received, this is the best option, next to not getting hurt at all."

"Guess you're the new doc, then?"

"You guessed right. Galen Stewart."

"Well, I tell ya, Doc. If I had my druthers, I'd just as soon not've got perforated at all."

"You think you might drink a little beef tea? I don't want you having too much to eat just yet, in case there's some internal damage I may have missed."

Bubba allowed as he could tolerate some beef tea,

and maybe a little coffee if the doctor would permit. Galen raised the young man up with some pillows, poured him a half cup of coffee, then went to find Beatrix for a cup of the beef tea she had been cooking all night.

They heard the door to the mud room open. Galen couldn't wait any longer. He jerked open the inner door.

There stood his wife, wearing a man's coat five sizes too large that came down to her ankles.

He never gave her a chance to say anything. He grabbed her and hugged her as hard as he could without doing damage. He heard her mumble something from inside the coat against his chest, then realized he was probably smothering her. He released his hold, only slightly, and kissed her frigid lips.

"You're frozen half to death. Come into the kitchen and sit by the stove. Beatrix! See to Bubba. I'll look after Lily."

He put a kitchen chair beside the stove, then pulled up a second so they sat knee to knee. "How the hell did you get home? We never heard the train come in."

"Wind is blowing east to west. It must carry the sound away. We've been stuck at the bottom at Rock House Hollow most of the night. The yard sent down a team of track walkers. They started fires along the rails, then scattered sand under the wheels. I swear, the men walked faster than that engine could pull, and we never really got to build up any speed. We'd go a few feet, then slip back." She was finally starting to warm up, and slipped out of the coat.

"Why didn't you call? We would have come pick you up."

"Because it's still an ice storm out there, and I didn't want our mule to break her leg."

He picked up the coat and held it up. There was an L&N insignia on it. "Whose coat?"

"Mr. Terry. He's laying over for the next couple of days, and said I could leave it at the depot for him. Oh, Galen, he was so good to me last night. Especially when that nasty preacher started up."

"Preacher?"

"From 'First Church' he said. He is an evil man. I tried to move away from him, and he grabbed my arm."

Righteous indignations welled up, but he tamped it down. His wife wouldn't forgive him if he went to fight her battles. "What'd you do to him?"

She held up her bruised knuckles. "I broke his nose."

"Good. Want some breakfast?"

"Oh my God yes. I haven't eaten since breakfast yesterday."

He went to the stove to see what Beatrix had. "How about some oatmeal?" He fetched a bowl and another coffee cup. She wrapped her hands around the china, trying to warm her fingers while her husband dipped out some of the oat porridge. He found a jar of sorghum on top of the warming shelf, and a pitcher of cream on the window ledge. He put it all on the table, along with the sugar bowl, so she could prepare it to her own taste.

He sat beside her as she ate. "Got my first patient last night."

"Mm-hmm. Anything interesting?" This was a conversation only two medical professionals could have.

"About an hour into the ice storm a man at the lumber mill fell into the saw blade. I spent last night sewing him back together. He's in the spare room."

"Glad you were here to look after him." She continued to spoon oatmeal into her mouth. "Where did you treat him?"

"I didn't have much choice. I used the dining room table."

"We need to set you up an office here in the house. You won't be at the hospital all the time, and I suspect people will come to rely on you. We'll have three doctors and four nurses here next week, when we get our first influenza patients. You will most likely wind up seeing private cases about half the time. They don't need to be in the contagion area."

"What about the sun room, in the tower? Lots of light with windows all around. We can use the parlor as a waiting room, if we move out the furniture, put in wooden chairs and take up the rugs. It will do until we figure out something different."

Lily ate a second bowl of oatmeal, then went upstairs to wash and change her clothes. She returned a short while later wearing her nurse's uniform, then found her husband sitting with his patient.

"Dr. Stewart, why don't you get some rest? I'll sit with your patient for a while. I promise to call you if anything changes."

He stood. "Bubba Lee, this is my wife, Nurse Stewart. She'll look after you while I go grab a shave and get a clean shirt."

The man in the bed perked up as soon as he saw Lily sit beside his bed. "No offense, Doc. But she's a whole lot prettier than you are."

Anne Arrandale

Chapter Seventeen

Bubba Lee went home two days later, with instructions not to lift anything heavier than a fork until he came back to have his stitches removed.

While Bubba recuperated, Galen and Liberty were busy rearranging rooms to make an office and treatment room. What Lily called the first floor "Tower room" was large enough to split into two rooms, one for the doctor's office, the other for treatment and procedures. Furnishings for the clinic were being held at the depot, and were pressed into service for the new office.

Ice continued to coat everything, stopping work on the clinic for the time being. Randall Whittimore came up to help Liberty build the wall to divide the office, as well as one to section off a part of the parlor for the waiting room.

Randall was painting the new parlor wall when someone knocked. Lily was busy in the kitchen sterilizing and wrapping instruments. "Mr. Whittimore, would you answer the door please?"

Randall answered. A young woman wearing a ragged, threadbare coat and a man's felt hat, stood leaning against the doorjamb. "Yes'm?"

She tried to cross the threshold, but fell into Randall Whittimore's arms.

"Miz Stewart! You'd best come quick."

Lily dropped what she was doing and ran. "Bring her through."

Randall carried her through to the office and laid her on the treatment table that had been borrowed from the clinic's supplies.

A closer look showed their newest patient was little more than a child. Her face was discolored, but it was hard to tell if the mottling was from bruises or from the bitter cold.

Randall went to get Beatrix to help undress the girl, then went back to his painting.

Under the skimpy coat and shapeless hat, Lily found a girl no more than seventeen. Judging by the rounding of her belly, she was about five months pregnant. Beatrix pulled up the girl's shirt and pointed. "Look here, Miz Stewart. Poor child's been punched and kicked. And those are fist marks on her face."

"Any idea who she is?"

Beatrix shook her head. "No, ma'am. But Bubba might. He's able to walk some. Can we ask him?"

"Not yet." Lily continued her external examination. She laid a hand across the girl's swollen belly and held it there for a long moment. "She's having contractions. Beatrix, make me a big pot of strong tea, and open a tin of condensed milk. This child needs sugar and something hot in her."

The housekeeper returned with the tea just as the girl was starting to regain consciousness. Lily raised the back of the table to help her sit up. "How do you feel, sweetie?"

She didn't answer, but looked around the room in apparent horror. "Where is this place?"

Beatrix tried to pat the girl's shoulder reassuringly, but the child recoiled from her touch. "You're at Doc Stewart's house honey. This here's his wife. She's a nurse. Don't fret none. You're in good hands."

The girl's eyes darted about the room like a frightened animal. She struggled to sit up, to push her way off the table, but a contraction caught her and she fell back with a groan.

Lily gestured to Beatrix to sit down. "Sweetie, what's your name?"

"Adelle."

"Well, Adelle. I'm Lily. This is Beatrix. Can you tell me what happened to you?"

The child shook her head violently. "Nope. Nope. Never tell what happens at home. That's one of the rules."

"All right. Adelle, do you know you're pre...going to have a baby?"

She nodded.

Lily held up a wooden pinard, the horn used to listen to the baby's heart. "May I listen to your baby's heartbeat? It won't hurt, I promise. I just put this end here against your tummy, then put my ear here."

Adelle cringed away.

"Would you like to hear my heart with it, to see how it works?" Lily put the pinard to her own heart and bent so Adelle could listen.

"Is that really your heart?"

"It is. And babies have heartbeats, too. Someone has hurt you very badly, Adelle. I'm afraid something may have hurt your baby. So I'd like to listen to his heartbeat. May I?"

Adelle nodded.

Lily placed the pinard against the girl's belly and listened. "Adelle, I need to look at your tummy, and put my hands on it, to see where the baby is. May I do that?"

The cornered animal look was back.

"Your clothes are all wet. How about if we take these things off, and you put on one of my nightgowns? Then you can be warm, and we don't have to mess up your clothes."

"Well, I reckon that'd be okay."

Beatrix ran to get the requested gown from the ironing she'd finished that morning.

As Lily helped Adelle undress she continued to talk, soothingly, but enough to get what little information she could. "Adelle, do you know when your baby's due?"

"The granny lady says 'baby's take nine months, but first baby's can come any time."

"And is this your first baby?" She pulled the clean pink gown over the girl's head.

She shook her head. "Had another last year. But he died after three-four days. Mr. Jackson said it hadn't been right."

"Is Mr. Jackson your husband?"

Adelle nodded shyly.

"Do you know when this baby got started? When you had your last monthly visit?"

Adelle shook her head. "Don't hardly get it."

Perhaps she got pregnant right after she birthed her last child. "Do you remember when your last baby was born?

"June."

"Did you get your monthly visit after your baby was born?"

She shook her head. "No. Mr. Jackson says if I bleed that means I'm 'unclean'. He don't like it when I bleed. I have to sleep in the shed then, and take a bath in almost boiling water when it's done before I can come back in the house."

"How old are you, sweetie?"

"I'm sixteen." She sounded proud in her accomplishment of reaching her sixteenth year, with a husband and two pregnancies.

Jaysus. This man sounded like a lunatic. "Adelle, sweetie, did Mr. Jackson hurt you?"

The girl closed her eyes. "Mr. Jackson is my husband. He can't hurt me. He can only correct me."

"And did he 'correct' you this time?"

She nodded shyly. "I reckon I said something wrong." Before she could say any more, another contraction hit. "I think maybe the baby's gonna come now."

"Adelle, I need you to lie back down on the table, so I can see what's going on with the baby. May I?"

Another nod. Adelle laid back on the examination table. Lily lifted the gown, exposing her distended belly. She palpated, felt with both hands as she discerned the position of the fetus. The girl must be around eight months along, and this baby was coming today, one way or the other.

"Beatrix, call the depot and tell Dr. Stewart I need him right now." Lily had delivered babies, but this one was going to be a problem, she could tell. She pulled the gown back over the child's exposed limbs and called for Randall. "Mr. Whittimore, go out to the shed, please. There are two small tanks there, strapped together, marked 'NITROUS'. Bring it here please. Quick as you can."

Randall ran. He returned carrying the requested items. "Doc Stewart's coming up the road."

Lily took the tanks and connected the rubber tubing to the mask.

Another contraction. A scream this time, a lone, keening wail of someone in excruciating pain of which they had no understanding.

Lily handed the mask to her patient. "Sweetie, when you feel a pain coming, take a few whiffs of this. It will help ease the pain without stopping your labor. Because this baby will be here tonight."

Adelle thrashed her head. "No, no. 'In sorrow she will bring forth children.' Mr. Jackson says so. Pain is my punishment for making him sin."

Lily was still trying to formulate a lucid response to such a ludicrous statement, she heard Galen come in through the kitchen. She called, "Dr. Stewart. Your patient is ready."

Galen stepped into the examination room, hands in his trouser pockets to warm them. He pasted on his best doctor smile.

"Good morning. I'm Dr. Stewart."

When Adelle turned her face away, Lily continued the introductions. "Dr. Stewart, this is Mrs. Jackson. Sixteen, second delivery. She's between eight and nine months along, and is in active labor. Contractions are about three minutes apart."

"No." Her voice was strained.

Galen pulled a chair up beside the exam table. "What 'no'? Are the pains coming faster?"

"No. Not Mrs. Jackson."

"You're not married?" He was doing his best to sound gentle. What he craved was to find whoever put her in this state and beat him into a greasy spot.

"No. Married." A pain was building. "To Mr. Jackson Conover. First Church."

Lily drew Galen aside a few steps. "That's the man who grabbed me on the train. He must have taken his anger out on her when he got home."

Dr. Stewart returned to his patient. "Adelle, how did you get here?" He couldn't imagine a man dropping his pregnant wife off and not staying.

"I needed help. Man at church works for you. He told me where your house was. I walked here, as soon as Mr. Jackson fell asleep."

Dear God in heaven. The bastard beat her until he wore himself out, then had a nap.

"Adelle, I need to examine you. My wife will be here the whole time. I promise, I won't hurt you, and I'll stop any time you say. But I'm afraid there might be something wrong with the baby."

She nodded and gritted her teeth, terrified of what he was going to do.

"Mrs. Stewart, will you sit here?" He left his seat and proceeded with his examination. Slowly, as if he was trying to gentle a fractious horse, he folded up the gown to her hips, then asked her to raise her knees.

Lily held the girl's hands as she clenched them in terror. "Sweetie, he's not going to hurt you. I promise."

"Mr. Jackson says it's sinful for a man to touch a woman he's not married to."

"Not for a doctor. That's his job. I promise, Dr. Stewart has delivered lots of babies. So have I in fact. We're going to help you. If you'll let us."

"You sure it's all right?"

Lily smiled at her sweetly. "Yes, it's all right. And I promise, neither of us will say a word to Mr. Conover or anyone else you were here."

Adelle finally allowed Dr. Stewart to perform his pelvic examination. When he had finished he asked Lily to walk with him as he washed. "I was afraid of this. Baby's breech. Her pelvis is tiny, and I'm afraid to turn the baby this far into the labor."

"Can you convince her to use the gas? I haven't been able to, and she needs all the help we can give her. That bastard Conover told her that birthing pains are punishment for making him sin."

"I'll do my best. Come on."

Galen took up his place again by Adelle's head. He spoke softly, trying his best to keep her calm. "Adelle, your baby is facing the wrong way. Instead of coming out head first, he's feet first. We can help you, but it's important you help us. Can you do that?"

"I'll try."

He picked up the mask she had discarded. "First, you need to breathe some of this. I promise, it won't hurt you. It will only help you relax a little, and maybe sleep between the pains. The gas won't hurt you or the baby, but if you don't use it, we may not be able to deliver him safely. Can you do that? For me?"

"You promise not to tell Mr. Jackson?"

"I promise. Now, when the next pain starts, I want you to take a deep breath."

She grabbed for the mask and inhaled deeply as the pain began. This one seemed to stretch on forever. She dropped the mask. "I need to push."

Lily was ready. Under normal circumstances, had she seen the girl before she went into labor, there was a chance the baby could have been turned. No, there was nothing for it but to deliver the infant as he presented.

One push, then a second, and the feet appeared. Nurse Stewart grasped the little feet between her fingers, waited for the next contraction and pulled. The infant slipped into her waiting palm and promptly squalled.

She cut the cord, then laid the baby on the nearby table, quickly suctioned the nose and mouth, and wiped the little eyes. A quick wrap with a flannel, and she placed the child in Adelle's arms. "Adelle, sweetie. Open your eyes and meet your new daughter."

Galen made short work of delivering the afterbirth. "We have another problem. The placenta isn't complete. I'm afraid the beating she took ruptured it, and that's what brought on the labor."

"Can you deal with it here?"

He nodded. "I can do a D&C. But you'll have to talk her into it."

"Adelle, do you know what an afterbirth is?"

She nodded.

"It's supposed to come out whole. Because you were beaten up, yours didn't. If any of it is left behind after the baby's born, the mother gets sick and can die. It's important we clean every bit of it up. Dr. Stewart can remove everything, but you need to give us your permission. I promise, you won't feel anything, because you'll use some of the gas. When you wake up, you'll feel good, and you can nurse your baby like you normally would. Will you let Dr. Stewart help you?"

She nodded sleepily. Lily put the mask back on her face, and took the baby from her arms. "Beatrix! Come get the baby please. Keep her extra warm. She's had a rough go."

The exam table was lowered, and the patient's feet placed in the steel stirrups. As soon as she was fully relaxed Galen took up the curette and the speculum to perform a routine dilatation and curettage.

The entire procedure only took minutes. When he was finished, he dropped the instruments in a basin, and packed the patient with gauze. "We'll have to send Bubba home. We need the bed for Adelle. I'm not about to let her go home to that monster she's married to."

As if on cue, the front door flew open. "Where is that whore?"

Anne Arrandale

Chapter Eighteen

Randall was still painting, or at least pretending to paint, in the parlor when Brother Conover burst in. He dropped the brush in the paint tray and started to fetch Galen, when the doctor came through the other door.

"Just who the hell do you think you are?"

Brother Conover drew himself up to what he considered his impressive height, trying to make himself taller than the doctor. "I am Brother Jackson Conover. My wife is being held here against her will. I demand you turn her over to me."

Galen whispered something to Randall, who headed for the kitchen, where Beatrix was holding the newborn.

"I'm Dr. Stewart, Mr. Conover. Your wife came here after the beating you gave her. She was in labor."

"Served the whore right."

"Oh, it did? She needed to be kicked and beaten?"

"I was stuck on the train with some whorish woman who struck me in the face. When I returned home, she questioned me about why I had blood on my shirt. She accused me of drinking and brawling. I had to discipline her."

"So some whorish woman struck you?"

"She did. The bitch hit me, after I only attempted to educate her on the proper role of women."

Randall reappeared. "Mr. Whittimore, ask my wife to step in here please."

"I don't want to meet your wife. I insist you produce my wife so I can take her home."

"Dr. Stewart, you sent for me?" Lily was still wearing the bloody apron she had donned before delivering the baby. She would never normally do such a thing, but she wanted the shock value.

"You! What are you doing here?"

"Why Brother Conover. How nice of you to drop by."

"This is your wife?! This...woman?"

Galen put his arm around Lily's shoulders. "Yes, Brother Conover. This is my wife, Nurse Lily Barnett Stewart. She delivered your daughter not half an hour ago."

"I want my wife. Now."

Lily smiled, knowing it would annoy Conover no end. "I'm terribly sorry. She's having a well deserved nap after birthing your child." She wondered how many times she would mention his child before he caught on.

Conover tried to push past them.

Galen stopped him with a heavy hand on his bony shoulder. "That's far enough. You may leave now."

"I am not going anywhere without my wife."

Still smiling, Lily said, "Galen darling, get the shotgun, would you? There's a pest that needs taking care of."

Conover sputtered and fumed. "I'll go to the sheriff."

"Please do. We look forward to seeing him. And I suggest you go find him before my husband has another patient to tend."

Conover stormed out the front door, promptly slipped on the ice on the top step, and wound up face first on the icy ground.

*****

Bubba Lee was discharged with explicit directions, in order to make room for Adelle and her daughter. Mother and baby were both sleeping soundly, utterly oblivious to the tumult caused by her husband.

Galen and Lily were sitting at the kitchen table when the sheriff knocked on the kitchen door. Galen set his cup aside and let him in.

"Afternoon, Joe. Come on in. Coffee?"

The sheriff allowed as he could do with a cup, and sat with them. "Good to see you, Galen, Miz Lily. Quite a bit of excitement this morning."

Lily passed a plate of biscuits to Sheriff Joe Fromme. The man was stout, with an impressive waxed mustache.

"I suppose you've come about my patient?"

"Hell of a job you did on Bubba Lee. Can't hardly see where he got cut."

"Now Joe, I know you didn't come out in the ice and cold to compliment my hem stitching."

Fromme laughed as he picked up another biscuit. "I got Jackson Conover sitting in my office fit to be tied. Claims you're holding his wife against her will."

Lily said "Adelle Conover arrived at my front door around seven-thirty this morning, desperately seeking help. She had been beaten and kicked by her husband, because he had a bad night on the train. She's bruised from her face to her hips. He knocked her down and kicked her repeatedly. Tell me, Sheriff, did he happen to mention she was almost nine months pregnant?"

Fromme blushed to his hairline at her use of the "P" word. "Why no, Miz Lily. Nobody knew she was in a family way."

"If she hadn't been here, both she and the child would have died. She's still not out of the woods, and there's no telling if the child will have any lasting effect from the beating her mother received, or from the fact that Adelle was almost starved. She's only sixteen years old, and this is her second pregnancy."

"Second? I don't reckon anybody ever knew her to be expecting. None of the ladies ever saw her in town, and I don't reckon anybody else did, except maybe at church."

Galen asked, "You know her family?"

He shook his head. "Well, I know 'em, but I wouldn't call 'em much of a family. Her folks died when she was just a little thing. Her older brother raised her. Used to beat the hell...excuse me, Miz Lily...used to beat her every chance he got. Nobody ever said, but I reckon he sold that child to Conover."

Fromme picked up a third biscuit. "How long you

reckon she should stay here?" Both men looked at Lily.

"She's had a really tough time, sheriff. And the delivery wasn't smooth. She's torn up. I want her in bed for at least ten days, maybe longer. And I'm still worried about the baby.

"By the way, sheriff. Adelle said her first baby lived a few days. Can you find out what happened to him? Conover's a violent man, and I don't trust him."

Fromme stood up and reached for his hat. "I surely will, ma'am. I'll make sure Conover don't bother you none. And I'll tell him to quit spreading that story around about you beating him up."

"Well, that's partly true."

"What? Miz Lily, don't tell me a little slip of a girl like you beat up Jackson Conover."

"No, I didn't beat him up. He accosted me when the train was stuck at the bottom of the ridge. I got up to leave and he grabbed me. I did give him a fair chance and told him to remove his hand. He didn't. I broke his nose. Ask Mr. Terry. He saw the whole thing."

Fromme was still laughing when he walked out the door.

Anne Arrandale

Chapter Nineteen

Lily sat at the kitchen table, going through the ledger book for the clinic. Even with the extra hands Galen put on to finish the work, and the bonuses they were paying, the project was still well under budget. Their first patients would be arriving tomorrow. The new staff was already on site, and Galen was giving them the "nickel tour".

It had been ten days since Adelle's confinement. The girl was doing fairly well. Galen had removed the gauze packing the day after the D&C, and Beatrix made sure she had ample clean cloth pads.

Her first day allowed out of bed, Adelle wandered into the kitchen carrying baby Abigail. "Miz Lily, can I get a cup of coffee?"

"Sweetie, get whatever you want. You don't have to ask permission." The girl was still like a frightened doe, ready to bolt at the least provocation. "Get your coffee and sit down. Talk to me. These numbers are driving me crazy."

Adelle sat. She took her first sip of coffee, then froze when someone knocked on the kitchen door. The girl started to run for cover.

Lily laid a calming hand on her shoulder. Baby Abigail started to fuss, and her mother bounced her, cooing "shoosh".

"I'll see who's at the door. You just throw a blanket over your shoulder and nurse the baby. It's good for both of you."

She peeked out the door, then let it swing open. "Come in, sheriff. Adelle, Sheriff Fromme is here."

Fromme hung his hat on the peg by the door, poured himself a cup of coffee and sat down. "You're looking fine, Miz Adelle. How's the baby?"

She mumbled "fine" and studied her coffee.

"Miz Adelle, when you had your little boy last year, how long did he live?"

"Three, four days."

"And did you see him after he...passed away?"

She shook her head. "Mr. Jackson wouldn't let me see him. Said he wasn't right and that's why he died. He wouldn't even let me feed him when he was born. Just took him away."

"Do you know what he did with the remains?"

"Yes, sir. He buried him in the barn, where the ground was soft."

Fromme swallowed the last of his coffee and retrieved his hat. "Ladies, I'm off. Miz Lily, I'm gonna be seeing Galen. He might be a little late for supper."

Lily understood exactly what Fromme implied. He was going to get Dr. Stewart to act as witness as he exhumed the body of Infant Conover, then perhaps discover a cause of death. It was best not to tell Adelle that yet.

*****

It was close to nine at night when Galen dragged in that night. He'd washed at the boiler in the mudroom, and put on the heavy robe, as they had their first night. He had been covered in dirt and didn't want to drag any of it into the house, particularly with a new baby in the house.

Adelle and the baby had already gone to bed. Galen thought that a good thing, considering what happened.

He sat at the table, staring at the bowl of soup his wife set in front of him. He took one spoonful, then pushed the bowl away.

She'd seen him like this only twice before: once when he witnessed the flyer blown in half in a crash; then when a patient survived surgery, but suffered a massive stroke. "Galen, honey? What happened?"

Her husband had never been much of a drinker. But he went to the cupboard and pulled down a bottle of contraband Bourbon Liberty had stashed there. He poured himself a shot, downed it, then poured another, this time in his coffee. He took Lily's hand as he sat.

"You know I went with Joe to dig up the Conover barn?" She nodded. "Well, the little grave was right where Adelle said it would be. Joe started digging, and it wasn't any time before he found it."

She squeezed his hand, trying to offer him her strength. "Wasn't it skeletonized after a year?"

He nodded. "Just a skeleton. He didn't even wrap his little body in a blanket. It was the saddest thing I've ever seen. But that's not the worst. The cause of death was obvious. His little femur was broken, and his skull was crushed. Lily, he held that baby by the foot and swung him against a rock."

She went to him, pressed his head to her bosom and stroked his hair. She kissed his brow, never knowing what to say. All she could do was hold him.

"Conover barrelled in just as we were finishing up. He went after Joe with a shovel. Joe grabbed up his shotgun and blew his face off.

"He didn't die. At least not right away. Maybe I could have saved him. I wouldn't." He looked up at her, his eyes beseeching, seeking absolution.

"Good. I'm glad you didn't. He didn't deserve saving. Think how many lives you saved by not interfering. He was an evil, malevolent man, who gave nothing to anyone, and had no right to expect anything in return. You did nothing wrong."

"That's what Joe said. I can't help but think how wrong I was by not doing anything."

"Galen, you are a good man. A gentle man. I watched you with Adelle. I'm always amazed, watching you be so gentle with patients, when I know the strength in your hands. You can set and manipulate human bones, amputate limbs, remove and replace a skull cap. I've watched you hold a human heart in your hands and almost by sheer force of will keep it beating. Then I see you calm a terrified child, and deliver her baby safely and save her life. You never order. You ask. All that, Galen Stewart, is why I love you."

Chapter Twenty

Thirty new patients arrived on the morning train. Every one of them had a diagnosis of influenza, half with secondary pneumonia. So of course, what they needed was a scenic train ride, then a two mile trip in a horse drawn ambulance in forty degree temperatures.

Some of the men from the original construction crew stayed on to work around the hospital. Randall Whittimore not only handled the maintenance crew, but helped Liberty with work around the Stewart's home. Tommy Purcell was doing all the cooking for the patients, and managed a kitchen staff now. He had his moments of staring off when the headaches took him, but they were few and far between now.

Lily spent that first day making rounds, discovering the course each patient's illness had taken, if they had recently arrived from Europe, and what their prognosis was.

She also had to stay on top of the nurses. Half of them were newly capped from Nashville's Catholic teaching hospital, and they seemed only too happy to snare a young doctor.

Galen spent most of his day trying to avoid two of the new nurses. They seemed determined to trap him in a linen cupboard. His wife, of course, thought the whole thing was hilarious.

About two-thirds of the patients seemed well on the way to recovery. Good nutritious food seemed the best treatment, along with clean water in copious amounts.

On the patients' third day, they had their first two fatalities. Mere boys, fresh from France. They had made it out of the trenches and across the Atlantic, only to be felled by a tiny virus. Those deaths hit the staff extra hard.

Hardly any of the patients were from the area. They had no family nearby, no one to visit them. Even with Lily's strict policy that masks be worn at all times, her patients would have been grateful for a soft word that came from a person who didn't stink of carbolic. Even though they were effectively in a large ward, each one was isolated behind long sheets of fabric.

One of the two room tents had been set up as an operating theater. It was small, intended only for occasional use. Galen had insisted it be fully equipped, much to the consternation of their superiors. Their current theory was that any emergency could be returned by train to the capitol. Galen disagreed with that, and he was able to put it to the test the first week.

A farmer from Wilson County came up with their first patients. His fever raged, and doctors in Nashville rushed to ship him north. No one had bothered with any other examination. On arrival, Galen insisted every single patient be examined, regardless of their medical history.

Hiram Coffey had been working in his tobacco

bed when he took sick. His son had found him sprawled face down in the newly sterilized bed, burning with fever. The local doctor had succumbed to the flu himself in February. So Hiram's son had taken his daddy to the hospital, where he had been transferred to Nashville, as the Lebanon hospital was filled to capacity already. Nashville in turn threw Hiram on the first train north.

Bob Roberts met the patients as they arrived from the depot. A perfunctory examination of Hiram Coffey showed no pulmonary symptoms whatsoever, but a temperature of 104°, and lower right quadrant rigidity and pain. Immediately, Coffey was removed from the contagion unit.

Dr. Roberts found his superior in the clinic office reviewing correspondence. "Dr. Stewart, I got a man with a hot appendix. Thought you might want to see him personally."

"Thank you, Doctor." Finally, some real doctoring. "You handle the anesthesia?"

"Certainly, Doctor."

"Good. Go find a scrub nurse. I want to talk to the patient and introduce myself before I root around in his gut."

Galen found Hiram Coffey in the isolation ward. He sat beside his bed. "Mr. Coffey, I'm Dr. Stewart. I've got some good news for you. You don't have influenza."

He groaned, "Well, I by God got something."

"You do. Your appendix has decided it needs to come out. If we do it now, you'll live a long, good life."

"And if you don't?"

"You'll probably die here when it ruptures, and I'll be sending a telegram to your family about where to send your body."

"So what're you waiting for?"

Galen found Lily at the mess tent, discussing dietary needs for the new patients with Purcell. He wasted no time. "Time to go to work. Scrub in."

They scrubbed.

The surgery took longer than expected. The appendix was on the verge of rupturing, and the infection had begun to spread into the large intestine. It took time to make sure they got all the necrosis, intestinal gangrene being nothing to sneeze at.

The patient was returned to the recovery area, where Lily and Pearl Escue, the nurse who had scrubbed them in, would keep watch for the next twenty four hours.

It was getting dark when Galen brought his wife a plate of food. He sat with her at Hiram's bedside while she ate the shredded pork and biscuits.

He picked up the board where had charted his vital signs. "Any change?"

She tried to swallow before she spoke. "He woke up around an hour ago. Said a few rude words he'll not remember, then went back to sleep."

"So, normal. That's good. Oh, you got a letter." He passed her a sealed envelope.

"Oh, look. It's from Raymond." She used her knife as a paper cutter and ripped it open. "That rat!"

"What's wrong?"

"He says Josey got married. He brought his wife

into the house. His pregnant wife, and him a seminary student. Then he told Raymond he'd have to move out. That house belongs to the three of us. Josey had no right."

"Well, right or not, he's done it. I'll send Raymond a wire and tell him he's welcome here with us. Hell, we can probably use the help. He's been studying accounting since his accident, right?"

She nodded as she took another mouthful of beans. "He has. Shorthand too. In his last letter he mentioned learning to type, just one handed."

"It's settled then. I'll arrange his ticket, and get him here within the week. He can keep the books, and handle some of that damnable correspondence."

Lily finished her supper and set the plate aside. "Speaking of help, I'm thinking maybe Adelle should stay on. There's too much housework for Beatrix on her own. She needs help, and Adelle has no place to go, except maybe to one of the Crittenden homes."

Galen picked up her coffee cup, took a swallow and passed it back to her. "That's a good idea, but we need to consider living arrangements. The Rogans have a cabin out back. There's another building originally set up as a shop that nobody uses. Liberty can move the equipment into the barn and he and Randall can get it ready. That way Adelle can have some privacy with her daughter."

"And Raymond can have the bedroom over the kitchen." She passed the cup back. "Have you given any thought to when this mess is over? When we send our last influenza patient home?"

"I have. Do you want to go back to Baltimore?"

She shook her head. "We've lived so many places, no place and everywhere feels like home."

"I was thinking about hanging out a shingle right here. The place is a medical wasteland. Half a dozen untrained granny women delivering babies, and old Doc Logan who spends more time pulling calves than doctoring people. The nearest hospital is twenty miles away."

"Good. But if you intend to treat patients in the office we'll need someplace different to live. While our home is lovely, it's really not suitable for operating a surgery."

"Considering we live in a home provided by Public Health, I think moving would be a good idea. Fortunately, we don't have to decide anything right now. First, we need to get through this damned pandemic."

Chapter Twenty-One

A slightly built red haired man stepped off the morning train in Coatesville three days later. Lily met him on the platform with a bear hug.

"Raymond! You're here."

"Why wouldn't I be? I said I was coming."

She hugged him again. "I'm just glad you're here. We really need your help." She patted his skinny frame. "And it looks like Beatrix is going to have fun fattening you up."

Galen tied off the reins and walked. "Who is this man my wife's manhandling? Can't be her baby brother. He's just a punk kid."

"Galen, good to see you, too." He offered his hand.

"Come on. Let's get your bags and get home. Liberty finally taught me how to drive, and I want to show him I can make it to town and back without putting the buggy in the ditch."

Within the hour, Liberty relieved Galen of the buggy at the door, promising to bring the bags in shortly. Lily showed her brother where things were, and left him to cleanse himself of his travels, so Beatrix could sponge and press his suit and launder his shirt later.

He pushed the kitchen door open and stepped inside. "So tell me, Big Sis, when do I get to go to work?"

Lily set a plate of Beatrix's breakfast cookies and a cup of coffee in front of her brother at the kitchen table. "Tomorrow soon enough? Today I figured you'd want to rest and settle in."

He looked down at his robe. "Well, I'm not exactly dressed for work right now." He bit into the cookie. "Mmm. These are really good. Anyway, you mentioned there were discrepancies in the original figures and what you have now. Give me both sets of books and I'll see what I can find out."

*****

Beatrix was putting their lunch on the table when Galen returned from the clinic.

Raymond set aside the ledgers and picked up his page of notes.

Between "pass the beans" and "want the last biscuit", Raymond asked the questions he needed answered.

"Galen, who kept the books before you came?"

"The foreman, I suppose. "

"You mean Mr. Whittimore? I've seen his name in the new books."

Lily answered. "No, that would be Al Hailey. Galen fired him as soon as they met."

"How much was he paid? Do you know?"

"Not for certain. We were given a quarterly budget from the Department. We arrived two weeks into the quarter."

"How many men were on that initial crew?"

"Seventeen, including Hailey. He and another man left that first day."

"And how much was each man paid?"

"Two dollars a day. Maybe three for the foreman."

Raymond took his last swallow of food and pushed his plate back, then went to fetch the books. He flipped open the long green book to the page he had marked.

"See here? According to this, Al Hailey was running a crew of twenty-nine men, paying three dollars a day, and five a day for his own salary. He even charged for the week after he was fired; the entries were already made and the monies disbursed."

Galen came behind his brother-in-law and read over his shoulder. "So the bastard was embezzling."

"In spades, brother. In spades.

Raymond kept running his fingers down the columns. "Look at the expenses. You said you had to replace tents, and I saw the purchase price of those. Do you know how much the original ones cost?"

Lily began thumbing through bills of lading. "Here it is. The original tents were provided by the Department, and we only had to pay the freight to get them here from Louisville." She passed the statement over to her brother.

"So why did Hailey make an entry for over three

hundred dollars for 'used tents'? He's also showing money expended for feeding the work crew. Any truth to that one?"

Galen shook his head. "None whatsoever. I hired a man to cook, and had to buy a stove and utensils before he could bake a biscuit."

"You know where to find this wonder of creative accounting?"

"No, but I bet the sheriff does."

Raymond nodded. "I'm pretty sure I saw a pie in the kitchen. Let me have some dessert, get dressed, and we can go see him."

Lily stood up to fetch her brother a plate. "No, we'll have him come here. If we all troop into his office everybody in town will start talking. It's nothing unusual for Sheriff Fromme to come by here for some pie and coffee."

"What did you do in the army? Were you a spy or something?"

Galen picked up his and his brother-in-law's plates. "Remind me to tell you about some of her more colorful exploits."

*****

Liberty brought Joe Fromme back with him after his trip to town to fetch the mail, and the box of medical supplies that had come in on the afternoon train.

Beatrix and her husband left the main house, at the sheriff's request. Not that either of them would purposely gossip, but what someone didn't know they couldn't repeat. It gave Beatrix a chance to help Adelle in her own cabin and to visit the baby.

Raymond had dressed casually, in shirt and trousers. With only one hand, he had trouble enough buttoning those two articles of clothing. A tie was out of the question without help. He already had the evidence laid out on the dining room table, along with his notes.

Fromme carried his coffee and slice of pecan pie into the dining room, where Lily made the introductions. "Sheriff Fromme, this is my brother, Raymond Barnett. Raymond is an accountant, and has been good enough to go through the books for the hospital."

Joe Fromme stuffed a large hunk of pie into his mouth and talked as he chewed. "I hope you're not expecting me to understand all those fancy numbers, Mr. Barnett. Anything more involved than buying a pound of nails hurts my brain."

"Raymond, please, Sheriff. And I promise. No fancy numbers. Straight forward, plain as the nose on your face, fraud and embezzlement."

"Well, let's get to it then. And call me Joe."

For the next two hours, Raymond went step by step through Hailey's ledger, as Joe asked questions. He sent Liberty to the hospital for Randall Whittimore, to corroborate the information.

"Randall, you know where Al Hailey lives?"

Randall shook his head. "No sir. I know where his mama lives in Bethpage, but last I heard Al had him a wife over to Siloam."

"Can you check with the other men still at the hospital?"

Lily had to know. "Sheriff, did you ever find any

proof of who stole our supplies and burned the tents?"

"Well, Miz Lily, it's this here way. I've heard a lot of supposing, and a lot of what ifs. But nothing for sure and certain."

Raymond was still looking over the book. "Sheriff, do you know a company called Mayne Buggy and Implements?"

He shook his head. "Ain't no such animal. There's Gallatin Buggy and Implement on Water Street by the courthouse, but no Mayne, not even in Lafayette or Scottsville. What was he supposed to have bought there?"

"It says 'fittings'."

"For a well pump, maybe?"

Lily answered, "No, Sheriff. I was the one who sent Mr. Whittimore to hire the well digger. When we arrived, the plan was to get water from the creek."

"And wasn't Dorris Mayne the other man Galen fired?"

She nodded. "He complained about needing to show up every day. Galen told him he didn't need to ever show up again. He took off with Hailey."

"Now, I may not know where Al Hailey lives. But I do know Dorris Mayne. He's a sorry waste of air, if you ask me. He's got a reputation for burning barns of people who make him mad."

*****

Joe Fromme found Dorris Mayne right where he expected: at the still buried in his barn. Mayne pretty much gave up without a fight, and allowed Joe to handcuff him and put him in the back of the repurposed ambulance that served as his jail wagon for the ride back to Coatesville.

They started back to town then Joe pulled the wagon to a halt. Al Hailey was strutting up the road carrying an empty quart jar. Joe jumped off the bench and stood beside the wagon. "Howdy, Al."

"Sheriff. What brings you all the way out here?"

"Just a little unfinished business. You going to see Dorris?" He pointed to the empty jar.

"Well, I...uh...I..."

"It's okay, Al. I've been knowing for years now that Dorris sold corn. So long as he don't poison nobody, it ain't no skin off my nose."

"Oh." Hailey chuckled. "Then yeah. I was headed to see Dorris."

Joe linked his arm in Hailey's, and started walking toward the back of the closed wagon. "Only problem, Al, Dorris ain't home."

"He's not?"

"Nope."

"You got any idea where he is?"

"Yep."

"Where?"

Still holding Hailey's arm, Joe released the catch on the wagon's tailgate, to show Dorris Mayne cuffed in the back. "Step right in, Al. We've got things to talk about back at the station."

The sheriff's station in town, a small stone building across from the depot, had jail cells in what was referred to as the "cellar", but was actually the ground floor. Few buildings had cellars in this part of the state, because it was necessary to blast through solid rock to build. Joe and his deputy parked Al Hailey in a cell, then escorted Dorris Mayne up the front steps to his office.

"Sit down, Dorris. You and me, we need to have a talk."

"Ain't got nothin' to say."

"Fine. How 'bout you just listen to me?" Mayne didn't say anything. "So, I looked at some numbers from Doc Stewart's clinic. When did you start a buggy and implement store?"

"Huh?"

"Yeah. Apparently, Al Hailey paid your 'store' seven hundred dollars for fittings. "

"That low down son of a bitch! He gave me a hundred, said it was for keeping my mouth shut."

Joe leaned back in his squeaky wooden desk chair, and grinned like a cat with a mouthful of feathers. "Thanks Dorris. That's all I need right now." He called his deputy. "Yo Dave. Take Dorris here back down, and bring up Al. Oh, and make sure they don't get to talk to each other. Dorris here's not feeling very sociable, anyway."

Dave Goode took the prisoner to the cells, removed his cuffs, and locked him in the cell at the far end of the building. At Al Hailey's cell closest to the door, he held up the cuffs. "Hands."

Hailey extended his wrists through the "pie hole", the gap where food was passed, and Dave snapped the cuffs in place. Once the cell door was unlocked, he used the links between the cuffs and pulled him up the steps and into Joe Fromme's office. Joe was still sitting at his desk.

"Al, come on in. Sit down. You and me, we need to have us a talk." It worked with Dorris, it may work again. Neither one of these boys were mental giants.

Just like Dorris, Al Hailey said, "Ain't got nothin' to say."

"Well, that's fine, Al. How 'bout you just listen? I looked over some books from Doc Stewart's hospital. There's some...let's say discrepancies in your bookkeeping."

He snorted. "What's that prissy citified asshole saying now?"

"You mean Doc Stewart? Just that you've been stealing the Public Health Service blind. Charging them for things that were never received, or if they were, you sold them off to someone else and pocketed the money."

"That's a goddamned lie! I never kept no books. I don't even know how to write in a ledger."

"Now, who said anything about a ledger? And what's this I hear about you giving seven hundred dollars to Dorris?"

"I never gave him no seven hundred bucks. I gave that lying bastard a hundred. He was supposed to keep his damned mouth shut."

"Now, Al, the way I figure it, there's a couple of thousand dollars missing from the hospital funds. I want to know where the money is."

Hailey was quiet for a long moment. Very softly, he asked, "If I give it back, will I get off?"

"Now, I can't promise that. That's up to the court. But if you give the money back, things should go easier on you."

"What if I don't have all the money, exactly?"

"Like how much, exactly?"

"I got about half of it."

"Un-huh. And what'd you do with the other half?

Hailey studied his boots. He mumbled, "Horse."

"What about a horse, Al? Did you bet on one?"

He shook his head. "Bought one."

"Oh, you bought a horse? Where is it?"

"At the house. In Siloam."

"You know, Al, that sounds like an awful lot of money for one horse. What else did you do with the money?"

"Racking horse and tack. Got him from Mr. Henry Gooch down Gallatin. Real showy."

"Now, you know I'm going to be checking in with Mr. Henry Gooch first thing in the morning, Al. Then I'll be confiscating that showy horse. Reckon the doc can use a good saddle horse, considering he's only got that little spotted mule to rely on. Now then, where will I find the money?"

He sighed. "My place. Go to my house, tell my wife to give you the fruit jars I put down the root cellar. The horse is in the barn behind the house."

Sheriff Fromme left Al Hailey in his deputy's care, and headed to the depot. He had telegrams to send.

Chapter Twenty-Two

It was Holy Saturday when Joe got official approval from the District Attorney in Gallatin for the deal with Al Hailey. His first order of business was to deliver the recovered loot to Galen.

He arrived at the Stewarts' home after breakfast, and knocked on the front door. Lily answered. "Sheriff Fromme. You never come to the front door. Come in, please."

"Well, Miz Lily, could you and Galen come outside? I've got something to show you."

Galen was in his office with Raymond. She ran to fetch him and the three went outside to see Sheriff Fromme.

Joe shook hands all round. "Well, folks, I've got good news. Al Hailey and Dorris Mayne have turned over most of the money they stole from the hospital. Here's the cash I was able to recover." He handed a fat envelope to Raymond. "Now, come around here."

He took them around to the back of the house, where Liberty was holding the reins of a showy bay stud horse, with a mane and tail that almost touched the ground. The horse carried a postage stamp sized saddle, and from the way he stood, he was indeed "showy". This boy was special, and he knew it.

"Doc, this is Mr. Henry's Morning Ranger. No, really. That's his name. Ranger here has a pedigree that goes all the way back to George Washington. Seems Al used a good portion of the money he stole to buy him. As soon as I have the paperwork from Mr. Gooch, I'll see you get it."

"Joe, what am I supposed to do with a thoroughbred horse?"

"Oh, he's not a thoroughbred. He's a Tennessee Racking Horse, smoothest ride you'll ever have. He's supposed to be broke to drive, as well as ride, but it'd be a damned shame to hitch this boy to a buggy."

"Joe, I don't ride. I'm just now learning how to drive the buggy."

"How'd you get to be as old as you are and never learn to ride?"

"Because I lived my whole life in the city. Oh, there were horse farms around where I grew up. I was never interested. In town, I could walk out my front door and hail a cab or get on a street car. Never had any need. And my wife doesn't ride, either."

Raymond hadn't paid any attention to the conversation between the sheriff and his brother-in-law. He laid his hand on the horse's rump, and walked around, running his one hand over flanks and shoulders. When he reached the horse's head, he stroked the animal's face, laid his head against him and allowed the animal to breathe in his scent. He said something to Liberty, who came around to the left, and, in a quick move, gave Raymond a leg up into the saddle.

Raymond turned the horse in a tight circle, sat up straight in the saddle, and gave Ranger his head.

Galen and Lily stood open-mouthed as her brother rode the little horse up and down the road in front of the house. After the first pass, the horse set his pace, with the ground-eating racking motion. On the third pass, Raymond pulled the horse into the yard, and drew him to a halt. He kicked his leg over the small pommel and slid to the ground.

"Raymond, where did you learn to ride?" Lily was shocked. Their father never owned a horse.

"Druid Hill Park. While you were away making the world safe for democracy, I was stuck in the house every weekend with Holy Josey. When it got to be too much, I'd go out to the park and rent a horse for a couple hours. It sure beat sitting in the Park's mansion staring at the birds."

Galen said, "That still doesn't settle our problem. The money belongs to the Department. The cash can be deposited in the account. I can't very well deposit a horse. And I doubt the seller would take him back."

Raymond had a solution. "Galen, do I get a finders fee for discovering Hailey's embezzlement?"

"Probably. I need to write to Dr. Happer and get his opinion. Why?"

"Because I was thinking that Morning Ranger here would be an appropriate reward."

Raymond held out his hand to his brother-in-law, and shook to seal the deal.

*****

May, 1919

Galen and Raymond were subpoenaed to court the first week in May. They testified as to the malfeasance of Al Hailey, and the recovery of the money.

Raymond was in his element, providing forensic accounting services, and explaining everything in terms that wouldn't make the judge go glassy-eyed.

In the end, both Hailey and Mayne were found guilty. Mayne was given a three month sentence, and Hailey, what was referred to as 11/29, eleven months, twenty-nine days, the charges having been reduced to a misdemeanor as the perpetrators attempted to make restitution.

Once the guilty verdict was in, Dr. Happer wrote to Raymond, thanking him for his hard work, and offering him a cash reward. Raymond wrote back, stating he would prefer the horse, laying out the actual fair market value of the unproven three year old, and pointing out that the original seller had actually cheated Hailey during the sale of the grossly overpriced horse.

Raymond got the horse.

Young Raymond Barnett also managed to make the acquaintance of Adelle Conover and two month old Abigail. Up until now, he had only seen her from a distance, and only knew her infant as a blanket-wrapped bundle.

He was in the barn late one afternoon, tending the horse he now called Hank, when Adelle walked in, carrying her daughter in a market basket. The weather was warm, and the baby was only wearing a gown, laid on a blanket on top of a folded quilt. She set the basket on a stripping table pushed up against a wall, assembled what she needed, and set about milking the cow. Apparently she hadn't noticed Raymond. The poor child was so fearful of men she wouldn't have come within ten yards of someone she considered a strange man. She was only now getting used to Dr. Stewart speaking to her.

At just over two month, Abigail was learning to coo and giggle, and discovering she had feet. Raymond found himself fascinated by the happy sounds, and left Hank to investigate.

"Hello sweetheart. You are a cutie, aren't you." He held out his pinky finger, which of course Abigail grabbed.

Adelle screamed, and made a mad dash to rescue her daughter from whatever ravages this man might have had in mind. She snatched the infant from the basket, clutching her protectively to her breast.

Raymond threw up his arms. "I meant no harm, really. I was talking to her. She's a sweet baby. Honest. I only wanted to talk."

It was then Adelle noticed Raymond's left hand was gone. "What happened?" She pointed at his arm.

He looked around and found an empty keg. He pushed it over and sat down, thinking he might be less threatening sitting than standing. "Two years ago, I was on a friend's boat. It was the Regatta. You know what a regatta is?"

She shook her head no.

"A regatta is a big race for sailboats. They have one in Annapolis every year. Anyway, I was on the boat, and we were getting ready to come about-- to turn around. One of the lines got wound around my arm. We hit the wake of the boat that turned ahead of us, I went over the side, and the line ripped my hand off."

"Did it hurt?" She sounded so childlike.

He nodded. "Not right away. It wasn't until later, in the hospital, that it really hurt."

"Can I see?"

Now was the time he had to put all his patience to use. Getting to know this young woman would be like trying to befriend a wounded animal. She could dart away at any moment. "Sure. If you want to." He unbuttoned his cuff and rolled the sleeve up to his elbow, then extended his arm for her inspection.

Adelle crept closer, sidling up to Raymond's outstretched arm. Clutching the squirming baby to her with one arm, she reached out tentative fingers and touched the pink flesh of the stump where his wrist had been. "It's smooth."

He nodded. "I know. That's because it's new skin. Kind of like what a baby has." Her fascination with his disability was a welcome change from the disgust he often experienced in others. That was why his brother had forced him from their family home, because his bride feared the young man with only one hand.

"Can I help you? It looks like the cow kicked the bucket over. Can I finish milking for you?"

She shook her head. "I can do it." She looked at where he sat on the keg. "Watch Abigail?"

"May I hold her? Or would you feel better if she was in her basket?"

Silently, she held her baby out to this man, who didn't seem so bad after all.

Raymond Barnett sat on the keg, holding the baby in the crook of his left arm, as he made up nonsense words, tickled, and kissed tiny baby toes, while her mother finished milking the Jersey cow.

This was the scene Lily discovered when she went to call her brother in for his supper. She didn't have the heart to interfere, but observed. Her brother, who had never been comfortable around women before his accident, was being absolutely foolish over this little girl. The mere fact that Adelle had willingly surrendered the baby to him, a virtual stranger, said much for his gentle nature. She went back to the house before Adelle saw her.

Adelle finished her duty, turned the cow out to her calf, and grabbed the full bucket. Raymond waited until she got closer before he spoke. "Take Abigail. I can carry the milk."

"I can take both." She was shaking her head so hard he was afraid she might jar something loose.

"I know you can. But you shouldn't have to. Not when I can help."

He stood slowly so as not to spook her. Abigail's basket was still sitting on the stripping table. He laid her on the blanket, picked up the basket and handed it to Adelle, then took the milk pail from her.

Every time he had seen Adelle she seemed to be scurrying, moving from place to place like a little mouse, hugging walls and staying in the shadows. Now, for the first time, she walked beside Raymond Barnett as he carried the galvanized bucket filled with milk. At the kitchen door, he stopped. "I know it's not very gentlemanly, but I find I don't have a spare hand. Can you open the door?"

For the first time in years, Adelle giggled.

*****

Adelle and the Rogans were in the habit of eating most of their meals in their own cabins, while the family ate in the dining room or the kitchen. Lily generally washed their dishes herself as a way to assuage her guilt over having household help and being otherwise useless in the kitchen.

Raymond's favorite topic of conversation over supper that night was his meeting with Adelle and the baby. "I met my girlfriend today."

Galen was unaware of the meeting in the barn, and assumed it was one of the clinic nurses. "Anyone we know?"

"Well, you should. She lives right here."

"Raymond, you can't mean Adelle."

He shook his head. "Her daughter. I spent about half an hour playing with Abigail while her mother milked the cow. She's a happy little critter."

Galen laid his knife and fork down on the plate. "Adelle let you hold her baby? Lily and Beatrix held her the day she was born, but I don't think anyone else has been within arm's length since then."

Never one to let a good story get in the way of a good meal, Raymond kept eating as he spoke. "I was tending Hank when Adelle came in to milk. She didn't know I was there. She set Abigail in a basket on the table out there. I stopped to talk to the baby, and her mother panicked. I threw up my hands...well, one hand and an arm. She noticed. I guess that made me less threatening. I was shocked when she asked questions."

Lily laid her hand on his disabled arm and gave him a reassuring squeeze. "She must really trust you."

"She must have. She's the only one who doesn't work in a hospital who asked to touch the stump." He helped himself to more vegetables. "Can you fill me in on why she's so skittish? I doubt she even knows."

Lily looked at her husband, who gave a short nod of approval. "I can tell you what's common knowledge. Adelle's parents died when she was very young. Her older brother raised her and beat her on a regular basis. When she was only fourteen, she was sold to a local preacher. She had her first baby at fifteen. Conover bashed the baby's brains out and buried him in the barn. She went into labor with Abigail after her husband beat and kicked her half to death. She walked from town in a raging ice storm and gave birth right here. Ten days later the sheriff went with Galen to dig up the barn. Conover attacked Joe Fromme, and Joe made Adelle a very young widow."

"So, she's only sixteen?"

Galen passed his brother-in-law another biscuit. "And you're twenty-two. So tread lightly."

The sun was dipping below the horizon when Raymond went to check on his horse and make sure he had some fresh hay and water. He passed Adelle's little cabin and saw her sitting on the step, playing with baby Abigail. He waved, and was surprised when she gave a small wave in return.

It didn't take him long to finish his business in the barn. He was closing the stall door when one of the barn cat's calico kittens started rubbing around his ankles. He scooped the kitty up and held her loosely, in case she decided to make an escape. He carried the tiny furball to Adelle's and asked if he could sit with her.

"No, no. Get it away!"

"What's wrong? It's just a little kitten." He rubbed the soft fur against his face to show how harmless she was.

The girl was clutching her infant so tightly in her panic, the baby whimpered. "No cats. Evil. Mr. Jackson said they steal the baby's breath."

Mr. Jackson must be what she called that bastard of a husband. "Adelle, do you trust my sister?"

"Sister?"

"Nurse Barnett. She's my sister, Lily. Dr. Stewart is my brother-in-law. Do you trust them?"

"Uh-huh."

"They're both in the kitchen right now. How about we go ask them if cats are bad."

Adelle and her daughter followed behind him to the kitchen. Lily was washing while Galen wiped the supper dishes.

"Lily, settle an argument for us."

The doctor and nurse exchanged shocked glances. "Sure. Come in, Adelle. Sit down. You don't need to stand in the doorway."

Raymond pulled out a chair for his guest and sat next to her. The girl seemed so at ease with him, while she was still skittish around Galen.

"Lily, my friend here seems to think this innocent little kitten capable of stealing baby Abigail's breath. Would you be good enough to tell her this is not true."

Lily sat down next to her brother and took the kitten. She made a show of loving on the little feline to show she was harmless. "Is that something your husband told you?"

She nodded. "When we got married, I had a little kitty. When the baby was coming, Mr. Jackson said cats steal babies' breath. So he took it out in the barn and killed it." She spoke matter-of-factly, as if reciting times tables. Then, as she looked into Raymond's face, a small, silent sob escaped and she buried her face in the baby's blanket.

Raymond wanted nothing more than to hug this child and hold her and take all her hurt. Then he wanted to dig up her dead husband and kill him all over again.

Lily was still holding the kitten. She set the cat in her lap and stroked her soft fur. Kitty started to purr, and curled up in a ball, settling in for an impromptu catnap. "There's nothing wrong with having a cat around a baby, Adelle. So long as kitty's healthy, nothing will happen to the baby. They sometimes want to sleep with the baby, but that's only because babies are warm and smell like milk."

Her hold on Abigail was starting to relax.

Raymond asked, "Would you like to hold her? She won't hurt you, and she's so soft."

Out of the blue, Adelle handed Abigail to Raymond. She held out her hands to Lily. "Can I hold?"

Very gently, Lily lifted the kitten from her lap and passed her to Adelle.

The girl's face lit up as she stroked the soft tricolor fur. "She's soft. She buzzes."

"She's purring." Raymond said softly. "Cats do that when they like you."

"Can she stay?"

Lily's heart was breaking for this orphaned waif, whose only experience with love of any kind had come in the last two months of her young life. "Of course she can stay, sweetie. Just remember, if she's in your cabin she'll need to go outside every so often. And you'll need to make sure you wash your hands after you hold her before you pick up Abigail."

She nodded. "I remember."

Abigail had fallen asleep against Raymond's shoulder. "The baby's asleep," he whispered. "Would you like me to carry her home for you? So you can carry the kitty?"

She nodded again.

Galen grabbed a lamp and led the way through the darkened yard to Adelle's cabin. He traded the lamp he carried for the unlit one on her kitchen table, then left.

Adelle climbed the two steps, still enthralled by her little pet. Raymond trailed behind her, amazed she was going to allow him into her sanctuary.

"Where should I put her," he whispered. "She's sound asleep."

"In here." She led him into the small bedroom, where a cradle waited beside the bed.

He laid Abigail in the wooden cradle Liberty and Randall had constructed. He straightened and turned to leave, and bumped square into Adelle. He caught her before she fell, then released her immediately, knowing his touch would be too much.

Back in the kitchen, making sure to keep a respectful distance, he asked, "Have you picked out a name for her yet?"

She shook her head. "You name her."

"How about Belle? Or Honey?"

Adelle's little face lit up with a broad smile. "Honeybee. 'Cause she buzzes." She held out her hands holding the relaxed, purring kitten.

Raymond put his hand under hers to hold her steady, and rubbed his cheek against the kitten's fur. "Hello Miss Honeybee." He kissed the top of the furry head and lowered his hand as he stepped away.

"Do you need anything else?" He hoped she did.

She shook her head.

"All right then. I'll bid you goodnight. "

He got to the door when he felt a hand on his arm. He turned just in time to feel her quick kiss on his cheek. "Thank you."

Anne Arrandale

Chapter Twenty-Three

July, 1919

"Hailey! Move yer ass boy. Them maters ain't gonna hoe themselves."

The county jail guard carried his shotgun high, braced on his thigh as he rode his mule along the edge of the field, supervising the prisoners at their work.

Al Hailey worked his way down the row, chopping weeds with his sharpened hoe. Behind him Dorris Mayne followed with a bucket, picking the rope tomatoes.

"I swear to my time, Dorris. I am gonna get even with that prissy, uppity doctor. I'll get even if it hare-lips hell."

Dorris was itching for some retribution of his own. "Ya know, Al, I'm outta here in two weeks. Maybe I can handle it. That is, if you make it worth my while."

This might be a good idea. He could pay Stewart back, and it would never come back to him. "You just might have a deal, Dorris. You just might have a deal."

*****

Dorris Mayne was released from custody a week later. He sneaked aboard a boxcar on the train back to Coatesville. From there, he had things to see and people to do.

He walked up the road toward the Stewarts' home. During his time in jail, Dorris had opted not to shave or cut his hair. He looked like a derelict, and he knew it. It suited his purpose admirably.

As he neared the Stewart house, he heard the telltale rhythm of a horse's hooves, moving fast. Dorris stepped to the side so he didn't get run down. A showy bay horse blew past him, speed racking for all he was worth, with that prissy Yankee Barnett perched up on his back. Bastard was riding Al's horse!

Dorris Mayne began to formulate a plan. Yeah, that just might work.

*****

Raymond stood in the kitchen, watching his sister figuring out the workings of the new pressure cooker autoclave the Public Health Service had sent. "You know, Sis, if the fair ever comes back, I bet I could win some nice prizes at the horse show with Hank."

She had spent the summer watching her brother work the horse, allowing him to build his strength gradually, and basically allowing the horse to have fun. The little stallion loved her brother, and she knew the feeling was mutual.

"Probably. Of course, having some championship ribbons wouldn't hurt his stud fees, either."

He put his arm around his sister's shoulders and gave her a squeeze. "Sis, if I didn't know better, I'd swear you were a country girl at heart."

She started screwing down the lid. "Maybe I am." She set the big pot on the stove, and waited for it to come up to pressure. "Galen's talking about buying a house here in town, so we can stay here when this epidemic is over. We hardly have any patients right now. If it stays like this the Health Service won't need our clinic anymore."

"Guess that means I'll have to find someplace else to go." He sounded so pitiful.

She refilled his coffee and sat beside him. "You're an excellent accountant. There's no reason you can't hang out a shingle and take on private clients. You can even work for attorneys doing the same thing you did for us."

He held up his damaged arm. "How many people would hire a man like this?"

"Raymond John Barnett, you are being ridiculous! The fact that you are missing a hand has nothing to do with your ability as an accountant. You forget, we worked with men who lost legs, arms, even faces. And those men still had abilities, a purpose. Many of those men still hold down jobs. So what's wrong with you?"

"Yeah. But they were wounded in a war. They have honor. Who wants somebody who lost a hand sailing some rich kid's fancy boat?"

"If you're so sensitive about it, why don't you have a prosthetic? A company in Nashville makes wonderful articulated hands."

"I tried. The hospital said they were all for the veterans."

"That was before you had a brother-in-law who's a doctor. He can fit you, send the molds off on the train with Mr. Terry, and we can have it back in no time. Then, if you're still sensitive about how it looks, wear a glove over it."

"Okay, Big Sis. I'll talk to Galen about it. If it'll make you happy"

"It will." She changed the subject abruptly. "So, I see Adelle talking to you whenever you're outside. She hardly talks to anyone, unless she absolutely has to. She really trusts you."

"I trust her, too. Maybe because we're both kind of broken."

"Oh, Raymond. You're not broken. Just a little dented."

*****

Dorris Mayne spent the rest of the day laying low. He had plans to make, material to gather. Good thing everything he needed was in Al Hailey's barn. No sooner had Al been convicted, his wife had hared off to Kentucky with some drummer. Rotten faithless bitch. No matter. Dorris planned to stay in Al's barn until he settled Stewart's hash.

Al said it right. He'd get even if it hare-lipped hell. Yeah, he'd see to it. And when Al got out, he'd see Dorris was taken care of. He said so.

Dorris Mayne dug through the loft of Hailey's barn. He found empty jars, and a couple of jars that held the shine Dorris made. Hmm. Al must have forgotten he had them, considering the day they got arrested he was coming to fill another quart jar. He could put this shine to good use. One for now, and one for tonight.

He settled down in the empty barn loft and broke open the quart jar of homemade liquor. He held the jar up to the light and looked through the clear liquid. He was right proud of this. His liquor was some of the best in two counties. His daddy taught him how to make it, and Dorris made improvements over the years, adding a coil here, some malted grains there, experimenting with the sugar content. It was a damned shame he couldn't sell it open and honest.

The first pull he took from the jar choked him. The second swallow went down smoother. Damn, it was some good stuff.

Two hours, and half a jar later, Dorris Mayne was staggering around the loft, trying to find the ladder. He was out of drinking shape, if a pint could put him on his ass.

*****

Raymond was in the barn saddling Hank. It wasn't easy, but he was getting better at doing up the girth. Liberty stood by in case he needed help, but his goal was to be self-sufficient. Once he had it secure, he led the horse to the mounting block. It had taken him time to figure out the best system for him, but he swung up into the saddle, picked up the reins and was ready for his afternoon ride. It was something he managed to do at least once a day, sometimes, twice, to keep Hank in shape, and to get himself in condition. He knew he had spent the last two years doing little of nothing but sitting behind a desk. Now he had an outlet, and he was determined to better himself.

As he rode into the yard, he saw Adelle sitting on the step, with baby Abigail on her lap. The baby was holding her head up on her own now, and loved to look around. He pulled Hank to a stop.

"Morning, Adelle."

She looked up and smiled.

"I'm going for a ride. Can Abby ride with me?" It was a long shot. But just maybe she'd allow it. "I won't go far and we won't ride fast. I promise."

Adelle walked to where he sat astride the little horse, and stroked the animal's flank. Once she assured herself the horse wouldn't shy she passed Abigail up to Raymond.

She surprised him. He had to juggle briefly, to arrange her so she was sitting in front of him, with her little feet on either side of the saddle, her back snuggly against him, his left arm holding her securely.

A click and a touch of his heels and Hank stepped out. The horse seemed to know he carried precious cargo, and walked slowly. Raymond took him around the house, to the constant giggles of baby Abby. She bounced in delight, kicking her heels on the leather, making it a little difficult for Raymond to hold her.

He reined in at Adelle's door, and waited for her to take her daughter back. Adelle's smile was as broad as her daughter's when she reached up to her. "Thank you," she whispered.

Leaning forward across the saddle so their faces were almost touching, he said, "Maybe one day you'd like to ride with me."

She didn't say yes or no. But he heard her giggle as she ran into Lily's kitchen.

Raymond turned Hank toward the road, leaned back in the saddle and called, "Rack on."

The horse was ready. He stepped out, starting with a racking walk, then at Raymond's cue in a ground-eating speed rack, his mane and tail flying in the wind.

They rode to the clinic, where Galen was seeing the few remaining patients, those who had been slow to recover. He tied Hank to a willow tree by the creek where he had sweet grass and fresh water, and went to find his brother-in-law.

Galen took the young man into his office. "Anything wrong at home?"

Raymond sat back in his chair, glad he had another man to talk to. "It's about Adelle."

"What's happened? Did anyone hurt her?"

"No, nothing like that. I want to make sure I don't. That's what I need to talk to you about."

He figured this was coming. "You sure you wouldn't rather talk to Lily about this?"

He shook his head. "No. You're her doctor. I figured I should talk to you."

"Don't tell me you need a 'birds and bees' talk?"

Raymond gave him a look. "Please. I'm twenty-three. I've been around."

"Okay. Then what do you need to discuss?"

"I think I want to marry her."

Now where did that come from? "And how does Adelle feel about it?"

"Oh I haven't said anything to her. I can barely say three words to her before she runs into the house."

"So what makes you think you two should marry?"

Raymond looked over his shoulder, half expecting someone else to show up. "It started the day we met. She took time to ask about this." He held up his amputation. "Then when I gave her the kitten, she kissed my cheek. Since then, she talks to me. Not much, just a word here and there. She laughs for me. And she trusts me with her daughter. Today, she let me carry Abby on Hank. And when I passed her back, I told her one day she could ride with me."

"How did she react?" Galen pictured the frightened mouse dashing back inside.

"She giggled, then ran into the house with Lily and Beatrix."

"Well, I'll be damned."

"What?"

"Raymond, let me tell you a story. Since Adelle came to us, I've found out a lot more, some of it from Beatrix that Adelle confided in her, some from Lily, and some from people in the community.

"Adelle can't read nor write. Her brother never bothered sending her to school. Her husband, Abigail's father, never made love to her. From the day he married her, every sex act was rape. She's never known love, until her daughter was born. Never had anything of her own, never even knew pleasure in any form.

"She was so uneducated, she believed everything he told her. That if he beat her it was allowable because he was her husband and it was his right. If she didn't cook his supper right he beat her. It took little of nothing to set him off.

"The day before Abigail was born, Lily had been on the same train with Jackson Conover. Conover decided my wife's soul needed saving. She wasn't having it and tried to move to a new seat. He laid hands on her, and she decked him." Raymond nodded. He remembered that wicked right cross. "The conductor intervened and stopped him from retaliating further.

"Like any other bully, he took his anger out on the only weaker person available to him. His pregnant wife. He beat her with his fists, kicked her over and over, and I'm pretty sure he raped her. His assault was what put her into labor. Thank God she was able to get to Lily. Had she tried to deliver at home, as she had with her son, she would have died. And I'm almost certain Conover would have buried Abigail next to her brother.

"What I'm trying to say is tread carefully. She's fragile. You've got to allow her to blossom into a person in her own right. She needs time to understand how the world works."

"Oh my God Galen. I want to hold her, and protect her from all the bad things in the world. How can I, when the people she most needed protection from were her brother and her husband?"

"That's something else. Adelle doesn't ever need to know this. She and Conover were never actually married. He performed the ceremony himself, and never even bothered filing a certificate with the county. She was so young and innocent she didn't know any better. So she's not even a widow."

Raymond sat and digested all this. "Do you think Liberty would show me how to hitch Hank to the buggy? I need to take Abby and her mama for a ride."

*****

Dorris Mayne gathered what he needed in an old tow sack, and headed back toward town close to sundown. If anyone saw him they'd figure he was on his way home from work. He walked slowly, not wanting to arrive too early. He had a job to do, and he didn't intend to mess it up. If he did, Al wouldn't pay him like he promised.

When he got near the clinic, he stopped to look around. Good. Only one guard on duty. When the guard was on the far side of the compound, Dorris nipped inside the cook tent. He found the big butcher knife Purcell used to cut up meat. He tucked that into his sack, then grabbed a boning knife for good measure. Maybe he'd stop back there later for some more fun, after he took care of that doctor who thought his shit didn't stink.

*****

Raymond spent the better part of the afternoon with Liberty Rogan. Their first order of business was to put Hank in harness and get him hitched to the buggy. When the little horse didn't balk at all, Liberty declared the sheriff was telling the truth, that he was broke to pull. Once he was in the traces, it was a simple matter to take Raymond out on the road and give him a driving lesson.

After half an hour, Liberty declared Raymond ready to drive on his own, with the admonition that the hardest thing to do would be to hold the horse back if he decided he wanted to "rack on".

Raymond pulled the buggy up into the yard in front of Adelle's cabin. He hopped down from the bench, went to her open door, and used his knuckles on the frame. "Miss Adelle, you home?"

His eyes adjusted to the dim light of the overly warm kitchen and saw her sitting at the table nursing Abigail. He turned away to protect her modesty. "Miss Adelle, would you and Abby like to go for a buggy ride with me?"

Raymond smiled when he heard Abigail's little burp, signaling she was finished. He had to strain to hear her mother's soft, "Yes, please."

He went and stood by the conveyance, waiting like the gentleman he was. She came out on the step, with the shawl Lily had given her around her shoulders, holding her daughter on her hip. He ran to meet her, and offered his hand to assist her down the two steps. To his great surprise she accepted his touch, even if she did pull away once her feet were on solid ground.

She smiled when she saw the little horse hitched to the Studebaker buggy. "Hank's pretty." He loved the sound of her voice even if he did have to strain to hear it half the time.

Raymond patted the horse's rump as he went by. "I think Hank likes to think he's handsome."

Adelle giggled, making Abby giggle too.

"If I could, I'd pick you up and set you on the bench. But I can't." He held up his amputation. "But if you give me Abby, I can hold your hand and help you in."

Abby went to him willingly, grabbing his nose as soon as he had her securely in his arm. He held her hand while she stepped on the wheel hub, then up onto the bench. He handed her the baby, and waited until she slid to the left side of the seat. He climbed up beside her, took up the reins, and clicked Hank into motion.

He kept the horse at a walk and they headed toward town. It was all he could do to keep his eyes on the road, when he kept sneaking glimpses at his two passengers. Abby rode on her mother's lap, giggling and bouncing as the world went by.

Adelle never wore her hair up. She had never learned how to do anything but braid it. Now it was blowing loose in the breeze. To Raymond, she looked like some Celtic goddess.

"Want to go faster?"

She nodded. "Yes, please. Faster."

They reached the depot. Raymond pulled the buggy around, so they were headed back toward the house. "Hold on to something."

She looped her arm through his and held on for all she was worth.

He snapped the reins over Hank's back and called, "Rack on."

Hank stepped out on command, pacing to match old Dan Patch. They didn't have far to go, but it was enough to make Adelle smile at him, and for now, that was enough.

He started slowing down as they neared the house. She let go of his arm but didn't move away. When he pulled the buggy up into the yard in front of her door, she didn't make an effort to climb down as he expected. Maybe she was waiting for him?

He stepped down, then held up his arms for the baby. She passed Abby to him, then took his hand to climb down. She reached as if to take the baby, but shocked him down to his socks when she put her arms around his waist and hugged him.

Knowing her tortured past he didn't offer to return her embrace no matter how much he wanted to. Instead, he held Abby in his arms and enjoyed the feel of her cheek against his chest.

"Thank you Raymond." She said his name!

"You're welcome Adelle." As she took Abby back, he took the biggest chance of his life and lightly kissed her cheek.

She giggled and scurried back into her cabin.

Raymond let Hank into the barn and unhitched him, then took up an old piece of sacking and rubbed him down. "Little man, you've had a busy day." He fetched a comb and started to comb out the horse's long mane. "I wonder if Adelle would like to braid this for you?"

*****

Supper that night was festive. Lily had instituted a policy of the entire household eating at least one meal a week together including the Rogans and Adelle. She had done it for the young mother's sake, trying to bring her out of her shell, to give her an idea of family life without abuse and hatred. Thus far it hadn't done much good.

Beatrix had fixed a beef roast with potatoes and some lima beans she had put up earlier, with sliced tomatoes from their garden patch. There was more food on the table than Adelle was accustomed to seeing in a week. She still wasn't used to such largess and only took vegetables. In the short time she'd been with them, Lily had noticed she rarely ate meat. She thought perhaps she had problems chewing, after the beating she had taken.

Raymond sat next to her, and watched the tiny portions she took. "Adelle, honey, there's plenty of food. Have some meat." He spoke softly, afraid she may bolt.

She shook her head almost violently. "For men," she whispered.

That was it. Raymond Barnett wanted more than anything to find the bastard who did this to her and kill him all over again. "Adelle, do you trust me?"

She nodded.

"Do Miss Lily and Miss Beatrix have meat on their plates?"

She looked around, then nodded.

He picked up a slice of beef from his own plate with his fork and set it on her plate. "This is yours. After you eat that, if you want more you may have it. You may have all you want, can't she Lily?"

"Of course, Adelle. You don't ever have to worry about what you eat here."

Galen set his silver aside, and wiped his mouth with his napkin. His voice was calm, fatherly. "Adelle, you're still feeding Abigail. You need a lot of good food so you can feed her. You don't want her to get sick, do you?"

"No Dr. Galen."

Raymond picked another slice of meat for himself. "Now that's settled, eat your dinner. I saw Beatrix has something special for dessert."

Dessert was indeed special. Beatrix managed to get some bananas when the train came in that morning. The store had vanilla wafers, so she took advantage and made a banana pudding. It had been in the oven setting the meringue while they ate.

Lily spooned out large portions into bowls and passed it around. Adelle looked at it, turned the bowl to study the dish carefully. She picked up her spoon, and very deftly lifted off the meringue and deposited it in Raymond's bowl.

He was puzzled. "Don't you like meringue?"

She leaned toward him and said, very confidentially, "Eww. Calf spit," and shivered comically.

Anne Arrandale

Chapter Twenty-Four

Dorris Mayne took advantage of the family's dinner hour to find a hiding place in the Stewarts' barn. The milk cow and the spotted mule were out in the pasture. The only occupant, aside from the odd chicken or two, was Al's showy little stallion. He hated what he was planning to do, but it would serve that prissy doctor right. That's what he gets for putting them in jail, and making them return money both men figured was coming to them anyway.

He crouched in an empty stall behind some hay bales. This would be the perfect place to start his mischief. He opened his quart jar and poured half onto the floor and into one of the hay bales. Hay fires smoldered a good long time before they flamed. Alcohol burned high and hot, and took fast. Yeah. This was perfect.

It was still too early to do what he intended. He had a good hour before the household settled down for the night. He took a long pull from the half filled quart jar and settled back. A pint should last him the hour he needed. It was going to be a good night.

*****

Tonight had been the best night Raymond could remember. Adelle had talked to him. They ate together. She made a joke. And she'd kissed his cheek and hugged him.

After dinner they sat on the settee in Lily's parlor while he told Abigail the story of the Three Bears. Adelle had hung on every word too. Clearly, she had never been told stories, either. He walked her to her front door, and not only had she kissed his cheek, she had allowed him to kiss her in return.

This, this was his best night ever.

He was standing in the mud room, trying to work the boot jack. Before he could pull his foot out, He heard Adelle scream.

"Raymond! Fire!"

He stomped his foot back into his boot and took off. It wasn't far to her cabin door, but he could see the red glow inside the barn where Mr. Henry's Morning Ranger was stabled. The horse inside his stall was frantic, kicking and neighing.

Adelle stood on her back step, holding Abigail. Raymond grabbed the blanket the baby was wrapped in, and dunked it in the horse trough. "Run for Lily, tell her to call the fire brigade." He put the blanket over his head and went to save his horse.

Adelle didn't stay to watch him enter the burning barn. She was already running through the back door. "Miss Lily! Miss Lily!"

Lily had never heard Adelle speak that loudly or say that much at one time. "What's wrong?"

"Fire. In the barn. Raymond said to call the fire brigade."

Galen was already ringing the telephone to have the operator alert the brigade at the fire hall.

Inside the barn Raymond had no trouble reaching Hank's stall. So far the fire seemed to be confined to the unused stall opposite. He pulled the blanket from his head, wrapped the horse's eyes to keep him from bolting, and led him outside. The mule and cow were in the pasture already, the buggy in the yard. The only thing they would lose would be some tools and some hay from last winter.

He led Hank around to the gate, opened it and slapped the horse on the rump to send him out where he'd be safe for the time being. His only concern with him being out all night was because he had a penchant for kicking the cow. At the back of the barn, in the red glow of the smoldering wood, he noticed what looked like a pile of rags. Could this be the source of the fire?

He walked over to it and moved it with his toe. The pile groaned.

"Galen! Out back."

Galen ran around the back of the barn. "What?"

"There's a man back here."

Galen joined his brother-in-law. They each hooked an arm under the unconscious man's armpits and dragged him around to the yard. Meanwhile Liberty and Beatrix were dowsing the fire with water dipped from the trough. They had the bales extinguished, but were still trying to put out the flames beginning to lick up the barn wall.

The sheriff arrived ahead of the fire brigade. Galen called to him. "Joe, we found him leaning against the barn wall. Drunker than a skunk. If Raymond hadn't found him, he'd be a human torch now."

Joe Fromme turned the man over and held his lantern higher. "Dorris Mayne. Figures."

The fire brigade arrived, their horse drawn truck making enough noise to wake the dead. They ran out their hose, pumped up the tank, and sprayed down the barn. It didn't take long for everything to be under control.

Lily had been standing beside Adelle, trying to stay out of the men's way. Once the fire was extinguished she realized the young mother was no longer beside her. It took Lily a minute to find her.

Adelle stood with her arms wrapped around Raymond as he held her baby. Lily called to him. "Raymond, is everything all right?"

He looked up at his sister, then placed a chaste kiss on the top of Adelle's head. "She saved us, Lily. 'Though she be but little, she is fierce'." He hugged her just a little tighter with his good arm.

*****

October, 1919

More influenza patients were arriving daily. The summer had given them a welcome respite, but as soon as the weather turned cold, and people were forced indoors, the virus got another foothold.

Public Health finally provided them with motorized ambulances. Raymond was drafted to work as an ambulance driver, after one of their regular drivers became sick himself.

When he wasn't ferrying patients to the clinic, he performed bookkeeping services not just for Galen, but for several businesses in town.

The money he earned he spent on Adelle and her daughter. He determined months ago, the night of the fire, that he was going to marry her, and be a father to her daughter. But he intended to properly court her, to allow her to grow joyfully to womanhood, rather than be forced to assume duties for which she may not be ready.

Galen and Raymond spent an afternoon with Adelle, talking about her marriage. When she discovered she and Jackson Conover were never really married, she cheerfully declared she's really Adelle Fraser, her maiden name. She no longer quoted the ravings of her ersatz husband. Now, her conversations were peppered with "Dr. Galen says" and "Miz Lily says".

Many of the patients coming in now were from surrounding counties. Lily was happy that wives and parents could at least visit now.

One of their new patients was one of the late returnees from the War. He was young, in his early twenties, with two kids and a wife already. The family lived in a shotgun house on a farm in Siloam, so the wife was able to visit every day.

When Raymond brought Matthias King in on his ambulance, the young man was on the verge of pneumonia. According to Dr. Roberts, who rode the ambulance as attendant, said the house was pitiful, one where both wind and rain had equal access. The kids had constant snotty noses and the wife seemed to make herself scarce as often as possible, leaving her sick husband to fend for himself. Once he got to the clinic his condition seemed to improve immediately, although he still wasn't out of the woods.

Matthias King sat propped up in his bed with Lily beside him. She was trying to get some beef tea into him. "Matt, please. You need to drink some of this. You want to get better don't you?"

"Come on, Miz Lily. My wife's supposed to be here. She said she'll bring some soup."

After hearing how the family lived, Lily could imagine what went into the soup. "That's fine. Tell you what: half of this now, then you have the soup your wife brings. If that stays down, maybe we can try something more substantial for supper."

"Substantial?"

"Maybe some custard or tapioca? And I think I saw some applesauce in Mr. Purcell's kitchen."

"Let me have that cup."

Lily walked down the aisle, her smile wide. She did appreciate a cooperative patient. She spent time checking with the other eleven patients in her ward who were at varying stages of recovery, except for one woman.

For some reason this influenza didn't seem to bother children or older adults for the most part. It proved, however, to be deadly for young men in their prime. Perhaps because women weren't forced into factories, or trenches, or troop ships, they didn't seem to be stricken near as frequently as young men. Her single middle-aged female patient was an anomaly.

Hulda Wattan was in her late forties, from a reasonably prosperous family in Oak Grove. She had become ill the day after hosting her niece's wedding. Gatherings of more than three or four people were still restricted but in the country, there weren't many who would complain. She put on a huge do for her brother's daughter at their family home, laying down dinner for seventy people, as well as a church service held in the family chapel. The next day seventeen persons had been laid low by the influenza. Three died within twenty-four hours, thirteen recovered, and Mrs. Wattan continued to sicken. Her son finally carried her to the Stewarts' clinic.

Since her arrival Mrs. Wattan had slipped into a coma. Her breathing had become stentorious, the rales in her lungs being obvious even without a stethoscope. Lily raised the head of the woman's bed in an effort to ease her breathing.

"Dr. Stewart, a minute please." She hailed her husband as he walked through the ward. "Would you check Mrs. Wattan please?"

Galen stopped and listened to the woman's lungs, and her heart. He took her pulse, then lowered the head of her bed to fully recline. He checked her heart again, then it came. She gasped, or tried to, then it was over. Hulda Wattan was gone.

He drew the sheet over her face and turned to squeeze his wife's hand. "I'm sorry, Lily."

She dashed at a tear that was trying to escape, and turned away. Crying could wait until later. She had patients to see to.

Lily found two orderlies to remove Mrs. Wattan. Galen would see that her son was called. Otherwise, there wasn't much they could do for her. Her son would call one of the local morticians to collect the remains. She was thankful their situation wasn't nearly as dire as that in Baltimore where newly arrived Irish immigrants were being paid five dollars and a bottle of cheap whiskey to dig mass graves.

She made her way back to where King lay. His wife was with him. "Mrs. King. I'm glad you could be here. Matthias has been looking forward to your visit today."

Eulalia King was painfully thin and haggard. She was younger than Lily by five years, but two children in rapid succession, a husband off to war for a year, and piss poor living conditions had added twenty years. "I brung Matty some soup. Is it okay?" She held up a rag-wrapped fruit jar.

"So long as it's not too fatty."

She shook her head. "No'm. I didn't have no meat. I just cooked up some onions and taters in milk. Is that okay?"

"That should be fine. Promise me you'll see Mr. Purcell at the cook tent. I'll tell him to see you get a piece of meat to take home for the children. Will you do that?"

She raised her chin. "Don't need no charity, Miz nurse."

"It's not charity. It's preventative medicine. If your children don't get enough to eat, they'll get sick too. We don't want that, do we?"

Eulalia shook her head. "I'll get it."

Lily left her patient to his visiting and headed to the mess tent. "Mr. Purcell?"

Jimmy Purcell stepped away from his butcher block. "Yes'm, Miz Stewart?"

"Mrs. King is going to stop by to see you. You've met her. Two little girls, none of them look like they've had a decent meal in a month? I told her to stop by and see you. Would you see she gets a nice piece of meat so she can fix her girls something decent to eat for the next few days?"

"Yes'm. I've got a nice ham shank on the board. What about some eggs? Mr. Jent brought us five dozen yesterday, and another five dozen today. We don't need nearly that many."

"Then why'd you buy them?"

He shook his head. "I didn't. Mr. Jent couldn't sell them so he brought them here. Said to consider it a donation."

"Good. boil up two dozen for her. That way she won't have to worry about breakage or how to cook them. I don't even know if she *can* cook. Today, she brought 'soup' that she made with boiled onions and potatoes and milk. Maybe you could give her a piece of cooked meat instead?"

"Yes'm. I just took a pork shoulder out of the oven. I'll cut her off about half of it. That should keep them fed for a day or two. How about some sweet potatoes and apples? I got two bags of each."

"Mr. Purcell, you fix her up with whatever she needs. But she's walking. Remember how much she'll have to carry."

"Well, unless Raymond could take her home?"

She laughed. "And Raymond can take her home."

Back on the ward, Lily found Matthias King sitting back against his pillows, snoring. "When did he fall asleep?"

Eulalia looked up from the jar she was sealing. "A minute or two ago." She held up the jar. "He et half of it."

"Good. I promised if he ate, and he kept it down, he could have some custard tonight. We're trying to keep him on soft foods for now. That's why your soup was good for him. Would you like to leave it so he can have some later?"

She set the jar back into the tow sack and set it beside the bed. "I reckon I oughta go now. Since he's asleep and all."

"Remember, you promised to see Mr. Purcell. And I'm going to have my brother take you home."

Raymond was in the back of his ambulance with another driver. The pair were busy cleaning, wiping down surfaces with a carbolic solution, something Lily insisted be done between every run. "Raymond, how much longer will you be?"

He dropped the rag into the galvanized bucket and jumped down. "How about now? What'd'ya need?"

"Eulalia King has a big parcel from the kitchen. She needs a ride home. Care to drive her?"

He nodded. "Sure. Give me a minute and I'll be right over."

Eulalia was waiting outside Purcell's cook tent with an armload of paper wrapped parcels when Raymond pulled up. He set the brake and jumped down, then hurried around to open the other door. He handed her up to the seat, ran back to his door and climbed in.

Two little girls were sitting outside the King home. They appeared to be around three and five. Sunken cheeks, hollow dark eyes, dirt smeared, and hair that didn't look like it had seen a comb since Christmas. Even in the late afternoon chill, they had no sweaters or even sleeves in their flour sacking dresses. When Raymond pulled up, the children didn't run out. They looked at each other, then cowered back against the house in the shadows. He could tell something was dreadfully amiss.

He carried the parcels into the kitchen for her and set them on the dry sink. Across the kitchen, long strips of fly paper hung down from the ceiling, some heavily crusted with dead bugs.

Before she could thank him, Raymond was out the door. The house gave him a bad case of the whim-whams, and he didn't intend to stay any longer than necessary.

Outside, the children were still sitting in the dirt, huddled together like frightened sheep. Raymond had to check on them. "C'mere, girls."

The pair sidled over to him, terrified of what he may do, prepared to bolt at any second.

He squatted down, so he was on their level. "Your mama has some boiled eggs in the kitchen if you're hungry."

Both girls shook their heads. Maybe food was so scarce in their home they knew better than to ask for anything until it was offered.

A child at heart, Raymond reached into his coat pocket and pulled out some wrapped sour balls. He spoke as if he was sharing the greatest secret in the world. "How about a piece of candy? It can be our secret."

Each girl selected on cellophane wrapped candy. Raymond had to stop the younger girl from putting paper and all in her mouth. He showed her how to pull the ends to unwrap the treat, then took the paper from them.

He patted their heads and headed back to his ambulance. Before he could climb in the seat, he heard the unmistakable sound of explosive diarrhea. He scanned the yard, and saw the older girl had soiled herself, and the younger girl was doubled over. He ran for the King's front door.

He opened the door and called, "Mrs. King, your kids are sick."

She sauntered to the door, stuffing a boiled egg in her face. "Oh, they're always doing that. Nothing to worry about." She closed the door in his face.

It may get him fired or arrested or both. He didn't care. He grabbed a child under each arm and put them in his ambulance. "Come on, girls. Let's go see your daddy." Neither girl objected.

It took fifteen minutes to reach the clinic. He pulled in front of the doorway and started yelling for his sister as he opened the door. She came out, confused as to what the emergency could be.

"Lily, I've got the King kids. They're deathly sick; I'm afraid they're dying. Their mother had them locked out of the house, wouldn't offer them any food. The older girl doubled up in the yard and has the screaming shits. I couldn't leave them there."

His sister only nodded, and guided the girls into the isolation area. Once there, she filled the canvas tub from the boiler, stripped the flour sack dresses off them and plopped both girls into the hot water. They looked stupefied, as if they had no idea what a bath was. Judging by their condition, they didn't.

"Raymond, find Galen and bring me back something to put on them. Then go see Mr. Purcell for some applesauce. Please?" She got a look in their hair. "And ask him for about a cup of lard, please. We have head lice, on top of everything else."

It took some scrubbing but she finally got a lifetime's accumulation of crud off the children. Raymond found some small size long-handled underwear. He cut the bottoms off, then Lily slipped them over the girls' heads. They would do for the time being. She took the cup of lard that had been softening by the stove and smeared it liberally on each little head, making sure to get the scalps completely covered, and all the way to the end of each strand of hair, then wrapping pieces of sheeting into turbans.

Lily was looking at their hands when Galen found her. He pasted his most pleasant "doctor smile" on his face. "Who have we here, Nurse Stewart? Not our usual patients."

"Dr. Stewart, these are Eulalia and Matthias King's two girls. Raymond drove their mother home. He found the girls hiding in the yard. Severely undernourished, abdominal pains, watery bloody diarrhea, dark urine, and white streaks on the nails. On top of everything else they've got cooties."

He picked up the older girl's hand and examined her fingernails. "Mees' lines. Arsenical poisoning. How the h...on earth did these babies get into arsenic?"

"Could it have come from the water? We know the family has little of nothing. No telling where they get their drinking water."

He shook his head. "No, this isn't organic arsenic. As little as they are, even they couldn't get this far advanced poisoning from drinking. And God knows they weren't bathed in it. No, either it's inhaled or ingested. Something or someone is poisoning them."

"I asked Mr. Purcell for applesauce, thinking that might help with the bowels. Now I see it won't. Suggestions, Doctor?"

He started to tick off on his fingers. "Milk. Bone broth as soon as Purcell can get a chicken. Apple juice for the bowel issues. Be careful with their hair. I expect it may start to come out in clumps any time. And make sure they're kept in isolation, so they don't pick up anything from any patients. For now, I think you and I should be responsible for their treatment."

"Should we move them to the house? It may work out better."

He nodded. "I agree. But first we need to notify Joe Fromme. Otherwise, Raymond may wind up charged with kidnapping."

Galen went to the door and called his brother-in-law. "Call Joe Fromme and ask him to come by here. Tell him we have an emergency."

Sheriff Fromme arrived half an hour later.

It didn't take long for him to make a decision. "Their father is a patient here, correct?"

"He is. He's sleeping right now."

"Wake him up. Tell him the girls are sick, and you need to take them to your house for treatment. They need to be where they can be watched around the clock. I think Beatrix and little Adelle would be more a comfort to these kids than a bunch of doctors and nurses in masks they don't know. Meanwhile, I'll see that Eulalia knows her kids are safe."

Lily made the call to Beatrix to alert her, then had Raymond bundle the girls in blankets for the short trip to the house.

Beatrix sent her husband to Jent's store, to outfit the girls in nightgowns, and one dress each, guessing at sizes. The first floor bedroom was kept ready for patients should the need arise. It was a simple matter to get it ready for their two new charges.

Raymond drove with Lily to take the children to their home. The girls were still stuporous, too weakened and exhausted to understand what was happening, no matter how thoroughly it was explained to them.

Beatrix met them at the front door. "You poor little lambs. You just come in here with Beatrix, and Doc Galen and Nurse Lily will get you all better. Now, I got some nice clean nightgowns for you, and we'll tuck you into bed." She turned to Raymond. "Adelle's in the kitchen cooking that bone broth Doc Galen ordered."

Raymond found her at the stove, adding onions to a pot of boiling bones from yesterday's roast chicken. He saw tears rolling down her face. "Honey, what's wrong?"

She sniffed, and wiped her eyes on her sleeve. "Onions." She looked toward the table. "Apple juice for girls."

Raymond broke the seal on the jar and poured out two small glasses. "Let me stir this and you take the juice into them, please."

Adelle delivered the juice with smiles for the two silent children, then returned to the kitchen, finding Raymond leaning against the dry sink. She passed him to stir the pot one more time, then to set it to the back of the stove so it didn't boil hard. As she dropped the spoon, he reached out and caught her hand. It was a simple thing for her to turn and step into his arms. He held her loosely, not wanting her to feel imprisoned.

She wrapped her arms around his waist and laid her head on his chest, very briefly. A quick kiss on the cheek and she was gone, back to Beatrix and the two children.

Seven month old Abigail was sitting up in her cradle in the corner. She spotted Raymond and held out her chubby arms to him. "DaDa."

God, that made him feel good. He picked her up and nuzzled his face into her sweet baby neck. "Soon, baby girl. Soon I can be your daddy." A check, a confirmation. "But first you need a clean diaper." He made quick work of changing her, and had her dry and clean before her mother returned.

Lily sat with the two King girls until suppertime. She alternated giving them apple juice and milk that she had Beatrix heat just to boiling for half an hour. She didn't want to take a chance on any contamination of any sort. Beatrix assured her the bone broth would be ready for them in the morning. For tonight, they'd have to be content with juice, milk, and perhaps some semolina.

Galen took over with the children at supper time. Both children were asleep when he relieved Lily of her duty. He ate a quick supper of cold meat and bread, and sat reading the medical journals he had been ignoring for the last several months.

The younger of the two girls breathed her last before midnight.

Careful not to wake her sister, Galen lifted her gently and carried her to his treatment room, laying her on the table.

He roused Lily from where she slept on the settee. "Can Raymond sit with the older girl? I want to do an autopsy. The question of ingested or inhaled is the difference between accident and murder."

She ran up the stairs to fetch her brother, then headed up to her room to throw on some clothes.

Galen had readied the room for the unofficial autopsy. He only intended to examine the lungs and the stomach contents. He would perform the procedure with a scope but it had to be done carefully. The state's medical examiner might need to perform a complete procedure.

Lily gathered as many lamps as she could and arranged them around the room. She swore their next treatment room would have electricity even if they had to provide their own steam generator.

Next she arranged the intubation instruments. No need for any sterilization tonight. Even with the simpler procedures it was going to be harrowing, particularly for Galen.

*****

Raymond sat beside the King girl's bedside, weeping silently. He knew death was an integral part of a doctor's practice or a hospital. But why did such a tiny child have to die so unnecessarily? He had been grief-stricken at his father's death from Dropsy, but that hadn't been sudden. He had watched as his father's feet and legs had swollen until he could no longer walk, then a few days later the great doctor strangled to death on his own bodily fluids, and no one could do a damn thing. Tonight, he slept while the little girl he tried to save died because he wasn't fast enough. If he had been more observant when he picked up the father, perhaps if he had paid attention he would have known they needed help then. Could those three days have made a difference?

Now, as tears streamed down his face he prayed as he had never prayed before, for the recovery of this child whose name he didn't know.

*****

"Ready when you are, Doctor." Lily had the rigid rubber tubing ready to be introduced into the child's lungs.

"You have the specimen jars ready?"

"Six. More if you need them."

He took the tube and passed it carefully through the trachea, until it reached the lungs. Lily took a large syringe, fitted it into the tube and aspirated what she could, then expressed the contents into a sample jar.

Galen withdrew the tube slightly, then guided it further into a lower part of the lung Lily took a second sample. Each jar was labeled and set aside.

A second tube was passed through the cadaver's nose to extract the stomach contents. It wouldn't be conclusive, and probably wouldn't show the last thing she had eaten, but it would be possible to detect a toxin.

Three stomach content samples collected and marked, and they were done.

Galen extracted the tubing, and set it aside. Lily had a sheet ready to wrap the body. Galen kissed the child's cold forehead. "I'm sorry, little one." She wrapped the body quickly, then extinguished all but two of the lamps.

"Go up to bed, Galen. I'll sit with the child."

He shook his head. "I haven't run a toxicology test for years. I need to re-read Sir Bernard Spilsbury's paper to make sure I do everything right. And I want Joe there when I do the test."

"All the more reason to get some sleep now."

They finally agreed they would both sit up with their young charge. Galen could read the British paper on testing for arsenical poisonings.

Raymond returned to his bed but sleep wouldn't come. Before sunrise he went out in the cold morning air. He fed the stock and spent time talking to his horse as he combed the animal's mane. He heard a noise behind him.

"Raymond?" Adelle's small, bell-like voice came from the darkness.

Raymond left the stall and found her standing by the cow's manger. "Adelle?"

"What's wrong?"

He shook his head and swiped at his eyes.

She laid her hand on his left arm and squeezed. Even now, after all these months, she was leery of him, afraid of what he might think or what he might do. Now, standing in this darkened barn, she seemed almost bold.

"Dell?" This was the first time he ever used a diminutive of her given name.

She stepped closer to him, still maintaining her contact with his arm. One hand reached up and wiped the tears from his cheeks. "What's wrong?"

Raymond grabbed her in both arms, holding her tightly, tighter than he'd ever dared. "She died, Dell. That little girl died tonight. I tried to save her, but I was too late." He wept onto her shoulder, ashamed of his tears, but needing her more than ever.

Adelle clutched at him, needing to be his anchor in his personal storm. No man had ever wept in her presence before, and certainly not over a child. No one had ever needed her before except her daughter, Abigail. It was a simple motion to turn and kiss the corner of his mouth.

He raised his head. "God, Dell, I'm sorry. I never meant..."

She took his face between her hands and brought his face to hers for their first, real kiss. It was soft, gentle, promising a future. Adelle was unsure how to proceed, needed him to school her, but was afraid to ask.

Raymond wanted nothing more than to carry her to her bed, and make love to her for the rest of the day. At this moment, in the midst of his sorrow, he needed her gentleness, but feared his passion would frighten her away. The bastard who fathered her children had been a rutting beast. He refused to be classed with Jackson Conover.

"Raymond? Will you love me?"

As they stood in the dark, and he considered how to answer her question, he realized she was standing barefoot in the barn, wearing her cotton nightgown with a shawl thrown around her shoulders, her long hair hanging loose down her back. "Dell, I do love you. More than you'll ever know." He kissed her lips again, gently, as she had kissed him.

He had to strain to hear what she said next. "No one has ever loved me. Will you?"

"Adelle Fraser, I love you more than life. What more can I do?" She had to tell him. It was too important that he not make a mistake.

"Raymond, I want to know how love feels. You touch me and I get...tingly all over. There has to be more. Show me. Now."

His good hand wound in her hair and pulled her close for a kiss, a real kiss this time. She opened to him shyly, not really understanding, but reveling in every sensation. He broke away, gasping to maintain control. "Not here. Not in a barn. In a bed."

*****

The sun was up when Adelle made it out to the barn to milk. Raymond left her, reluctantly, to find his sister. "Lily?" He found her dozing on the settee in the parlor.

"Huh? What's wrong, Raymond?" She pushed her hair out of her face and struggled to sit up.

He sat beside her. "Not a damned thing, Big sis. I'm getting married."

"Married? You and Adelle? Really? When? Oh God I've got so much to do."

"Hang on. The Methodist preacher gets in tomorrow. We want to go then. Have you got something Adelle can wear? Her clothes would fit in the last century."

"I have the dress I was married in. It's out of style, but no one here would know the difference. It's purple and lavender, and I think it would fit her." She hugged her brother. "Raymond, I'm so happy for you both. Of course, you know Beatrix is going to want to throw a big party."

He shook his head. "No. Family. Joe Fromme, maybe Randall Whittimore. The Rogans. I'm afraid more than that would terrify Adelle. Maybe later, after she's more comfortable, we can have a garden party. Besides, what about your patient?"

"She seems to be improving. I got some broth in her a little while ago, and it stayed down. The question is what do we do with her when she's better. She can't go back home."

He patted her arm. "We'll worry about that when the time comes. Now, where's that brilliant husband of yours? I'm gonna need a best man."

Galen was napping in the chair beside their patient's bed. Raymond gave his shoulder a shake and gestured for him to step away. Once they were away from the bedside Raymond asked, "If you're not busy tomorrow afternoon I'd like you to stand up for me."

"Well, sure, any...wait, what? Stand up? You and Adelle?"

Raymond's smile was too wide to form a word. He nodded like a fool.

Galen clapped him on the shoulder. "About damned time, boy. Couple of times, I was afraid you were going to start a grass fire the way you looked at each other."

*****

They ran the tests on the samples collected from the King girl late that morning. Joe Fromme sat on the stool in the corner, not really understanding what exactly was going on.

The lung samples showed definite evidence of inhaled arsenic. It would have been slow to act, making them gradually sicker. But when he tested the stomach contents the presence of ingested arsenic was unmistakable.

While the sheriff was with Galen, Eulalia King came to visit her husband. No soup this time. Instead she stopped by the cook tent and got some hot tea. Lily saw her stirring sugar into the tea, then offering small sips to her husband.

Joe pulled her into Galen's office when her visit was done. "Miz Eulalia, what are your daughters' names?"

"Euphonia. She's the older one. And Henrietta. Why?"

"You knew they were sick. Doc Stewart has been caring for them?"

She nodded.

"Henrietta died last night."

He expected hysterics, weeping, screaming. He wasn't expecting coldness. "What'd that uppity bitch and her brother do to her?"

"You mean Nurse Stewart and Raymond Barnett? Raymond tried to save your children's lives. He did save Euphonia's. Doctor and Nurse Stewart worked around the clock trying to help them. Euphonia woke up this morning, and is taking broth. Henrietta never regained consciousness. Do you know why they got so sick?"

She shook her head. "How should I know? They're kids. They get into everything."

"They were poisoned. It had to have come from your house. Dr. Roberts and I will be going to your house to see what the source of the poison is, and how it came to be inside your kids."

Before Joe could finish his interview, he heard a commotion. Bob Roberts was calling for assistance.

"Dr. Stewart! King's arresting. Come quick."

By the time Joe Fromme got to his bedside, Matthias King was dead.

Galen grabbed the tea cup from the floor beside the bed. It still held half a cup of the tepid liquid. He carried it directly to the laboratory, where he ran the test for arsenic. It came back positive.

Joe Fromme arrested Eulalia King for murdering her husband. Once she was confined to the cells in Deputy Goode's care, he left with Dr. Roberts for the King home, to seek out the source of the poison.

They rode there in the sheriff's buggy. The door was standing open when they arrived. Fromme hurried to the door and called, "Hello the house." Someone was moving around inside. He gestured to Dr. Roberts to stay put, drew his revolver and started inside.

A man wearing a cheap ditto suit and boiled shirt stood at the dry sink, washing dishes in the basin. "Who the hell are you?"

The man dropped the enamel plate he was holding and turned around. "I could ask you the same thing."

"Sheriff Joe Fromme. I repeat. Who the hell are you?"

The man wiped his hands on his pants and offered his right hand to Fromme. "Rolandus Gilmore." The hand was rejected. Gilmore reached in his breast pocket and pulled out a card. "First State Life. I come by every month to collect Eulalia's premiums. I heard her husband was sick. Figured I'd help before she got home."

Joe took the card. "How long has Miz King had insurance on Matthias?"

"She bought the policy just before he joined up. When he got home, she took out policies on both kids, and herself, too. Keeps the premiums up, too. A lot of folks don't."

"Un-huh. How much are the premiums?"

"Two cents a month for both kids, for five hundred dollars coverage each. Three cents a month for Missus, and a nickel a month for Matthias. She has seven fifty coverage, he has two thousand dollars."

"Okay. Have a seat at the table, Mr. Gilmore. Don't touch anything else. Dr. Roberts and I have work to do."

Bob Roberts walked into the kitchen. "Where's the fly paper? When I was here to pick up Mr. King there were at least six strips of fly paper hanging from the ceiling. They're gone." He opened the pantry cupboard. There was a square bottle on the shelf. "Here's why Matthias slept so well. 'Dr. Pierce's Compound Extract of Smartweed.' Stuff is mostly opium and alcohol. I bet she put it into his food." He reached further back, behind jars of beans. "Unopened rolls of fly paper. This brand hasn't been made for about ten years, but stores can still sell it until their stock is gone. 'Active ingredient: Arsenic'." He kept digging. "Ant poison. 'Active ingredient: Arsenic'. I believe these are what we need, Sheriff."

Joe Fromme still held his revolver on Gilmore. "Mr. Gilmore, you'll be coming back to the station with us. You and me need to have a talk."

*****

Raymond took the train to the county seat that morning. He wanted a marriage license so no one would question his marriage to his Adelle. It was a quick trip, and two dollars well spent. He was home in time for supper.

When Adelle brought the milk into the kitchen Lily took Abigail from her, passing the baby to Beatrix. "Raymond told me you're getting married. What are you going to wear?"

Adelle looked down at her threadbare dress. "Don't have much."

Lily held out her hand. "I have a beautiful dress you can wear. Then we can go up to Mr. Jent's and get you some new shoes."

Lily's lavender dress was almost a perfect fit. It was a little too long to be fashionable, but considering this girl had never shown so much as an ankle in public, it would do.

Lily also gave her underclothes, something she was unaccustomed to wearing. She giggled at the idea of a brassiere, but agreed to it when she saw how much better the dress fit with foundations.

The hat Lily wore in Belgium when they married had been lost somewhere during her travels. Beatrix produced a piece of ecru lace that would serve as her veil. Veils were no longer symbolic of virginity. Now they were merely fashionable for weddings.

Shoes at the Jent Mercantile presented a small problem. Plenty of work boots, but only two pairs suitable for a wedding: old fashioned pearl grey high buttoned boots and Mary Jane's with a two inch Louis heel. Lily made sure Adelle tried both on. She settled on the high buttoned boots since the girl was terrified of trying to walk in heels.

The morning of her wedding dawned bright, cold and clear. At almost eight months old Abigail was eating real food now, although still reliant on her mother two or three times a day. Adelle fed her, then went to see her future sister-in-law for help to get ready. Lily set up the tub for her in the mud room, locked both doors and helped her bathe and wash her hair.

"Miz Lily, is it okay that I'm happy?"

Now where had that come from? "Stop with the 'Miss Lily'. We're going to be sisters in a very short time. From now on it's just plain Lily. As to being happy, why shouldn't you be?"

"Never have been. It feels...funny."

"Can I tell you a story?" Adelle nodded. "I met Galen when I was fourteen, right after my mother died. My hair used to be as long as yours, almost the same color, too, all brown with lots of red in it. The day we met, I was absolutely bald"

"Oh no! Did your pa shave your head?"

"No, no. I had diphtheria. So did my mother. It killed her. I lost all my hair. It grew back, like this." She fluffed her curly white hair. "Anyway, Galen had to examine me after I lost all my hair. I didn't see him again for a year, until my father brought him to the house for supper. When he treated me like a patient I thought I'd die. You see, the first time I saw him I had decided I was going to marry him.

"I tried to go to medical school, to be a doctor like my father. The professor wouldn't let me in his class. I swore my life was over then, that nothing would ever be the same. I was sort of right. That was the day I joined the trained nursing program. I didn't see much of Galen again until just before I graduated. The day I graduated from the nursing program was the first time I was alone with him. We didn't meet again for months, because he went away to war the very next day.

"After that we would be together for a few months, then be apart, sometimes for a whole year. But we always found our way back to each other. Since the war ended this is the longest we've ever been together. And it's the first time we have ever been able to admit we were married. See, the army didn't approve, so we had to keep it a secret.

"So yes, sweetie. You are allowed to be happy. It's about time, wouldn't you say? For your whole life, you've been pushed around by men. Never been allowed to be Adelle. You had to be a good girl for your parents, then for your brother, then for Conover. Before you were allowed to have a childhood you had your own baby. Now you get to be Adelle. I'll tell you a secret. You can be any Adelle you want to."

"I want to be Adelle Barnett. Is it okay that I want to marry Raymond?" She sounded worried.

"Yes, Adelle, that is the absolute best. You make my brother very happy. Does he make you happy?"

She nodded hard enough to make herself dizzy. "Lily, what does 'love' feel like?"

Oh crap. How does one explain that? She screwed up her courage, much as she had when she had to scrape maggots off the dead sheep her first day in France. "Let's see. 'Love'. It's when you want to be with that person more than anything in the world. When his happiness is more important than your own, not because you're afraid of him, or something might make him mad, but because when he's happy, you can be happy. But sometimes, he'll get mad at you. You'll get mad at him. And that's okay, too. You'll have some fights, but I can promise Raymond will never raise a hand to you in anger. You'll fight with words. The only thing you have to guard are your words, because words can hurt worse than a slap. Never say anything to each other you can't take back."

She picked up a towel. "Let's get you out of the tub. My brother won't want to marry a prune."

"What happens if we fight? Won't he love me anymore?"

Lily wrapped a towel around the young woman who had grown so much since Lily delivered her daughter. "I'll tell you another secret. After an argument, you make up. And you'll love each other even more. Making up can be the best part."

Adelle pulled on the fluffy robe and Lily led her up to the master bedroom. The purple dress was laid out on the bed already, along with the undergarments. "Lily, what are you going to wear if I have your dress?"

Poor kid. She had two blouses, one skirt and a

dress to her name. Raymond would correct that in short order. "Let me show you." She pulled out a green dress that was cut similarly to the lavender one Adelle would wear. "Would you like to help me get dressed? I don't think Beatrix would approve of this." She pulled her corset from the drawer. It still bore the small chocolate stains her husband had left there in Belgium. "I can't do the laces up by myself, and it's been so long since I wore it."

"Why?"

"Because Galen likes it. He *really* likes it."

They were still laughing when Adelle was figuring out how to do up the laces.

*****

Raymond and Adelle stood before Mr. Sullivan at the altar of the Methodist church to exchange their vows, with Galen and Lily as their witnesses. The bride and groom were almost embarrassingly happy throughout the ceremony.

Beatrix and Liberty were at the house, preparing for the small party. Mr. Terry, the conductor, had managed to sneak a case of champagne from Nashville into the depot, which was currently resting in Galen's buggy. Terry would join them for a glass later, along with Sheriff Fromme and Randall Whittimore. Those were the people in whose presence Adelle was comfortable, and Raymond was insistent she not be distressed, particularly on her wedding day.

Outside the church at the foot of the steps, waited a brand new high wheeled gig, hitched to Mr. Henry's Morning Ranger. Hank's mane was braided with ribbons matching Adelle's dress. The happy couple came out of the double doors of the church and Adelle stopped short. "Raymond, what's that?"

"It's ours. Now I don't have to use Galen's buggy. And I can hitch this one up myself."

He handed her up into the gig, ran around to the other side and climbed in. A fur rug was under their feet, but Adelle was too excited to feel the cold. Raymond took up the reins, snapped them across Hank's rump and they were off. He didn't take her back to the house yet. He wanted to show off his new bride. They rode through town, down to the clinic, then returned to the house to meet their family and friends.

After their small party Raymond handed his bride back into the gig. This time, in the fading daylight he headed Hank north of town. They were going to the small spa hotel at Epperson Springs at which they were to spend two nights, a wedding gift from Galen and Lily. Lily gave Adelle more lingerie and several dresses from her own wardrobe.

The hotel was the biggest place Adelle had ever seen. Forty rooms, all in one building. Granted, the place stank of sulfur, but the waters were supposed to be beneficial.

Raymond handed the gig over to a groom at the front door and handed their valise to a bellman. He led Adelle through the front door, to start their new lives together.

*****

People stayed at the Stewart home long after the happy couple left. While they were standing in church during the exchange of vows, , Galen had slipped his arm around his wife's waist. He gave her an extra squeeze and looked at her, the question in his wide eyes. She smiled and gave him a small nod. For the rest of the day he kept his arm around her, seemingly afraid of letting her out of his sight.

By the time the sun was down Galen was in a right state. "Will they never go home?"

Lily looked around at those assembled. Euphonia had been transferred to the clinic for the night, where Bob Robert's and the nurses would care for her. Abigail was spending the night with the Rogans. They'd have the house to themselves. She tapped on Galen's wine glass with the handle of her fork. "Ladies, gentlemen, I hate to be a poor hostess. But it's getting late and some of us have to work tomorrow."

Having observed the doctor devour his wife with his eyes all day everyone recognized it was time to leave. Mr. Terry wondered if he could convince Mrs. Terry to turn in a little early tonight.

Once the house was empty Lily took her husband by the hand and led him up the spiral stairs to their tower room. Galen was unbuttoning the back of her dress as they climbed. He grumbled, "Whose idea was it to take the room on the third floor, anyway?"

Lily giggled as they climbed. She pulled the pins from her hair as she walked, letting the curls fall around her shoulders. She reached the third floor landing and opened the door.

Galen grabbed her, swept her into his arms and carried her into their bedroom, kicking the door shut behind him.

*****

April, 1920

The district attorney accepted the test results from Galen, and released the two bodies of father and daughter for burial. Lily arranged for their internment at a local church yard.

First State Life insurance paid the claims on Matthias and Henrietta, but not to Eulalia. They paid instead to Euphonia, the five year old, for her maintenance and upbringing.

Both Eulalia and Gilmore went to prison. They planned the crime together, with Gilmore providing the arsenic with the intention of sharing in the payout. It appeared this wasn't his first time.

Euphonia continued to stay with the Stewarts. Joe Fromme came to the house one Sunday afternoon and sat at the kitchen table with a slice of Beatrix's pie and a cup of coffee.

"Galen, now that your clinic is closed y'all reckon you'll go back north?"

"I wanted to talk to you about that. You know any houses for sale in town?"

He nodded. "As a matter of fact I do. The railroad manager used to live here in town up until a few years ago. You know that big white house on the Lafayette Road across from the station?"

Galen nodded.

"Railroad's selling it. Cheap too. It's got ten acres, groom's quarters over the stable, and what used to be called bachelor's quarters in the back. If you want to see it, ask at the depot."

The men talked about the opportunities of setting up a regular medical practice in town. Then, apropos of nothing, Joe said, "The Baptist Children's Home has been in touch. Seems Eulalia wants them to take Euphonia."

Galen didn't bother getting up. "Lily!" She came running. "Nia's mother wants to send her to an orphanage."

Lily dropped into a chair. "Over my dead body. Tomorrow we go to Gallatin and start the adoption."

"Guess that's your answer, Joe."

Fromme left soon after.

Lily stood with her arms around her husband in the kitchen. He asked "Are you sure about adopting Nia?"

"Of course. She's bright. She learns quickly. Haven't you noticed how sweet she is with Abigail, like a little mother. I suspect, even as young as she was, she had to assume responsibility for her sister."

She leaned back a little to make sure she had her husband's full attention. "Besides, she'll make an excellent big sister to our September baby.

"Lily?"

"Yes, my love?"

"Are you...are we...September?"

"Yes, my love."

He hugged her tighter, lifted her feet from the floor and spun her in a circle. "I love you, my darling girl."

Notes on the Book

The title comes from a song by the same name, by Jos. E. Howard and Philander Johnson, came out in 1916, and was a number One record in 1918. The refrain is:

Somewhere in France is the Lily,

Close by the English Rose;

Somewhere in France is a sweetheart,

Facing the battle's chance,

For the flow'r of our youth fights for freedom and truth

Somewhere in France

You can find a recording on YouTube at https://www.youtube.com/watch?v=eGybyL8hXEo

No matter how gross and disgusting the treatments seemed as recorded here, they were all standard medical practices of the period. In fact, maggots are still used for treating gangrene when all else fails.

Imagine the meatball surgeries of M*A*S*H, only without antibiotics, or much in the way of anesthesia, painkillers, and limited sterile procedure other than lye soap and boiling water at times. There were no vaccines for anything but smallpox. Things like morphine (called Morphia by the British) heroin (Diamorphine) cannabis were all included in over the counter medicaments. The Pure Food and Drug Act was in place, but the stores and manufacturers were permitted to sell out their existing stock. Meaning the stuff was still around, ten years after the law was passed.

Bayer, the German company, owned the patents on Morphine, Heroin and even aspirin. Other countries were able to compound their own Morphine and Heroin. No one had managed to reverse engineer aspirin, which was about their only fever reducing drug. They were forced to rely on quinine, which helped a little. But more people died from sickness and infection during WWI than from injuries received on the battlefield.

Much like during the Covid19 pandemic, many people refused to admit anything was wrong. Nashville actually refused to keep track of influenza deaths, claiming those deaths were not a public health issue. They actually loaded people onto trains and shipped them to outlying counties, where they were treated in tent hospitals like the one described here.

The horse Raymond got, Mr. Henry's Morning Ranger, was after my great grandfather, Henry Gooch. He really had a racking horse to pull his buggy, and lived in a fine great house in Galllatin. Unfortunately, he had to sell off the land piecemeal, until there was only ten acres and the house left of the original estate.

Before you ask, Coatesville is a fictional town. But the things that happened there, and at the front, are "torn from the headlines".

Thanks Hon.

Made in the USA
Middletown, DE
16 November 2022